I0534505

On the Take in Waikiki

BOOKS BY TERRY AMBROSE

Seaside Cove Bed & Breakfast Mysteries
A Treasure to Die For
Clues in the Sand
The Killer Christmas Sweater Club
Secrets of the Treasure King

McKenna Mysteries
Photo Finish
Kauai Temptations
Big Island Blues
Mystery of the Lei Palaoa
Honolulu Hottie
North Shore Nanny
A Damsel for Santa
Maui Magic
The Scent of Waikiki
On the Take in Waikiki

License to Lie Series
License to Lie
Con Game
Shadows from the Past

Anthologies with Stories
Paradise, Passion, Murder: 10 Tales of Mystery from Hawai'i
Happy Homicides 3: Summertime Crimes
Happy Homicides 4: Fall into Crime
Happy Homicides 5: The Purr-fect Crime

On the Take In Waikiki

Terry Ambrose

COPYRIGHT

On the Take in Waikiki

ISBN: 978-0-9968914-4-8

Copyright © 2020 Terry Ambrose

All rights reserved.

Cover design by Dar Albert

AUTHOR NOTES

Homelessness is a significant problem in Hawaii. I'd originally decided to tackle this subject by writing about a common scenario in the islands, a visitor who runs out of money and can't get home. However, after I started researching the problem I discovered another, more intriguing, avenue. How to solve the seemingly unsolvable problem of homelessness itself?

Kinohi Village was inspired by a real-life project that was the brainchild of businessman Duane Kurisu. That real-life project, Kahauiki Village, is a partnership between government, business, and the aio foundation, of which Kurisu is the founder. Kurisu's idea was to recreate a part of Hawaii's history, the plantation lifestyle. This would create a place where more than 150 homeless families with children could live, thrive, and support each other.

The most significant difference between Kahauiki Village and my fictional subject is that the real village was not mired in controversy or scandal. In fact, the project became a model of efficiency and effectiveness, showing how a public-private partnership can benefit all of the interested parties. It's a place where people not only get housing, but can also find nearby jobs, onsite child care, transportation, and much more. Kahauiki Village brings all of these elements together by involving the surrounding businesses and the community itself into a mutually beneficial partnership. The entire project is an amazing and inspiring example of what can be done when creative minds go to work. If you'd like to learn more about this creative solution visit kahauiki.org.

The corruption referenced in this book is also a very real part of Hawaii's past. The yakuza had a strong hold on construction on O'ahu in the 1960s and 70s. That hold diminished over time as new gangs rose to power. McKenna's description of the yakuza's influence and demise is an accurate depiction of Hawaii's history. Another part of that history is related to the pay-to-play practices that were common in the construction industry. Once again, the description in the book is accurate, including the reference to Kukui Plaza, which involved one of Hawaii's longest serving mayors, Frank Fazi.

On a sad note, Flour and Barley was a real restaurant in the International Marketplace. It had excellent gluten-free pizza that was, quite honestly, the best I've ever had. Another victim of COVID-19, the Honolulu location has closed. I can only hope the owner decides to open new locations at some point in the future.

ABOUT THE AUTHOR

Once upon a time, in a life he'd rather forget, Terry Ambrose tracked down deadbeats for a living. He also hired big guys with tow trucks to steal cars—but only when negotiations failed. Those years of chasing deadbeats taught him many valuable life lessons such as—always keep your car in the garage.

Terry has written more than a dozen books, several of which have been award finalists. In 2014, his thriller, "Con Game," won the San Diego Book Awards for Best Action-Thriller. His series include the Trouble in Paradise McKenna Mysteries, the Seaside Cove Bed & Breakfast Mysteries, and the License to Lie thriller series.

You can learn more about Terry and his writing at terryambrose.com.

1

FIFTY MINUTES. THAT'S HOW LONG it took for things to go south. And for this to become the Meeting of Five Regrets.

Benni Kapono, the light of my life, girl of my dreams, and all those other romantic clichés, had suggested we attend a talk about genealogy. Due to a recent letter I'd received, I'd grown leery of researching my roots. So leery I now regarded dredging up my family's past as the last thing I wanted to do. My downfall was Benni's disappointment when I'd said no. Obviously, Regret #1 was that I'd caved.

The presenter was Sue Ito, the daughter of Kenji Ito, one of Benni's clients. Justifiably proud of her dad, Sue also had five slides about how he'd come from nothing, built his business, and how his foundation had raised millions to benefit causes ranging from feeding families to housing the homeless. A great guy, but, seriously? Five slides? This was supposed to be about genealogy, not an ad for Ito Development.

The talk should have been interesting. Tracking people down. It's what I used to do for a living. The difference was, I'd been a skip tracer. My job had been to find deadbeats, not dead people. Slide after slide about online databases, old news stories, birth and death certificates lulled me toward Regret #2—a meeting stupor.

So there I was, out like a light. In front of everybody, including the speaker and all those people in the rows behind us. Yeah, Regret #2 was a big one.

Benni jabbed me in the ribs and hissed, "Behave yourself, McKenna. At least try to act interested."

"Sorry, it's a lot drier than I thought it was going to be." Even with my brain only half-awake I knew the words were trouble. And yet, out they came. Hoping to score a quick recovery, I whispered, "I'm good now."

Benni rolled her eyes and ignored me. Someone snickered. A chorus of shushes made my cheeks flush hotter. I sat up straight, took a few deep breaths, and began an internal mantra. *Stay awake, McKenna. Stay awake, McKenna. Stay...*

I suspected the snicker had come from the dufus who'd been eyeing Benni from the minute we walked in. It wasn't his fault she was island gorgeous with full dark hair, almond eyes, and a smile that could melt the coldest heart. I, on the other hand, was a typical, retired haole—a white guy with more salt than pepper in my hair and no otherwise remarkable assets.

Fortunately, the meeting ended about ten minutes after the dozing incident. A number of the twenty-or-so attendees rushed forward to talk to the speaker. Benni stood, brushed back a strand of hair that had fallen forward, and gave me what people in the islands call stink eye. Holding out her hand, she asked if I was coming. Feeling like I was four and we were about to cross the street, I committed Regret #3.

"Where?" I shot back.

In retrospect, I was acting more like a four-year-old than either of the two little girls who had sat patiently through the entire presentation. They were quietly munching on cookies while I was busy alienating the woman I loved.

I pushed down my natural tendency to get snarky when cornered and stood. Leaning close to Benni, I whispered, "I'm sorry. I've been behaving badly tonight."

Her brown eyes flashed. "You were rude, McKenna. Sue and her father are my clients, and you fell asleep in her presentation. Really?" She huffed, grabbed my hand, and pulled me forward. Then she asked the question I'd been dreading. "I thought you wanted to be here. Why'd you fall asleep?"

As part of Regret #1, I had professed my interest in genealogy. It had been a tactical and strategic error driven by my desire to make Benni feel better. It was time to fess up and face the consequences of my actions. I grimaced and kept my tone low. "After my life imploded in LA, I moved here to start over. You're the one who helped me realize I couldn't simply leave the past behind. I thought I was ready, but when I saw that first slide with the full family tree, I realized I didn't want to dredge up my family roots."

Benni's eyes widened, then misted over. She whispered, "But you told me you were interested in your family."

"I'm sorry, but the truth is, I don't know if I can face it."

I rubbed the back of her hand with my thumb. She didn't pull away, but did turn sideways to avoid looking at me. I didn't blame her—I'd just leveled with her in a room full of strangers, and the hurt was obvious.

We inched forward when the overly enthusiastic couple who had spent an inordinate amount of time gushing over the wonderful presentation migrated toward the little countertop area to raid the tray of cookies and grab glasses of punch.

Benni's brow creased and she regarded me. "Can I just ask you one more question? Are you afraid, or do you really not want to know where you came from?"

"I came from LA." Oh, crap. Regret #4. I was doomed to sleep on the couch in my own apartment if I let this go any further. "I'm sorry, Benni. I don't know what's gotten into me tonight. That was uncalled for. I realize you're just trying to understand. My problem is that I made a break with the past and I'm good with that. Your family has been in the islands for generations. You have ancestors from China, Japan, the Philippines, and Europe. I think that could be fascinating to dig into."

The fine line of Benni's jaw tightened along with her cheeks. I didn't blame her for being unhappy with me right now—I wasn't happy with me either. I'd avoided the truth when I shouldn't have, and now I was letting my defense mechanisms run amok.

"I've really messed up. Haven't I?"

"Yes," she said quietly, the hurt even more apparent in her voice.

"I love you," I whispered and rubbed the back of her hand again with my thumb.

She let out a long, exasperated sigh. "I love you, too. But you can be very difficult at times, McKenna."

"I know. Can we talk about this at home? I promise to tell you everything."

She agreed and we waited in silence. I was thankful for the time to regroup as we inched forward. When our turn came, Sue and Benni exchanged a hug, then Sue turned to me and wrapped her arms around my neck.

"You're McKenna, yah? Benni's told me about you. *Mahalo* for coming. I could tell things were dragging a bit." She pulled away and glanced at the door before she answered. "Guess I was getting a little distracted."

"It wasn't you," I lied. "This has been a long day."

Sue smiled weakly. "That's kind of you. Anyway, I'm glad you could make it. I understand you were a skip tracer in LA. Maybe we could compare notes sometime? I'm always interested in new research techniques."

"I'm pretty out of practice." It wasn't necessarily a lie, but my techniques were old school and, as I said, not really applicable to dead people.

"Nonsense, McKenna." Benni took my arm and gave it a little shake. "He'd be happy to help. Wouldn't you?" She smiled sweetly.

Point taken. Do this, and all is forgiven. You'll have a ride home…and a place to sleep. Don't, and you'll be getting cozy with the cookies tonight.

"Uh, sure. Why not?" I said.

Benni squeezed my hand and mouthed a silent thank you, but Sue missed my not-so-enthusiastic offer of help altogether because something across the room had her attention. I cheated and peeked to see what was so interesting. Actually, there was nothing.

The walls in the meeting room, a standard white found in most commercial construction, were devoid of decoration. The slat windows weren't any better. They looked out at another commercial building. At least a gentle breeze drifted through the open windows, keeping the room from growing stuffy despite the fact that we were in the middle of July. When Sue's attention wandered again, I realized she was watching the door.

Benni reached out, laid a hand on Sue's arm, and asked, "Where's your dad?"

Sue bit her lower lip. "I…I don't know. He said he would be here. But, you know, with all the work he's been doing over at Kinohi Village—maybe he just got tied up."

"I've heard a lot of good things about that project," I said.

Sue's face lit up. Like Benni, she had brown, almond-shaped eyes, high cheekbones, and a friendly smile. "You've heard of it?"

"Who hasn't? Benni's told me about it, but I've also caught it on the news. It's going to provide long-term housing for something like seventy homeless families once it's done."

Benni nodded enthusiastically. "You've been paying attention. Good job, McKenna."

"The project could get bigger if the community keeps supporting it." Sue stopped and motioned to the mom with the two little girls. "I want you to meet someone."

Mom held both the girl's hands as they approached. Though I'm terrible at kid's ages, I'd put the younger one at about three and the older about five. Sue introduced the mom as Amy Stone.

Amy shook my hand, but followed the island custom of exchanging a hug with Benni.

"Your daughters are precious," Benni said. "I remember when mine was that age. What are their names?"

"This is Anna." Amy put her hand on the shoulder of the older girl. "She's in kindergarten and has decided she wants to be an airline pilot when she grows up." Amy rolled her eyes and smiled. "I told her she'll have to wait until she can reach the controls before she can do that. And this is Emily. We're still working on picture books."

Anna smiled politely, but held back. Emily, on the other hand, stepped forward. "Why did you fall asleep, mister? Were you tired?"

Amy gasped. Her hand shot to her throat and she immediately apologized. Benni was doing a terrible job of holding in her laughter while she gazed at me expectantly. The room felt hotter than it had all night.

I was not about to match wits with a three-year-old. Not on purpose, anyway. I cleared my throat and knelt in front of her. "Well, sweetheart, when people get old they sometimes need naps." I stood, looked at Amy, and added, "She's adorable, even if she is a little too observant."

"Sorry," Amy gushed. "Emily is my little extrovert."

"Amy's on the waiting list to get into Kinohi Village," Sue said. "You've been in a shelter now for...how long?"

"Two months. I won't lie, it can be difficult."

I prayed I wasn't gawping her. Two months? In a shelter? With two kids? I hadn't seen that one coming. How did I respond? You clean up well? You don't look homeless? Thank goodness, Benni saved me.

She reached out and gently touched Amy's shoulder. "I can only imagine. If you don't mind my asking, what brought you here tonight?"

"Last week, Kenji came in where I work. I'm a barista at a coffee shop and he comes in all the time. He was gushing about how proud he was of Sue and her work. He was worried nobody would come, so I decided to show my support." She scanned the assembled crowd, many of whom were now talking or gathered around the goody table. "It doesn't look like I was really needed. You had plenty of interest."

Emily tugged on her mother's hand and gazed at up at her. "Mama, I'm tired. Can we go now?"

Amy scooped up her daughter and kissed her on the forehead. "I'm sorry Baby Girl. Let's get you both…" She stopped, winced, and said, "Home." Tears brimmed in her eyes and she forced a smile. "Someday, we'll have one. Thanks to your father's vision."

As Amy walked toward the exit, I felt myself willing Kenji to walk through the door.

It was Regret #5.

He didn't.

2

AN UNCOMFORTABLE SILENCE CAME OVER our little trio—Sue was worried about her dad, Benni about Sue, and I had a growing sense of apprehension I wished I could dial back. The truth was, Benni and I were getting married soon and I should be focused on the wedding, not on dealing with a man who might or might not be missing. Maybe this was nothing more than an Ito family squabble.

Out of desperation to break the silence, I asked, "Has he ever done this before?"

"No," Sue said adamantly.

Benni's expression was solemn. "Kenji's very reliable."

"And he's always punctual," Sue added.

"Maybe it's just a calendar mix-up," I offered. "I'll bet he thinks it's tomorrow night."

My suggestion fell on deaf ears. Both Benni and Sue raised their eyebrows and checked the entrance again. I breathed a sigh of relief, just sure that the missing man-of-the-hour had walked in. I smiled, turned around, and muttered, "Crap." It wasn't Kenji.

Chance Logan stood in the doorway. A rich kid with a troubled LA past, he was not only one of my tenants, but had become my sidekick during the murder investigations I'd been dragged into. Other than the obvious age and physical differences between us, the biggest distinction might be that Chance had been eager to help me solve those murders. I, on the other hand, always seemed to go kicking and screaming. Chance spotted us, waved, and started in our direction. I made a show of tapping an imaginary watch on my wrist. "You're late."

"Island time, brah. Island time."

Seriously? I leaned forward and lowered my voice. "Watch who you call brah. The locals hate it when haoles think they speak the lingo. Anyway, what's up? You missed the whole thing. What happened?"

"I'm here now." His cheeks flushed slightly, then he eased past me and exchanged a quick hug with Benni before turning his charms on Sue. They did quick introductions. He was smooth. She, enamored.

"Wait. You're Kenji Ito's daughter?" Chance frowned at me. "You didn't tell me that, McKenna. Kenji's asked me to join the board of the island food bank. That's a pretty important detail you left off."

My cheeks were again feeling warm, but this time it wasn't because I was embarrassed. "I haven't seen you much lately. I didn't know." I considered a little dig about not being a mindreader, but too many wisecracks had already backfired on me tonight. "I'll try to do better next time."

"No worries," Chance said, then turned to Sue. "I'm sorry I missed your presentation. Something came up at the last minute.

I wish my girlfriend could've been here. She's fascinated with family histories." Without missing a beat, he grinned and said, "So, tell me all about it."

"It was a very informative presentation on genealogical research," I said.

Chance nodded enthusiastically. "Nice. How long have you been at it, Sue?"

"Several years. I started at my dad's insistence. I was fresh out of high school and needed a job. He had me spend the summer working for him and documenting our ancestors. It was quite an enlightening experience."

"Was he hard to work for?" I asked.

Sue paused, then shook her head. "I wouldn't say hard, no. He's understanding, but he can be demanding and makes sure things get done. He's got a good balance of yin and yang."

"You're lucky," Benni said. "My dad's all yang."

"Sounds like it," Chance said. "I remember you told me once that he could be hard as nails."

I don't know why I was, but I was surprised Chance knew about yin and yang. I shouldn't have been. Chance had a black belt in some sort of kung fu voodoo, which could be where he'd learned about the whole yin-yang thing.

"My dad is very much about doing things by the book." Benni laughed and cocked her head toward Sue. "Kenji, on the other hand, has a way of seeing things from both sides. I think that's why he envisioned Kinohi Village. He has empathy for the homeless, but he's got solid business sense."

Chance stroked his chin and frowned slightly. "I haven't been around him that much, but from what I've seen, he's not the kind of man who would intentionally disappoint his family."

I didn't think it possible, but the worry on Sue's brow deepened. "He's not."

"So where is he?" Chance asked. "I'm surprised he's not here."

"He said he was coming. I'm getting worried about him," Sue said.

"McKenna thinks he's missing," Benni added.

What? No. No, no. "I never said that." Well, maybe it's what I'd been thinking, but no matter how good a businessman and father Kenji might be, he hadn't even been gone a day.

I knew where Chance would want to go with this—he was itching for a case even though he was still working towards his PI license—through a detective agency I believed to be completely bogus. I mean, seriously—what legitimate detective would call his business the Phillip Marlowe Online Detective Agency?

The other thing I knew was that if Chance got involved, he'd want me to help. What worried me most was how easily he could sell our pro-bono services to Sue. Chance might have screwed up a bunch of careers before he came to the islands, but he had a strong background in BS-onomics.

Enough was enough. I had a wedding to focus on. And one last opportunity to keep the inevitable from happening. "Personally, I think you're making too much of this, Chance. There's nothing to indicate Kenji didn't forget or change his mind."

"There is," Sue said adamantly. Still babbling over her shoulder, she returned to the table where she'd left her belongings, pulled out a notepad, and extracted a small piece of paper. She returned with it and handed it to Chance.

"My dad gave me this yesterday. He would have called if he wasn't going to be here."

Chance read the paper, then handed it to me.

I'm in a rush right now and can't stay, but wanted you to know tomorrow night will be a tremendous success for you. I will be there for sure! I wouldn't miss it for the world. Love, Dad.

Now I knew how it felt to go down on the Titanic.

"What time yesterday did he give you the note?" Chance asked.

"In the afternoon. He came into my office, but I was on the phone and couldn't break away. He scribbled it out and left. It was the last time I saw him."

"And you haven't talked to him since?"

"I tried calling, but just got voicemail."

Chance paused, gave me a curious side glance, then returned his attention to Sue. "Has anyone else seen him?"

Benni shifted to one side and extended one leg forward. "Not that I know of. I called his office. Dana said the last thing she knew he was on his way to see me."

I'd heard Benni mention that name before, but couldn't place the conversation. "Dana?"

"She's the receptionist. What's strange is that Kenji called me in the morning and confirmed a meeting for the afternoon, but when I showed up at his office, Dana told me they were in the middle of laying utilities on the project. She said there must have been a problem, so I tried calling Kenji to see if he wanted to reschedule. When he didn't answer, I left a message. He hasn't called me back, McKenna. I'm worried about him."

"That's why you were so insistent on coming here?" I asked. "Because you thought Kenji would be here?"

"No, I wanted to be here for Sue's presentation."

13

"But you figured if you saw Kenji you could ask if he wanted to reschedule?"

"Exactly. Him not being here is *da kine* suspicious. Yah?"

Da kine is one of those placeholder words we use in Hawaii. It has a lot of different meanings, but in this case the context was clear—Kenji not being here was very suspicious.

Chance held Sue's gaze as he spoke in ominous tones. "So your dad stopped by your office yesterday afternoon, wrote out that note, then just disappeared?"

The color drained from Sue's face and she clamped her hand over her mouth. "Do you think something's happened to him?"

I couldn't blame her for being worried. The way Chance had summed up the situation, even I was beginning to think the worst.

Benni reached out and gave Sue's shoulder a reassuring squeeze. "Chance is just being melodramatic. He and McKenna see boogeymen everywhere."

"I wouldn't go that far," I protested.

The term boogeymen implied evil spirits and apparitions. The evil we'd found had been very real. Real people. Real murder. Despite the fact that I, too, was now on the Kenji's-in-trouble train, this was not something I wanted any part of just before my wedding. I tried mentally telegraphing Chance to knock off the melodrama, but he ignored me. It was time to throw the Hail Mary pass. "Maybe you should report this to the police, Sue."

"It's too early," Chance said. "Sue, I'm not saying anyone has tried to do him harm because it's way too early for that, but McKenna and I could do a little checking to see if we can find him."

Okay, let's call it the Meeting of Six Regrets. Chance and I were going on a field trip. To find a missing businessman. In a city of 300,000 people. With ten million visitors a year. Sure. Why not?

3

IT WAS AFTER TEN BY the time Benni and I got home. We were getting ready for bed and although I was dead tired, I wasn't sleepy. Too many thoughts raced through my head about Kenji, the wedding, and even what was going on with Chance. Leaning against the bathroom doorframe, I watched as Benni removed her makeup and applied some sort of overnight magic cream that she swore kept away wrinkles.

When she finished, she rested one hip against the counter and crossed her arms over her chest. "What are you doing, McKenna? Why are you watching me like that?"

"I was just admiring the most beautiful creature I've ever laid my eyes on." It sounded pretty darned good to me, but it made Benni burst into laughter.

"Don't think you can be a stick-in-the-mud all night and then get lucky with one goofy compliment." She paused, bit her lower lip, and smiled. "You think I'm still pretty?"

I stepped forward and put my hands on her waist. "Yes. I do. And I will until the day I die."

She turned suddenly serious. "Do you ever...think about that?"

"Think about what?"

"Death. Dying. With all the murders you've investigated..." She quickly added, "I don't want anything to happen to you."

I wrapped my arms around her. Felt the rise and fall of her chest against mine. I never wanted this to end. But the truth was, we were twenty years apart, and, statistically, my death would occur long before hers.

"I think that's one reason this whole genealogical research thing is getting to me. Both my parents are gone now and I don't know what to expect because they never talked about other family members. I have no idea if I come from a family with good genes or bad."

"Good genes or bad? For real?"

"Yeah, what if I have an infidelity gene. Or I'm predisposed to be an ax murderer? Or..."

"Oh, stop it, McKenna. You need the facts before you start imagining all sorts of family mayhem. Try doing some actual research. It might help. I can understand you being scared. It's a big deal to dive into the unknown."

If only it were still unknown, but that stupid letter—I should just destroy it. Yes. Best idea of the night. Shred it and never tell a soul—even though I'd promised to tell all now.

Easing Benni away, I took a long, slow breath to quell the tension building inside me. There was an elephant in the room. Actually, two. And we were ignoring the largest one—Kenji's disappearance. Maybe it was best if we didn't talk more about that tonight.

"I'm less scared than I am angry," I said. "I'm angry with my parents for not telling me more. I'm angry because I never had grandparents hovering over me, spoiling me. I'm angry at myself because I never questioned their silence. I think that's the real reason I didn't want to go tonight. I…can't seem to get past…"

Benni slipped back into my arms. The feelings roiling inside me subsided and the tightness in my body softened.

"I wish you'd have told me before," she said. "I wouldn't have made you go."

"I'm sorry. You shouldn't have to deal with my baggage."

Holding my hands, she stepped back and gave me a you're-being-silly look. "Don't you see? Your baggage is my baggage now. Unless, of course, we're talking about airports. Then you can carry your own. And maybe one of mine."

We both laughed, and I suddenly felt stupid. Of course what she said was true. She couldn't, wouldn't, ignore my problems. Nor would I ignore hers. How did I not realize that sooner?

"You really do live with aloha, don't you?" I asked.

"Of course. Mrs. Nakamura drummed that into all of us in fourth grade. For me, it resonated. Maybe because my parents were so strict. And when I moved to the Big Island, our community was so filled with aloha that it just became my way of life. I tried to teach Andi to live the same way when she was growing up."

"You did a great job with her. I'm sure she's made you proud."

"She has. Her career in music is taking off." Benni's voice faltered. "I just wish she could be here for the wedding."

Uh oh. Make that three elephants. Kenji, the letter, and Andi. I could destroy the letter and Elephant #2 would simply disappear. But Andi, that was a real conundrum. I'd used every excuse in the book to keep us from hiring musicians. Short of telling Benni her daughter had secretly contacted me, was coming to the wedding, and wanted to sing for us, what could I do? I hadn't given up on keeping the secret, but it was becoming more difficult by the day.

Feigning forgetfulness, I said, "Oh that's right. She's on that national tour. Anyway, I'm sure she still carries a lot of aloha in her heart."

"I hope so."

I had to change the subject. And fast. "Living with aloha is hard for me. I chased deadbeats all my life, it's hard not to be cynical."

"You don't have to analyze it, McKenna. And you'll never be perfect at it. I make mistakes all the time. But as long as you try, that's all you can ask of yourself."

"Are we still talking about living with aloha?"

Benni gave me one of those half-smirk, half-shrug smiles that said, maybe not. "We might have gotten a little beyond that."

I waited, listening to my heart beat, all in an attempt to ignore Elephant #1. It didn't work. "I have a feeling this also has to do with Kenji Ito and his project."

"It does."

Looking around the room, I thought about the different directions my life could have taken. None measured up to this.

"What's going on, McKenna?"

"I was just trying to imagine what things would be like if I wasn't managing the Sunsetter Apartments. I wouldn't have this place. I never would have met your brother. He never would have introduced us."

"Life has a way of working itself out. This was all meant to be."

Meant to be. Did that mean what I think it did? I frowned and regarded myself in the mirror. I was a few inches taller than Benni, my slight frame a product of physiology rather than lifestyle. My brown eyes always reminded me of mud pools, perhaps because they masked what lay beneath—sometimes, even from myself. "Ever since I met you, I've felt like I've been on a journey of self-discovery, but that I'm only halfway there."

"We're all on that journey. It's just that most people don't realize it. At least you know you're heading somewhere."

"Like Kinohi Village?" I quipped and immediately realized I'd opened the door to let Elephant #1 roam the room.

A long silence settled between us. The lines of Benni's jaw tightened as she studied my face. After what felt like an eternity, she broke the silence. "Is all this coming out because you don't want to become involved?"

"What? No. Chance and I will do some digging tomorrow."

"You're sure?"

"Positive."

"That's a relief. Kenji's not the kind of man to miss something so important to one of his daughters. He told me about this time when the family was here on O'ahu and he was working construction on Kauai. Sue and her sister were in elementary school. They both had a school program during the same week, but on different days. Kenji flew back-and-forth every day that week so he could be there for each of them."

"So you're saying he's a reliable guy, and I shouldn't think he just took a night off."

"Finding out what happened to him is one of those things you can do for their family...for me...to show some aloha."

"Honolulu's a big city. There's a gazillion tourists here all the time. Do you have any suggestions about where Chance and I should begin?"

"Start at Kinohi Village. That's Kenji's baby. But, you and Chance need to beware. Some of the people out there won't be happy to have a couple of haoles showing up."

I sighed and watched the ceiling fan spin in lazy circles. Sometimes it felt like life did exactly the same thing. "Oh, perfect. Just what we need, angry locals. Been there, done that."

Benni slipped past me, turned the fan speed down to its lowest setting, and slid into bed. "I don't think they're angry so much as they're suspicious. You know how it is."

Did I ever. "Yah. I learned the hard way when I came here that racial stereotypes run strong in the islands. I'd never experienced that until I moved here. Now, though, I get it. All you have to do is read the history of how outside money transformed the islands."

"At least you came here with an open mind."

I turned off the light and we snuggled together, Benni resting her head on my shoulder while I simply enjoyed the moment. With a contented sigh, I whispered, "I love you."

"I love you, too."

Slivers of light peeked around the perimeter of the blinds at the window's edge. Overhead, the ceiling fan continued it's lazy, counterclockwise circles. My eyelids drifted shut. Finally, I was at peace.

Fingertips came to rest on my stomach. I gasped. Benni's hand inched lower.

"You're my haole," she cooed. "And I don't hate you."

Holy cow, if this was what it meant to live with aloha, sign me up as a true believer.

4

I AWOKE JUST BEFORE SIX to the sound of slippahs clip-clopping along the concrete walkway outside our bedroom window. To the rest of the world slippahs are known as flip-flops. Their popularity varies widely, but in Hawaii they're a footwear staple. It took a few months for me to get used to the idea of almost never wearing real shoes, but once I adapted, I realized my feet were much happier. The other upside to slippahs is they make it a lot easier to follow the island custom of removing your shoes when entering someone's home.

Benni had already made a pot of coffee and was sitting on the back lānai by the time I was out of the shower. I poured myself a mug and went to join her. The screen door opened, but the track felt rough. The pitch of Benni's voice rose an octave as she slipped into a little Pidgin.

"Hey, Mr. Apartment Manager, you gotta do da kine maintenance. Yah?"

I chuckled, then knelt down to inspect the track and located the spot where a few grains of sand and a tiny bit of corrosion were causing the friction. I knew what I had to do. Standing, I gave Benni a kiss and sat next to her. "You're in a good mood this morning, I'll clean and lube it today. Feels like I'm doing that every week now."

"Stop complaining. I saw you had it marked on the calendar before I came out here. And it's been more than a month, not a week."

"I should be able to get to it this afternoon. Chance and I will go to Kinohi Village first thing, then I've got a prospective tenant for number six."

The trade winds caressed my face. I breathed in the salty air, letting it fill my lungs as if it were a magic elixir. Beyond the lānai, a wide stretch of sandy beach led to a deep-blue ocean dotted with whitecaps. Truly, paradise.

We spent the next half hour finishing our coffee and having breakfast, which consisted of some fresh fruit and a couple of gluten-free muffins. For me, 'going gluten-free' wasn't trendy or hip. I'd done it because I had to. Celiac disease was an ever-present complication in my life, one that I'd learned to live with.

Shortly before eight, Benni tried calling Kenji and got no answer. She left for work a few minutes later. On her way to her car, she said good morning to someone. A few seconds later, there was a triple knock on the door and Chance entered without waiting for an invite.

"Howzit, McKenna?" He waved his hand in a shaka sign, his thumb and pinky extended, the middle fingers folded over.

I handed him a mug of coffee and cocked my head toward the dining table. "Have a seat. Benni has a client meeting on the North Shore."

He took a healthy drink from his mug and gave me a thumbs up. "Not a fun drive at this hour."

"I would never do it."

"That's because you don't drive."

"Exactly. I suppose if somebody held a gun to my head I might."

"Only might?" Chance grinned.

I recognized that look. He wasn't going to let this go. And neither was I. "I'd have to think about whether it was worth it."

Chance cradled the mug in his hands and pursed his lips. "You're right. You'd definitely have to consider how many lives would be at stake. And I don't mean yours. What about the poor people you might run down? Or the guy with the gun? He'd probably shoot you just to stop the car."

I gave him a mock glare, mostly because he seemed extra sharp this morning. "You know what? You can be a real pain sometimes."

"I learned from the best." Chance winked and downed what was left in the mug. He cocked his head toward the front door. "Ready to roll?"

"Definitely. By the way, I need to be back here by eleven. I have an appointment with a prospective tenant."

"Then what are we waiting for? Get your stuff and let's go."

The drive to Kinohi Village was uneventful. Well, as uneventful as you can get when you're riding in a bright red 1984 Ferrari 308 GTS with the top down and the exhaust rumbling. The Ferrari definitely made a statement—*I'm here, and I have money*. It seemed like an odd statement to make on the way to a project to house the homeless.

"Have you thought about getting rid of this car?" I asked.

"I'm not ready yet. It's such a great machine."

"And the kind that was driven by your idol."

He sneered at me, downshifted, and goosed the gas to blast through a yellow light. When he eased off the accelerator, he said, "That has nothing to do with it. It's a great car."

"You're repeating yourself, Chance. Great machine. Great car. If I didn't know you better, I'd say you were grasping at straws."

"I admit I had a Magnum fetish when I got here, but that's done." He huffed, then added, "I've matured."

"Right. That's why you've started showing up late for everything."

"It's a personal thing. Don't worry about it." Chance came to a stop before the entrance, which was blocked by a small army of people carrying signs. "Holy smokes."

"What's all this?" I asked.

"Read the signs. They're protesting against the project."

"Duh. That was a stupid question. What I meant was, how are we going to get through?"

"Like this." Chance nosed the Ferrari into the crowd.

The sign-wielders weren't happy with our intrusion, but with the exception of one man, they parted to let us pass. The one, however, a man with a receding hairline and a scraggly goatee, stood in front of the car glaring at us. "Take your money and go home, haoles."

"Isn't that just the pot calling the kettle black? That guy's as white as you or me." I was tempted to stand up and shout at him about learning to live with aloha. Then again, that wasn't the best way to make the point.

"It's cool, McKenna. Chillax."

Chance maintained eye contact as he inched the Ferrari forward. The other guy must have decided his legs were more valuable to him than his ego and moved aside. Thirty seconds later we were past the human roadblock, but engulfed in a plethora of construction noises, the loudest being the backhoe to our right with its diesel engine and constant beeping every time it moved.

I took another look over my shoulder at the protestors. "Benni said there were people out here who didn't like haoles. I wonder if those are the ones she was talking about."

Chance pulled the Ferrari to a stop and shook his head. "I don't think so."

"Now what?" I asked as I turned to face forward. "Oh, crap."

A burly man wearing a yellow hardhat scowled at us from the front end of the Ferrari. The pair of two-by-fours he carried over his shoulder seemed more like toothpicks than construction material. From the way he was pointing at us and barking in Pidgin, he was not a guy used to being ignored.

"I don't think the nudging forward trick is going to work with him," I said.

Chance shook his head. "Not unless I want a new hood ornament."

The backhoe shifted into idle, the decibel level dropped, and the void was filled by an orchestra made up of construction equipment. A whining table saw filled in for the string section; pounding hammers provided the percussion; the list went on and on.

I returned my attention to the two-by-four guy. He was big, but I'd bet Chance was faster. I chuckled. "You can take him."

Chance hung his head and closed his eyes. "Let's try and do this peacefully. Okay?"

"Fine by me. But since this little adventure was your idea, you can talk to him."

"No way. We're doing this because you roped me into attending that meeting. This is your fault. You go. If he beats you to a pulp, I'll come rescue you."

"Roped you…" My comeback was cut short, first by the backhoe, then by the big guy jerking his thumb in the direction of a trailer about fifty feet away.

"Hey! You two! Dis hardhat area!"

"He wants you to park over there." I pointed at the empty spaces in front of a construction trailer.

As we passed the worker, Chance called to him. "Mahalo, brah."

"Stupid haoles," the man grumbled, then turned and stormed away.

"Just when I thought you were making friends," I said.

We made it to the trailer without further incident, but on the way my phone buzzed with a message from Benni.

"What's up?" Chance asked.

"Benni called Sue and told her we were going to be here. Sue recommended we talk to Julie Edgeworth. She's the project manager."

"Did she say where we'd find this project manager?"

"The project trailer, maybe?"

"You're a riot, McKenna."

"Come on, let's see if someone can point us in the right direction."

We exited the Ferrari, which was already more dusty rose than red, and started toward the door. At the base of the stairs, Chance stopped and regarded me.

"For the record, we are not beating up anybody while we're here." He turned and went up a couple of stairs.

27

"It was only a suggestion," I muttered, then gave him a mock karate chop to the back of the neck.

"I saw that, McKenna."

"Jeez, some people have no sense of humor," I grumbled under my breath.

"Heard that, too."

I kept my mouth shut and my hands to myself as we entered the trailer.

5

THE INSIDE OF THE TRAILER was a model of utilitarian functionality. The furniture, an unqualified success in the no-frills department, consisted of two gray metal desks with laminate tops, mismatched chairs with worn seat cushions, and filing cabinets straight out of a World War II war room.

A woman wearing a pale blue tank top and snug jeans emerged from the back room. She carried a white hardhat with the name Edgeworth stenciled on label-maker tape. Still peering at us as though we were lost and needing directions, she laid the hardhat on a nearby desk. "Can I help you?"

"My name is Chance Logan. This is my associate."

I extended my hand. "McKenna. And you are?"

She did a double take and shook my hand. "Julie Edgeworth. Are you Benni Kapono's fiancé?"

"I am."

"Benni's been a strong supporter of the project since the beginning," she said with a smile. "She's a delight."

29

"I feel the same way about her." I gushed, then switched to a more businesslike tone. "I'll tell her you said that."

"Has she told you what the project's all about?"

"To some degree. A way to keep families from having to live on the streets."

"Actually, this is more of a holistic approach. Not only do the residents get housing at a fixed rate, but we have enough contacts in the community so that nearby businesses are hiring those who need jobs. We have on-site day care. And the residents have neighbors they can trust. It is, quite literally, a village."

"I understand you've had inquiries from the mainland about how this project can be duplicated elsewhere," Chance said.

Julie seemed impressed and pleased that at least one of us had done our homework. Maybe more than pleased. There it was —the playing with the hair, the longing gaze—she was captivated by Chance's attention.

"We have." She beamed up at Mr. Tall, Fair, and Handsome. "Benni's told me all about you two and your adventures."

Chance gave her an aw-shucks shoulder shrug, then turned on the brilliant smile. "I hope what she told you was good."

"It was." Julie's cheeks brightened, but she seemed to realize we'd veered way off topic. "How can I help?"

"We've been asked by Sue Ito to help find her father," I said. "Benni told us we should talk to you."

Julie blew out a breath. Her eyes ping-ponged between us, and when she spoke her tone was somber. "Kenji hasn't been around here since yesterday morning. The last thing I knew, he said he was going to Sue's presentation that night. He's so proud of all the work she did researching the family tree. He wasn't there?"

"He never made it," Chance said.

Julie tilted her head to one side and scrunched up her face. "Something must have come up. I wish I had more to offer."

"How long have you known Kenji?" I asked.

"About six months. He's a good boss. I owe him a lot. If it wasn't for him, me and my family would be on the streets for sure. I was laid off from a previous job." She stopped and sighed, then continued. "Even with my degree in accounting the only work I could find didn't pay nearly enough to feed our family."

"The islands are tough," I said.

"I'm one of the lucky ones. Most of my friends work two or three jobs. My husband does that. We didn't have much to start with, and we'd burned through all our savings by the time I started here." She cocked a hip against one of the desks, crossed her arms over her chest, and surveyed the room. "This office may not look like much, but it's been my family's lifeline."

To my side, Chance was making agreement noises. Not that he'd ever known a day of poverty. Chance was a trust-fund baby. He'd never know hard times unless he went broke buying fancy toys. But, he had done some local charity work, which might be where he'd learned about the less-privileged side of society.

"What were you doing before this?" I asked.

"Some construction, waitressing, anything I could to bring in money. Kenji took a huge chance on me. I hope that when this project finishes, he'll keep me on."

I pointed to a photo at the end of the desk she was using as a hip rest. Julie, two young girls, and a man sat on the steps of a treehouse. "Is that your family?"

A smile lit up her face when she gazed at the photo. "My husband and the girls. Those are our front steps. Our house isn't much, but the rent is good. The neighbors get kinda noisy at times."

31

I inspected the photo more closely. The house appeared to be in the middle of a rainforest. "Neighbors? It doesn't look like you would have any."

Julie laughed. "We call them neighbors. Mostly chickens and birds, but we have some feral cats, too. The nearest people are down the road and we never hear them."

Since we'd entered the office, I'd seen nothing that would help us find Kenji. There were no personal items or photos other than Julie's. This was turning into a major dead end, and I had a prospective tenant meeting in just over an hour. It was time to see if we could salvage this trip. "You have no idea where Kenji might be?"

"I wish. I've got some questions for him about the project."

"Like how to keep your workers busy?"

Chance didn't appear happy with my pointed question, but Julie laughed.

"Oh no." She waved a hand toward the trailer window. Outside, workers milled around like ants swarming a scrap of food. "Most of these guys are from companies that are donating materials and services. They know exactly what they're here to do. We also have volunteers out there. Some of them are tenants who've already been able to move in. In fact, our volunteer coordinator is due back in a few minutes. What goes on inside the project isn't the problem."

"Those guys out front?" I asked.

"Yah. Our big problem is what to do about them. They affect the public perception. At first it was just one guy, but it keeps growing. Pretty soon, we might not be able to get supplies in. I don't think any of the crew will quit no matter what goes on out front. They're like me. We all need the money and the benefits too much."

Through the window, I could see the line of protestors. The guy who had blocked our way wasn't in view, but I'd bet he was still there. "One in particular was very aggressive. I think his sign said, Riffraff Go Home or something like that."

"Receding hairline? About forty? Perpetual scowl?"

"That's the one. What's his problem?" Chance said as he ran his fingers absently over the edge of the desk.

"His name's Graham Tynsdale. He's the organizer. Kenji calls him a professional activist. I call him a sign for hire, but the bottom line is he's a jerk."

"Are you saying he's getting paid to picket?" I asked.

"We're pretty sure. He's protested other causes. Kenji said he'd like to hire an investigator, but I told him he should save his money. What's it matter why the guy's here? He's got a right to free speech. You know, all that good stuff."

"Being paid to exercise your right to free speech seems a bit of an oxymoron, but then, money does make the world go round. Is there anyone else we could talk to? Maybe some of the workers? Residents?"

"Why would you want to do that?" Julie snapped.

Whoa. Talk about a short fuse.

"Sometimes those random pieces of information turn out to be helpful," Chance said.

It was the first time Julie had exhibited anything other than friendly cooperation. Then again, maybe the friendly attitude had just been an act. "Chance is right," I said casually. "It could be helpful."

Julie's jaw tightened, then relaxed. "Okay. Missy Jonson is headed this way. She's our liaison with the tenants. Maybe she can tell you something. She's also a good example of how people get here."

As if on cue, the door opened and a petite woman entered. She was around thirty, had the dark hair and eyes that dominate the islands, and wore a sling carrier on her chest in which a miniature person wearing a pink sunbonnet was napping. When Missy looked our way, she did a double take. She and Chance eyed each other until Julie broke the silence.

"Missy, these men are trying to find Kenji."

My curiosity was killing me. It was almost as though she knew Chance. Stepping forward, I said, "My name's McKenna. This is my associate Chance Logan. Do you two know each other?"

Missy snuck a peek at Chance, flushed, then gave me a friendly smile. "We've never actually met. I only know him as one of the food bank guys." Her gaze flicked past me to settle on Chance. "Thanks for being a volunteer there."

"It's no problem. I like to help out where I can."

Was that where Chance had been lately? Doing volunteer work? In the past, if he talked about his role, he always downplayed it. But last night, he'd let slip he'd been invited to join the board. Another mystery? From the way he was fidgeting, it was as though Missy had revealed some sort of embarrassing secret. I suddenly realized I'd just learned something new about my former movie-star friend—he was more comfortable on the silver screen than he was in the spotlight of personal attention.

Julie asked Missy to tell us her background and explain her role as coordinator. Missy seemed perfectly comfortable telling us she'd divorced her husband about a year ago, had four kids, and that her husband stopped paying child support when he left Hawaii. She'd turned to living on the streets after being evicted from her apartment.

She stroked the back of her little girl's head and laughed. "My ex's final contribution. When he found out I was pregnant again, he said he was leaving."

"That's why you divorced him? Because he left?" I asked.

"He wasn't much help anyway."

The deadbeat dad. Got it. "I'm sure being a single mom is challenging, but at least here you've found a future."

"What happened to me could've happened to anybody. I want to be a good mom and provide for my kids, but between rent, utilities, and daycare, it's more than I make. All it takes is one little thing. Yah?"

"The director told me your story one day," Chance said. "McKenna, Missy's being kind to her ex. She's better off without him."

Missy took a few deep breaths and her jaw tightened. "I won't lie. Things were rough for a while. They're better now."

Sensing that Missy would prefer to move on to a new subject, I said, "Let's hope you can get back on your feet now that you're living here. Julie told us you had a bit of a run-in with Graham Tynsdale?"

She peered at me for a minute, then recognition dawned on her face. "Oh, the protestor guy." Her little one stirred; Missy responded with a soft cooing and pressed her lips to the baby's head. "I don't know what I can tell you other than he's a nasty man. He accused me of stealing from the system just because I'm living here." She gritted her teeth and took a long breath. "Sorry. The whole thing was very upsetting. Personally, I think that guy is unstable."

Other than revealing something about Chance's inner philanthropist, the conversation with Missy wasn't much more productive than the one with Julie. Both were overly positive in their praise of Kenji, which, in my opinion, was useless because it meant they were trying to protect him. The question was, from what? Back in my skip tracing days, I'd learned perfect people didn't simply disappear. They stuck around and dealt with the bad things in life. What we needed was someone who knew Kenji's other side. Someone who would give us the dirt. Like one of those workers milling around outside.

We might get nothing new, but we wouldn't know until we spoke to some of them. There had to be something that would lead us to Kenji, even if it was the sort of dirt his supporters wanted to keep hidden. What we needed was someone like the two-by-four guy. There's no way he'd sugarcoat his thoughts about Kenji, assuming he had any. And providing he didn't try to beat up the haoles just for entertainment, it was worth a try.

6

IT WAS NEARING TEN WHEN Chance and I followed Julie out of the office and into the work area. We'd been equipped with hardhats and a stern warning to stay close for our own safety. But the truth was, not being able to wander freely made me want to do exactly that. With only about twenty minutes before we needed to leave for my tenant meeting, we were short on time and opportunities to make this trip worthwhile.

Julie guided us around the perimeter of the active construction, prattling on with Chance about the value of Kinohi Village while I tuned out their conversation. Off to our left, two carpenters were doing repairs on one of the homes. One of the men was the two-by-four guy. Between the construction noise and animated discussion going on next to me, it wasn't easy to make out their words, but I was sure I heard the two-by-four guy complaining about someone not showing up for work that morning.

Before I could say anything, Julie made an abrupt turn into a nearly completed section of the village. I was beginning to feel we were getting something akin to a timeshare sales pitch instead of the opportunity to speak with any sort of valuable information source. The feeling grew stronger when Julie introduced us to a plumbing contractor who was finishing installation of a kitchen faucet. He worked for a small company, one I'd used myself the last time I needed a plumber. But, for the life of me, I couldn't figure out why we were talking to him. Sure, he'd heard of Kenji. Yes, he'd met him a couple of times. No, he had no idea Kenji was even missing.

When Julie said we could talk to one of the painters, I explained that I needed to leave. Chance hemmed and hawed, claiming we had plenty of time. I countered that I had something else I needed to do on the way back.

Chance huffed and rolled his eyes, but acquiesced. "Okay, McKenna. I'll run you home. I can always come back later."

"No worries," Julie said. "Just be sure to check in with me when you get here."

We promised to return our hardhats to the office, which seemed to satisfy Julie. She turned back to the plumber and began coordinating the schedule for two of the other homes. Rather than going back the way Julie had brought us, we followed a pathway through several of the homes where a crew was busy installing landscape irrigation.

"McKenna," Chance whispered. "Have you got a few extra minutes? We could talk to those guys."

"I've got time, but they're a waste. We don't need contractors. They just work for a company and show up wherever they're told to go. We need to talk to the ones who don't have everything filtered by a third party."

We stopped at a junction where the sidewalk went straight and a dirt path led to the right. Chance checked over his shoulder and snorted. "Gotcha. Julie the Gatekeeper."

"Exactly. I'm sure she's only trying to protect her boss, but that's not going to help us. Let's try the guys on the construction crew."

Chance seemed to catch my drift and shook his head. "Oh, no, McKenna. We are not searching for that guy who was yelling at us when we came in."

"We don't have to. He's right over there!" I darted off the paved walkway and followed the dirt path into the construction melee. The two men had finished and were gathering up their tools when I approached.

The two-by-four guy spotted me and pointed his finger. "Hey! You. You can't be here. Construction area. No visitors."

I raised my hands and slowed my pace. "I come in peace. We're investigating the disappearance of Kenji Ito. As we were walking by, I overheard one of you say someone didn't show up for work today. Were you talking about Kenji?"

Instead of getting an answer from either of them, the two-by-four guy signaled his partner, the one I'd started to think might even answer the question, to pack up their tools. The man ignored us and did as he'd been told. The two-by-four guy let out a disgusted snort, then said, "We don't know nothing about da big boss. Now beat it. We got work to do."

Chance, who had been inching up next to me, took hold of my sleeve. "Sorry, guys. My friend gets a little carried away. Let's go, McKenna. We're not welcome here."

The second man perked up at the mention of my name. He closed the lid on the toolbox and stood. "Wait a minute.

McKenna? I heard that name before. You know Alexander Kapono?"

"He's my fiancée's brother."

A smile replaced the scowl on the man's face. "Hey, Mondo, this guy's okay. He worked with my cousin. They had some big adventure solving a murder. How you doing, brah? I'm Freddie. This here's Mondo."

While Freddie had gone all fanboy, Mondo didn't appear quite as impressed. He wasn't overly friendly, but he was no longer hostile. I handed each of them a business card. "Just in case either of you think of something else. Or need an apartment."

Freddie read the card and his head bobbed up and down. "Awesome, brah."

"So who didn't show up today?" I asked.

"Third guy on our team," Freddie said.

Mondo pocketed the card without even glancing at it and grumbled, "He got fired."

"That's the word," Freddie added. "I heard Kenji got rid of him 'cause he was making noise about how this whole project was a way for the company to make some big bucks."

Mondo signified his agreement with a thumbs-up. "Da big boss is ruthless."

That could be a natural consequence of running a big company. Or…I craned my neck forward, letting my gaze drift between them. "Was he ruthless enough for someone to want to do him harm?"

The two men exchanged a glance, but it was Freddie who answered. "He got some enemies. Some people don't like him." He snuck a peek at Chance, then one at the Ferrari. His face lit up and he smiled at us. "I heard you was working with some

40

haole who drove a red Ferrari. If you guys are involved, this must be some kinda murder investigation or something. Yah?"

I held up my hands again. "Let's not jump to conclusions, Freddie. It's too soon for that. We're just trying to find out what happened and why Kenji's gone missing. That's all. What's it like working here?"

"Don't tell nobody I said this, but it's getting kinda tense around here," Freddie said. "I ain't never felt like I been under so much pressure. They say they don't want nobody cutting corners, but one guy got hurt on the job 'cause of that."

"What happened?" I asked.

Freddie exchanged another of those who's-going-to-go-first looks with Mondo, then inched closer and lowered his voice. "Guy got electrocuted 'cause there was power on where there wasn't supposed to be. Another time, a water valve got left open. Place flooded and most of us couldn't work for a couple days."

"Why do you think those things happened?" I asked.

"Somebody not paying attention. I got a cousin works for Tommy West. There ain't nothing like that going on over there. I asked my cousin to see if he could get me on, but they don't got no openings right now." Something behind us must have caught Freddie's attention because his smile fell. "Uh oh."

"I can't afford to get fired. I got a wife and baby to support," Mondo growled. He jabbed his finger in my direction, then jerked his thumb over his shoulder. "You two, dis construction area. We don't need no haoles messing in island business!"

Mondo hadn't finished his tirade when Julie began yelling at us. "Mr. McKenna! You can't be here!"

"Just leaving," I called back, then mouthed a silent mahalo and darted away with Chance right behind me. Julie followed us like a yappy little dog all the way to the office. After dropping off our hardhats and escaping Julie's wrath, I told Chance I really did need to get back to the Sunsetter Apartments. We made our exit, all the while under Julie's watchful eye.

On the way home, I tried getting Chance to open up about his volunteer work, but he carefully avoided answering by countering with questions about the case. I finally gave up and we discussed what our next move should be. The bottom line was, we weren't sure and needed time to regroup. Our mood remained somber for the rest of the trip.

We pulled into the parking lot a few minutes late. I promised to touch base with Chance after my tenant meeting, then hurried toward my apartment. As I was passing a planter bed covered in lava rock, I noticed two small stones had somehow strayed onto the walkway. I bent down, picked them up, and tossed them back into their respective places.

Still hoping I'd beat the new tenant here, I double-timed it the rest of the way, but a man wearing a ratty tank top and shorts was already pacing in front of my door. "Aloha," I called out. "I'm McKenna, the manager."

When the smell of marijuana hit me, it was so overpowering I thought it might knock me off my feet—or send me on a little day trip myself. Holy cow, this guy was loaded. From a substance that was illegal in Hawaii.

The man wrinkled his nose at the sight of my extended hand and stuffed his hands under his armpits. "Don't do that. DNA."

Talk about feeling socially awkward. I pulled my hand back and muttered, "Excuse me?"

"No touching. Might transfer DNA. Could get collected."

This guy spoke faster than the rat-a-tat-tat of a machine-gun. He was loaded and looneytunes. He'd never fit in at the Sunsetter

Apartments. Not on my watch, anyway. I had to get rid of him. Fast.

"Of course," I said cautiously. "You're...Mr. Smith?"

"Right. That's right. Smith."

"Well, Mr. Smith, are you familiar with the laws regarding possession of marijuana in Hawaii? I'm afraid..."

Smith cut me off with another machine-gun volley of words. "Got an exemption. Organization I work for is above local laws. Special rights. Privileges."

Correction. Loaded, looneytunes, and delusional. "Mr. Smith, this isn't going to work out. I'm sorry."

The staccato in his voice became even more choppy. Almost indignant. "Can't stop me. Rent where I want."

The hairs on the back of my neck bristled. I was not taking orders from this clown. "Really? Well, you haven't even filled out an application yet, Mr. Smith. If that's even your name."

Smith's attention darted in several directions before it settled back on me. "Identity. Must protect it. People watching."

Oh, he wanted to play hardball? If Mr. Smith wasn't going to take a simple no, and if refusal to rent wasn't going to rid me of him, I had a secret weapon. It was time for McKenna's Skip Tracing Secret #2, *When in doubt, lie.* "So you work for a super-secret government organization and need to remain anonymous. Yah?"

"All secret. Can't discuss."

The nice thing about paranoia is that it feeds on itself. And I had just the burner to turn up the heat. I pulled back from Smith to suck in some clean air, then moved a little closer and whispered, "You're a spy?"

Smith's eyes darted everywhere. He couldn't seem to focus for more than a millisecond.

I waved my arm in a wide circle to indicate the apartment complex. "We have all the big organizations represented here at the Sunsetter, Mr. Smith. It's kind of like spy central. We've got the CIA, FBI…KGB."

"KGB? No. Disbanded."

I made a big show of checking for eavesdroppers, then shook my head and whispered, "You fell for that? That's exactly what they want us to think, Mr. Smith. By the way, we've even got an old lady here who's a deep cover Mossad agent."

Smith began to back away, the fear on his face obvious. I almost wanted to feel sorry for him, but I was now in the groove. I raised my voice so he would be sure to hear me. "She looks Japanese, but that's only her cover. She's really Israeli."

Smith broke into something resembling an off-balance, not-able-to-think-straight run.

"It's a terrific job of cosmetic alteration!" I called after him as he ran toward the parking lot.

I breathed a sigh of relief. With Smith gone, the air felt fresh and clean again. And, with Smith most likely out of my life forever, I felt positively jubilant—until a woman cleared her throat behind me.

"Mr. McKenna. Am I the one of whom you were speaking?"

I spun around, faced Mrs. Nakamura, and tried, unsuccessfully, to bury my fear. The old bat had always scared me, but for the first time since we'd met, I wondered if there might have been a nugget of truth in my lie. Maybe she really was a Mossad agent.

7

MOST OF MY DAYS ARE actually quite boring. The next hour, in fact, was filled with the bane of our modern existence, paperwork. So, when my phone lit up with a call from Benni, I was delighted. At least, until we got to the reason she'd called.

"It turns out my cousin just got hired on out here," Benni said. "We got a chance to talk and when I told him about the wedding, he offered to provide the entertainment. He and his sister do a lot of weddings up here on the North Shore. They're very good. What do you think?"

Uh…how about, it's a terrible idea? How did I stop this without saying, your daughter wants to surprise you by flying in for the wedding? And without revealing Andi had changed her travel dates on an international tour to be here? Or that Andi's visit was a surprise wedding present? "I thought you wanted something more…professional."

"They are professional. They're booked solid for the next few months, but he said they'd find a way to fit us in. He plays

45

guitar and they both sing. This will help us to keep things small and intimate, just like we wanted."

I sat on the couch watching the ocean through the screen door. The trades were blowing at a leisurely pace, filling the apartment with the scent of the ocean. If only the solution was something simple like opening a window to air out a stuffy apartment. I ran my hand through my hair. Time. I needed time to figure this out.

"What's wrong, McKenna?"

What was wrong? Plenty. This little development had the potential to derail Andi's trip to Hawaii. The only thing I could do was come up with a way to buy time—or call Benni's cousin and explain the situation.

"If you think they'll do a good job for us, let's get them booked. Why don't you get me a number so I can finalize details with them?"

"That's not a problem. I'll see him again this afternoon and take care of it. Are you sure you're okay with this? You don't sound okay."

Why was it Benni could always see through my facade? "I'm fine. I just had a run-in with Mrs. Nakamura."

"Oh my God, Auntie's a sweet old lady. What did you do to her now?"

What did I do? Why did this have to be my fault? "Technically, I didn't do anything to her."

"You didn't answer my question."

Crap. Cornered. Benni and Mrs. Nakamura weren't related, but here in the islands, it was customary to refer to an elder in one of two ways. I chose the formal approach, a choice I'd made because my own fourth-grade teacher had scared me to death. Benni, on the other hand, had been one of the old bag's star students and still fondly recalled her days in class. Now on a first name basis, Benni called her old teacher Auntie Asuka and they got along famously.

"Let's just say I might have had to exaggerate her...um... status."

"Status? What status?"

"We can talk about this later. It's not a big deal."

"What are you not telling me? And why are you being so evasive?"

Avoidance was only making things worse; I had to deal with this. Now. "Well...um...you remember that prospective tenant meeting I had this morning?"

"I take it things did not go well?"

"The guy was pretty wacko."

Benni's voice rose a half octave as she started rattling off questions. The only two I understood clearly were, "Did he get violent? Did he hurt Auntie?"

"Nothing like that," I said. "There's nothing wrong with Mrs. Nakamura, and she's not moving."

"Not moving?" Benni exploded. "What did you do?"

I swallowed hard, took a breath, and dove in. "This guy tried telling me he worked for some super-secret government organization. He was going on about how nobody could know his real name or that he lived here. There was no way I could rent to him. He'd upset the other tenants the minute they met him. So I might have tried to leverage his fear."

There was a long pause, during which I watched a small wave crawl toward shore. When she spoke, Benni's tone was firm.

"How exactly did you exert this leverage?"

"I might have told him we had a few spies living here."

"Might have?"

"Okay, I told him we had spies from a bunch of different agencies. I also told him we even had an old woman who looked Japanese, but was really a Mossad agent."

Benni remained silent for a few seconds, then laughed. "Where do you come up with this stuff, McKenna?"

"It was…an educated guess."

"And Auntie overheard your—explanation?"

"She snuck up behind me."

"Really? You're going with an eighty-year-old woman wearing slippahs snuck up behind you and you didn't hear her?"

"She's a ninja, I tell you!"

Benni sighed, then said, "I have to go. Try not to irritate any of the other tenants today, would you? I'll talk to Auntie tonight and smooth things over."

After we said our goodbyes, I sat for a few minutes watching the waves roll in. There was still time to work on the screen door track, but I needed lunch first. If all went well, I could have the door done before the sun started beating down on the lānai. While I prepared a salad, a piece of fruit, and a muffin for lunch, I considered going over to talk with Mrs. Nakamura. I was the apartment manager. Why should Benni have to shield me from my own tenants?

I'd definitely screwed up. Had gotten carried away with my own lie and pushed it too far. I resolved to march over there, tell the truth, and apologize—after lunch. And maybe after the screen door.

Before I could get to either of those, though, the landline rang. It was an unknown number, which usually meant it was a rental inquiry. "Sunsetter Apartments, McKenna speaking."

A deep voice growled through the line. "You the guy left the card at Kinohi Village?"

My throat went dry immediately. This wasn't Freddie. And it wasn't Mondo. "I am."

"You want to know about Kenji Ito, be at the Airport Tavern tonight at six. Come alone."

"I don't know where that is."

"You'll find it if you want the information."

I moved quickly to the kitchen counter, yanked a pad from the basket along with a pen, and wrote down the name of the tavern while I spoke. "How do I know if this will be worth my time? What kind of information have you got?"

"You wanted dirt on Ito? I can give you lots."

"Like what?" I shot back. If I could keep this guy talking, he might tell me everything without me even needing to go see him.

"Like why he fired Joe Taylor. And because you got nosey, bring a hundred in cash."

The line went dead. It was so tempting to dial him back and press for more details. Not that he'd talk for free—I doubted if he ever intended to. Why waste my breath? He'd called the time and place. It could be the break Chance and I needed to get the real story on Kenji. And hopefully, find him. I dialed Chance's number.

8

WHILE I WAITED FOR CHANCE to arrive, I checked the reverse directory for my mystery caller's phone number. There was nothing. Which meant the guy was smarter than I'd thought. When Chance arrived, I recapped the conversation. He was, of course, eager to take action.

"So that phone number's for a burner?"

"Most likely. I can't tell for sure, but the reverse number lookup was a bust. He sounded like a shady character."

Chance's head moved up and down as he seemed to come to some sort of decision. "Normal people don't need burners."

"Right again. We can call it da kine unusual, yah?"

"Totally. I agree that this could be helpful, but I also think we shouldn't rule out the basics."

"Follow the money," I said.

"Exactly. Mr. Marlowe always says if it's not about love, it's about money. So unless Kenji's wife decided to get rid of him, his disappearance is most likely related to money."

It had been quite a while since Chance had quoted the mysterious Mr. Phillip Marlowe—not Chandler's fictional detective, but the man who ran the agency Chance hoped would eventually get him his private investigator's license. I'd given up on the idea of convincing my friend that the Phillip Marlowe Online Detective Agency was a scam, and instead had learned to accept the nuggets of wisdom from this metaphysical mentor, which were sometimes even helpful.

"This doesn't have to be an either-or proposition, Chance. Let's not rule out any options yet. The money angle is good. It could give us some insight on how legit Kenji was. And I think I know the perfect person to check that out—Benni."

"I like that. She's savvy, has access, but will she do it?"

"Let's find out." I dialed Benni's number, got voicemail, and left a message. "I'll ask when she calls back. What about this meeting tonight? Are you interested?"

"Of course, but he said to come alone. Right?"

"Those were the instructions. He also said to bring a hundred bucks. I was thinking I could meet him on my own, but you stay nearby."

Chance got a distant look in his eyes as he considered the situation. "Okay. I'm good with that. I'll get Lexie and we can double date for dinner. We'll wait outside if you need any help."

My phone rang. It was Benni returning my call. "Sounds good to me," I said just before I tapped the screen to answer. "How's it going up there on the North Shore?"

"I'm on my way back." Benni spoke loudly. In the background, I heard the steady drone of road noise.

"When do you think you'll be here?" I asked.

"According to the GPS it should only take me another thirty-four minutes, but you know how that goes."

I did. We'd played this game before, trying to outguess the GPS. The humans lost unless something happened en route. "You okay if we go to dinner with Chance and Lexie tonight?"

"Sure. What's the occasion?"

"We have a lead on Kenji. I'll tell you more later. But I also have a request for you to do something. Chance and I think we should be following the money."

"What money?"

"We've heard conflicting stories about how much Kenji was making off Kinohi Village. The stories could be nothing more than rumors, but to be thorough…"

I let the words hang in the air, but the response I got wasn't what I expected.

"I don't have time to talk about this right now. I'm going into the tunnel. I spoke to Auntie and…"

The call ended abruptly. Before I even laid down the phone, there was a knock at the front door.

"Yoohoo, Mr. McKenna?"

It felt like I could no longer breathe when Chance stood to greet our visitor. I shook my head and waved at him.

"It's Mrs. Nakamura," I hissed. "Don't…" But it was too late. He'd already exchanged greetings and was opening the screen door. I was doomed. What had Benni not told me? I did the only thing I could do. Stand, smile, make nice. "Aloha, Mrs. Nakamura. Come on in."

Her flowered muumuu, typical attire for the old woman, ruffled in the gentle breeze. She clutched a worn cloth bag from Hilo Hattie's in her arms and the bottoms of her feet barely made a sound as she walked, barefoot, across the entryway tile. "How fortuitous that I caught both of you at the same time. Young

Chance, you will be needing this information, too, I think. Are you not planning on marrying Miss Ashbrook soon?"

Just when I thought I might be off the hook, Mrs. Nakamura tossed a crooked smile at Chance, pivoted quietly, and skewered me with her teacher-knows-best stare. I was in fourth grade all over again, paralyzed by fear and awaiting death by embarrassment. The most humane thing I could do for myself was to get my punishment over.

"I'm so sorry about what I said earlier." My voice came out sounding more like a squeaky screen door than that of an adult.

A smile spread across the old lady's thin lips and she waved her hand in front of her face. "Do not be silly. It was nothing."

How could it be nothing? We were talking about the queen of rules and etiquette. The woman who had schooled more island keiki than you could count. "But Benni said she talked to you and…and, now you're here…"

Her laugh sent more chills through my spine. It was one of those devious, evil, I'm-going-to-eat-your-flesh laughs. The kind villains spend years perfecting.

"Mr. McKenna, you have quite the guilty conscience. I found your antics very entertaining. In fact, I found your description most amusing." She paused and reached into the Hilo Hattie's bag. "Quite the imagination," she mused as she rummaged around. Suddenly, her eyes lit up and she pulled out a brochure and shoved it in my direction.

I looked down at the bony hand. The talons clutched a glossy trifold brochure. I could almost smell the money it had cost to produce. Professional photography. Impeccable artwork. Huge marketing bucks. I swallowed hard, took her offering, and read the front page out loud. "Elegant Island Weddings. What's… what's this for?"

That earned me another of those evil laughs. "Your wedding, of course. Benni told me you were resistant to using a professional organizer. I must assume you want to limit the size of the wedding to save money."

"Uh…"

Chance, who was standing in the safe zone behind the old bat raised one eyebrow and grinned at me. "Well, McKenna? Are you being a cheapskate again?"

Mrs. Nakamura turned and wagged a finger at him. "Now, now, Young Chance. It is impolite to tease another over their financial limitations. Mr. McKenna has not had the same privileges as you in life." As quickly as she'd turned on Chance, she whipped around to face me. "But Mr. McKenna, surely you do not wish to diminish your bride's most memorable day by…" She paused, grimaced, and added, "Penny pinching."

Chance bit his lip. He was obviously enjoying watching me squirm. My big problem was that my brain was still processing the entire situation—Benni telling Mrs. Nakamura I hadn't wanted to use a wedding planner, leading her to believe I was the one who was opposed to a large wedding—and the old broad actually trying to do something about it.

"Mrs. Nakamura," I stammered, quickly scanned the brochure again, and tried to hand it back to her. "I don't quite know what to say. But the truth is, Benni's the one who wants the small wedding."

"Men are so gullible." Mrs. Nakamura tittered as she shook her head. "Mr. McKenna, do you know nothing of young women? They all want a fairytale wedding." The claw pushed my hand—and the brochure—back toward me.

I didn't even have to open the thing to know what was inside. A fairytale wedding? Sure. And more than a year's worth of paychecks.

"I'll think about it," I said numbly. Benni's father had made it very clear he didn't approve of this wedding and we were the ones paying for it. But something like this? I could be paying for one of these services until the day I died. Maybe longer.

"Mr. McKenna," Mrs. Nakamura's voice softened. "I do not wish to be intrusive, however, I do not want you to have any regrets afterwards. I always told my students that there are some things in life one must do correctly. After all, there will be no do-overs for your big day. Will there?" The old woman bared her yellowed teeth in something resembling a smile.

I snuck a peek at Chance. He was nodding agreeably. If my face hadn't been so numb, I might have scowled at him. Right now, it was impossible.

"You've given McKenna a lot to think about, Mrs. Nakamura." Chance stepped to the side, basically inserting himself back into the conversation.

"Young Chance, you are such a good friend to Mr. McKenna." The old lady reached up and patted Chance on the cheek. "I wish you had been in my class. I'm sure you would have been a delightful student."

"You might have found me quite a handful," Chance said. "My parents spoiled me and I was always acting out."

"I would have tamed you," Mrs. Nakamura said with a wink.

My jaw dropped and I suddenly realized what I should have earlier in the day. "Mrs. Nakamura, did you ever have a student by the name of Kenji Ito?"

"Ah, Kenji Ito. Very bright boy. Shrewd. And a bit of an entrepreneur."

55

"You remember him that well?" I gaped at her. Once again, the old woman's memory astounded me.

"Quite clearly, actually. I kept him in detention for a week. One of the other boys wagered with him that he could not break into the principal's office. He was, of course, discovered. However, he was very proud of the fact that he had succeeded in his mission."

How much more did she know? I watched Mrs. Nakamura for signs of a reaction as I spoke. "You've heard of Kenji's project at Kinohi Village?"

"Of course. A very admirable endeavor."

"We've heard rumors that he might have started the project to further his business profits, not as a way to help the homeless. Do you think they could be true?"

Mrs. Nakamura sighed. "Ah, Mr. McKenna. I am but an old woman who remembers Kenji Ito as a young boy. I could not attest to his motives for such a project. However, I will leave you with a simple question. Can a lion cub grow up to be an antelope?"

The old woman backed away, cackling to herself as she waved one of those knobby claws at me.

9

WITH MRS. NAKAMURA GONE, IT should have felt like a weight had been lifted, but it didn't. Her comment left me more unsettled than ever. "Do you think that lion cub thing was Mrs. Nakamura's way of saying Kenji could be crooked?"

"I don't know. She was pretty cagey."

"Yeah. A riddle instead of an answer. There's only one way we'll find out. We have to find him. Why don't you go home and grab your laptop? Let's see what we can dig up."

"A little online brainstorming session? I like it. Be right back."

Chance headed for his apartment while I began a search using just Kenji's name. The list included everything from public records companies with 'real results' to pitches for services like Find a Grave. When Chance returned, I told him what I'd found in my first search. He suggested I try again, but this time include the word corruption in the search field.

57

I said I had another idea and would let him try the corruption angle. For my search, I added the words, 'construction projects'. This time, the list included jobs going back ten years. Not only were Ito Development's projects included, but some of the results also included information about the company's competitors. Over the years, the jobs and the company had grown in size—along with one of Ito Development's competitors.

"What do you know about West Construction and Engineering?" I asked. "I've seen their name around town, and now I'm seeing it in these results."

"That's Tommy West. His old man started the business and was happy being a small-time general contractor until Tommy came home from college with big ideas and a degree in engineering. He talked his dad into bidding larger jobs. Next thing you know, they got a couple of huge projects. They do a lot of inter-island stuff now."

I regarded Chance with raised eyebrows. "Well, aren't you just an encyclopedia of Hawaiian businesses?"

"Not really. Lexie temped for them one summer in college."

"Do you suppose this Tommy West knows anything about Kenji's business practices? Maybe we should talk to him."

Chance gave me a thumbs-up just as my phone rang. I recognized Benni's ring. "Hey, are you almost here?"

"Actually, I'm at Ito Development. I called Sue and told her about your follow-the-money theory. She said to stop by."

"That was fast. I'm surprised she didn't have to think about it."

"She's taken over in her dad's absence. Sue's actually got full power of attorney for exactly this kind of situation."

"So…Kenji made plans to have his daughter take over the company if something happened to him? Wasn't he kind of young to be planning for his demise?"

"It's a contingency plan, McKenna. The company has hundreds of employees. Kenji always felt things couldn't grind to a halt just because something happened to him."

I had a prickly sensation on the back of my neck and chose my next words carefully. "What happens if Kenji passes away?"

"I don't know what Kenji's will states, but I'm sure he planned ahead. Sue would manage things until the estate was settled. Oh no…he's not dead, is he?"

"Of course not," I lied. Actually, the thought, along with another far more sinister one, had not only crossed my mind, but taken up residence in that place where nagging doubts hid out in our brains. "When will you be back? We have that dinner, you know."

"No worries. Dana's setting me up with a user name and password for the accounting system. I'll be able to access the program remotely. It won't be much longer."

We ended the conversation with the usual I-love-you exchange and a promise from Benni that she would drive carefully. Chance, who had been waiting patiently during the call, was watching me with raised eyebrows. "Well?"

"We're good. She's got access to the books."

"I've got something, too. According to this news story, a woman named China Gaardner spoke at the City Council meetings when they were talking about Kinohi Village. She was a staunch opponent and was there for every discussion. She always claimed Ito Development was gaming the system to make inordinate profits."

If this were twenty years ago, I might believe that accusation. In those days, Hawaii's construction industry had been riddled with political contributions and outright bribes. But today? All the big jobs were competitively bid. How could you rig that? Maybe this China Gaardner just had an ax to grind with Kenji. Or worse. I laid my phone on the table, closed my eyes, and took a deep breath.

"Chance…Benni said something I think we should talk about."

"I know what you're going to say. I've been thinking that this is sounding much less like some guy taking a break from life than it is…something else."

"Maybe we need to change our approach. I don't have to tell Benni yet, but I'm wondering if we should be trying to find out who wanted Kenji out of the picture. What do you think?"

"Much as I hate to say it, I have to agree. Let's just hope we're wrong and he's still alive."

And that brought me to the other thing Benni had told me. "What about Sue?"

"What about her?"

"She might inherit the company."

Chance took a long breath and regarded me. Furrows creased his brow, but softened when he shook his head. "I don't see her as the greedy type, McKenna. Why don't we leave her out for now? We can always circle back and include her later."

"Sounds reasonable." Actually, it felt way better than that. It felt like a relief. "The last time anyone saw Kenji was about forty-eight hours ago. I'll text Benni and have her tell Sue to put in a missing persons report."

I sent Benni the text, then Chance and I spent about thirty minutes digging. We hadn't found anything of substance when the front door opened and Benni burst in.

"Hey, you two," she called as she dashed into the bedroom. She returned a couple of minutes later carrying a paper bag.

The aroma was divine. My stomach growled, which reminded me it was closing in on two o'clock. "I hope you brought us lunch. I just realized we worked straight through."

Benni's smile fell and she winced. "I wish I'd have known. This isn't gluten-free, so don't even think of touching it, McKenna." She handed the bag to Chance. "Pulled Pork Sandwich. You might as well enjoy it."

Chance opened the bag, breathed in the aroma, and sighed. "I'm sorry, McKenna. Actually, I'm not." He unwrapped the sandwich, eyed it for a few seconds as if he was trying to decide where to start, then jammed one end into his mouth.

My stomach might be growling protests about being left out, but my mind knew the consequences of eating something with gluten. Even armed with that knowledge, between Chance's moans of ecstasy, his eye rolling, and the sauce oozing down his fingers, I could barely focus.

"How about a banana, McKenna?" Benni raised her eyebrows and gave me an impish smile as she walked into the kitchen.

"You're enjoying tormenting me, aren't you?"

"No, sweetie. I love you." She gave me a little smile and a wink. "I don't want you to suffer at all."

"No worries about that. The eating machine over there devoured your sandwich in three bites."

"That was so good." Chance licked sauce from his fingers and smacked his lips.

Benni bent down to kiss me. "I'm sorry." She stood, smiled, and added, "But I brought you a lead. Her name is Kelly Atkinson and she's a photographer who's been documenting the development of Kinohi Village. She's got a ton of photos, everything from the project planning stage up to today."

"That's awesome," Chance said. "Do you know how to contact her?"

Benni pulled a scrap of paper from her pocket and handed it to me. "Maybe this will make up for the sandwich."

There was a name and phone number in Benni's handwriting. Nothing else. "No address?"

Benni punched me lightly on the shoulder. "Do you need me to do everything for you? You're the big-time skip tracer. Find her yourself."

"Not a problem," I said. "Just like old times." I dialed the number and waited. When a woman's voice answered, I said, "Is this Kelly Atkinson?"

"Who's calling?" The voice was abrupt, sounding much like a harried server in a restaurant trying to juggle the competing needs of her customers, the chef, and her coworkers.

"My name's McKenna," I said, doing my best to sound professional. "Is this not Kelly?"

"I'll get her." Again. Abrupt.

On the other side of the table, Chance had wiped his fingers clean and was tapping on his keyboard. What was he doing? Trying to get results on the Internet? We'd see about that. "She's getting Kelly." Though I knew nothing good would come of it, I couldn't resist a quick dig. "How are you doing there, Chance? Running into too many results?"

"Just you wait, McKenna," he grumbled.

"Is that a challenge?" Benni asked with a grin. She pulled out her phone and tapped the screen.

Oh, God, she was working for the other team? Not fair.

Benni held out her phone for Chance to see. He winked at her and typed faster. With a final jab of the Enter key, he spun the laptop around just as Kelly answered.

Rats. He had a news story that included her photos. The headline read, *Local Photographer Determined to Keep Developer Honest*. And now, I had a dilemma. I knew nothing about this woman. Based on the headline alone I could reasonably assume she disliked Kenji. Was she another one trying to bring his project down? Meeting in person, it would be possible to read her. On the phone, there were too many opportunities for deception.

"Hi, Kelly, my name is McKenna. I'm doing some research on Kinohi Village and understand you've been taking photos to document the project. Do you think there's a time when we could meet to discuss your work?"

"How did you hear about me?" Her tone was buttery smooth.

I cheated and peeked at Chance's laptop. "There was a story in the Star-Advertiser with your photos. If possible, I'd like to see more of them. There may be some we'd find of interest."

"Who did you say you were with?"

"I didn't."

There was a long pause before she answered. When she did, her tone was no longer velvety, but was tinged with suspicion. "I have a very busy schedule. Give me your number and I'll call you when things ease up."

I was definitely feeling the heat of the competition I'd started. Talk about embarrassing. I couldn't lose this little battle. "How much do you charge for a wedding?" I blurted.

63

Benni's jaw fell. She buried her face in her hands and shook her head. Chance appeared to be in shock, too. Apparently my question had taken them by surprise.

"Excuse me?" Kelly blurted. "I don't really do weddings."

I studied the screen. There were photos of all types—buildings going up, group shots, and candid individual photos. "I'm getting married soon and I'm supposed to find the photographer. From what I've seen of your work, you could easily transfer your skills."

"There have to be a hundred wedding photographers on island. Why me?"

"They've all got their agendas." After so many years on the job, it wasn't hard slipping into the persona I'd used to track a skip. "You know how it works. They do a hand shot here, bride gazing longingly at the groom there, blah, blah, blah. We might want to change it up a bit. It's going to be a large wedding. Come on, what do you say? I'll pay you for an hour of your time even if you decide not to take the job."

Kelly huffed. "Fine. Come by this afternoon and I'll squeeze you in." She rattled off an address, which I jotted down on the same paper Benni had given me. "What time will you be here?"

I glared at the banana peel on the table. "We just finished lunch, so maybe two-thirty?"

"Sure. Bring cash. And don't be late."

10

ON THE WAY TO SEE Kelly Atkinson, we made an ATM stop. I held down the fort in the Ferrari while Chance hit the machine. When he returned, he flopped down into his seat and held up a crisp Benjamin Franklin.

"Here's your money for the snitch, McKenna, but when are you going to learn that I'm not your personal piggybank?"

I snatched the bill out of his hand and stuffed it into my wallet. I considered a snappy retort, something like—when you stop acting like one, but decided that wouldn't help my cause. "I'll work on it. Wait, is your dad monitoring your finances again?"

"No. But it seems so much of our lives is focused on money. I don't want to wind up like the rest of my family, which has been all about making money for generations. I'd like to do something other than chase the almighty dollar."

"At least you know who your family is." Not that I was very enthusiastic about knowing mine.

65

The Ferrari's engine roared to life. Chance maneuvered us back onto the road, then said, "You're still down on doing genealogical research?"

"Benni's got deep roots here. I can be happy helping her."

Chance frowned and tossed a reproving glance in my direction. Even to me, the answer reeked of a lie—the one I'd lived much of my life. Someday, perhaps, I'd deal with that baggage. For now I simply wanted to shove it back in the closet.

Any picture I'd formed in my head of Kelly's studio evaporated when we pulled up in front of a small house surrounded by apartment complexes of all sizes. In some ways, this lone single-family home reminded me of a delicate white rose in a sea of red hibiscus.

The Ferrari came to a stop at the curb, and Chance leaned over, practically in my lap I might add, to inspect the house. "You sure this is the right place?"

I checked the street sign, then the numbers on the front of the house. "It's right."

"Let's get a side view."

"Okay, but Alder's one way. You'll have to go around the block."

"Gotcha." Chance circumnavigated the block so that we ended up parked across the street from the house on Alder. It was gawk time again. The depth of the house and lot had not been visible from Kamalie. Now, however, it was obvious that not only was this place huge, but it also had an attached apartment over a one-car garage.

"Wow, that's a surprise," I said.

Sounding like an interested homebuyer, Chance popped open his door and eagerly said, "Let's go check this out."

The perimeter of the lot was closed in with a three-foot-high chain link fence. A scraggly hedge on the inside had seen better days. Drapes fluttered inside open windows, allowing the trade winds to act as a natural air conditioner.

Climbing the front steps, I wondered how this single home had survived the conversion of the neighborhood to condos and apartments. Perhaps the answer was simply that it's location and size made it a jewel impossible to part with. Standing on the front lānai by the screen door, I cringed at the sounds of someone assaulting the keys of a piano.

"That sounds terrible," Chance whispered.

"No kidding. Torturing a piano like that should be illegal."

Chance rapped his knuckles on the old screen door. The wood rattled in its frame, making a noise loud enough to quell the sour-note serenade. The shadowy figure of a woman came into view.

"Yes?"

I recognized the tone. It was the woman I'd spoken with before Kelly. Not friendly then, not friendly now. Based on her voice and what little I could make out through the screen door— hair bleached platinum blonde, thin build, no visible wrinkles—I assumed she was in her late twenties or early thirties.

"We're here to see Kelly," I said. "I called earlier."

The woman huffed and hooked her thumb over her shoulder. "Around back. Over the garage."

When we didn't scurry off her lānai like a pair of frightened animals, she glowered at us. "What? Did you need something else?"

"No, we're good." I said and turned to make my getaway.

"Wow. Grumpy," Chance said as we exited the gate.

"If you played piano like that, you'd be grumpy, too," I snickered.

We followed the sidewalk in the direction the woman had indicated. The piano practice had resumed by the time we made it through another gate and up the stairs. At the second-floor landing, we came to a wooden door with an old-fashioned doorknob, a skeleton key for access, and a modern deadbolt for security. On the opposite side of the landing was another door, this one for the main house.

"Nice little setup," I said quietly. "A five-foot commute to work."

"I agree," Chance said, then tapped a few times on the apartment door.

"Just a minute," a woman's voice called from inside.

As we stood there, I realized why they hadn't bothered to install a screen door. The little alcove between the main house and the granny unit was shielded from the trades, but exposed to the afternoon sun and felt like a sauna.

The door opened and a young woman, late twenties or early thirties, stood before us. Her auburn hair had blonde highlights and she wore it pulled up in back. Her green eyes flicked back and forth between Chance and me. For once, I was surprised that a woman didn't swoon at the very sight of Chance's mug.

"My name's McKenna. This is my associate, Chance Logan."

"I'm Kelly." She shook hands with each of us. "Come in. It's hot out there."

When we were both inside, she closed the door and stepped past us into a small studio. It wasn't elegant, but certainly functional. There were multiple tripods, screens to reflect light, and a couple of inside-out white umbrellas on stands. A desk to our right contained a laptop computer and a large monitor.

"You have some expensive equipment," I said.

"Some of it is. I'm saving up for a new camera. Some jerk stole a lot of my equipment from the back of my car while I was at Sandy Beach taking sunrise photos. Thank God I had another regular gig, otherwise he would have crippled my business for months." She shook her head, closed her eyes, and took a deep breath. "Sorry. It still upsets me."

"Is most of your work outdoors?" I asked.

"I really don't do much studio work. Portraits are super boring. And I don't think I'm a good fit for your wedding. It's not my thing."

"Actually, we only wanted information."

She grimaced. "Whatever. You brought cash?"

Chance handed over one of the hundred dollar bills he'd gotten at the ATM along with one of his business cards. Kelly ignored the card, but held the bill up to the light and sighed. "At least I can eat this week—and maybe even put a little away. What do you want to know?"

"As I mentioned on the phone, I'm interested in your photos of the Kinohi Village project." I let the statement hang in the air and hoped she'd go for the bait.

"Are either of you a cop? Is this some sort of shakedown to get me to back off?" She turned away and began fiddling with a nearby camera. "If it is, it won't work."

"We're not cops," I said. "We've been asked to find Kenji Ito. He hasn't been seen in two days."

Kelly cocked her head to one side and frowned. "He's missing?"

"Yes."

She let out a sinister chuckle. "Maybe the heat got to him."

What did that mean? Truth or dare time. "Somehow, I don't think you're referring to the weather."

"No. I'm talking about the kind that comes from people asking questions someone doesn't want asked."

"We need something more specific," Chance said, his voice firm and determined.

I'd seen this side of the kid before. His ability to go from meek-and-mild to intimidating in a heartbeat would serve him well if he ever truly got his PI license. Since he'd taken over the bad-cop role, I might as well go with his opposite.

"Come on, Kelly. We're not here to accuse you of anything. We're trying to find a missing man. I'm sure you don't want any harm to come to him. Are you willing to help us or not?"

The pale white of her cheeks colored slightly and she bit her lower lip. "Okay. Fine. I don't know anything about the project for sure. But I do have sources that tell me Kenji was always out to make a buck. One of his construction jobs was for low-income housing. His company was always late on deadlines and the work was shoddy. From what I hear, that's typical."

Kelly certainly seemed to have 'sources,' but I couldn't help wondering how reliable they might be. Chance apparently had the same idea.

"That's pretty detailed information." Chance stared at Kelly, his blue eyes cold and determined.

"I...got a tip," she stammered. A moment later, her words came rushing out in a torrent. "And someone I know lived there. She said they had a lot of problems with plumbing leaks, circuit breakers blowing, and the security lighting cutting out. She worked nights and she got super scared once because there were a lot of shady guys hanging out. In the end, she found a better place."

"How well do you know this person?" Chance insisted.

"She's reliable."

The way Kelly bit her lip, I couldn't tell if she was irritated or embarrassed because we'd caught her fudging the truth. Either way, the types of problems she was describing could happen anywhere. It was nothing earth shattering. "Is this friend the reason you've been documenting Kinohi Village?"

"I'm one of the few watchdogs out there," Kelly snapped. "If I don't keep an eye on him, he could rip off the city for millions and nobody would know until it's too late."

Really? Kenji Ito, Criminal Mastermind. It hardly seemed possible. Then again, maybe we hadn't dug deep enough.

11

KELLY OBVIOUSLY HAD OPINIONS ABOUT Kenji, but so far the few gripes she'd voiced sounded like nothing more than normal maintenance issues. For that matter, I'd had plumbing leaks and security lighting go out at the Sunsetter Apartments. Her arguments were sounding very conspiracy-theoryish—long on rhetoric, short on facts.

"Why don't you show us your photos?" I asked. "You can explain as we go along."

She turned to face her laptop. "It's your money." It only took her a few seconds to find what she wanted, a folder on her computer. Photos soon began to appear on the large monitor. "You want all of them?"

"How many have you taken?" I asked.

"Maybe a thousand. Each day when I get done shooting I classify what I shot. If you want, I can show you the ones I consider good. Most of the others are duplicates or experiments."

"What kind of experiments?" I asked.

"Sometimes it's just tracking someone while they work. I'll usually shoot those with one or two seconds in between. I compare the series, flag the best one, and reject the others. Everything gets backed up to a local hard drive and mirrored in the cloud. That way I don't lose anything and if I realize I want one of those rejected photos, I can find it."

Given that we had less than an hour to finish up here and get home, I suggested we go with the ones Kelly thought were the best. Chance agreed, and Kelly, who had warmed to the idea of someone showing interest in her work, seemed to have a change of attitude as she angled the monitor in our direction.

"This one was taken the night of the City Council meeting when Kenji pitched the project. I could only get him from the back, but he must have known he was going to get approval. There was almost no discussion and the council only allowed a little time for public comments."

"The council gets an agenda and reports ahead of time," I said. "And they've been talking about ways to end the homeless crisis for years. Are you sure it wasn't just a matter of right project at the right time?"

Kelly shook her head vigorously. "There were some very unhappy people who attended that meeting."

"I don't suppose you were taking their pictures, were you?" I asked.

"As a matter of fact, I was."

Kelly scrolled forward until she found a photo of the audience. It was nothing but a sea of faces.

"That's just an crowd shot," Chance said. "We need something that tells us more about them."

She craned her neck forward and ran her mouse over a series of thumbnail photos, then clicked. "There's this one."

I immediately recognized the face of the organizer from the Kinohi Village protest. The man Julie had called a sign for hire. "That's Graham Tynsdale."

"He's a real jerk."

"You know him?" I asked.

"No. But I've seen him before, so I got his name." She clicked in the program's search field and typed in 'Tynsdale'. A picture of him standing on a street corner holding a real estate sign appeared on the screen. "He's a regular at that location."

"Imagine that," I said. "He really is a sign for hire."

"He was very loud and obnoxious in the meeting," Kelly said. "At one point, the mayor threatened to have him ejected if he didn't show more respect."

"Was he alone?" I asked.

Another photo filled the screen. Graham was talking to a man sitting next to him who wore a loud aloha shirt and a scowl equal to or better than Graham's. The woman next to the guy with the loud shirt leaned toward them, apparently very interested in the conversation.

I pointed at the man and woman in the photo. "Who are they?"

"No idea." Kelly began scrolling through photos until she got to some of the picket line in front of Kinohi Village. "But there they are again. That's the woman who was at the City Council meeting, and behind her is the man."

Sure enough. There they were, both carrying signs. Kelly zoomed in on the woman. Her mouth was open as if she'd been caught in mid-chant.

"Let's see the man," Chance said.

Kelly brought up the man's image. He wore a scowl on his face and his sign read, *Keep our neighborhood safe!*

The statement seemed ludicrous to me. That land had been lying vacant for decades and had recently become some sort of convenient garbage dumping ground. Kinohi Village would bring in people who not only wanted to keep the place in good condition, but who also wanted to be productive members of society.

"And you have no idea who those protestors are?" I asked.

"Nope. I never intended to use these photos for anything more than background."

That seemed unlikely to me. She'd gone to a lot of trouble to capture people up close. She'd attended a City Council meeting. Been at Kinohi Village on a regular basis. Something didn't track in her logic.

"Can I get a copy of that photo?" Chance asked.

"I guess." Kelly clicked an icon, then asked where he'd like it sent.

After giving Kelly his phone number, Chance watched his messages until the photo came through. He gave her a thumbs up, then asked her to continue. When we shifted into the construction zone, there were shots of plumbers, electricians, and carpenters. Kenji appeared in a number of the photos. The most interesting of the batch was one in which Kenji was talking to two workers while a third stood off to the side. Of the four men in the photo, I recognized two. Kenji stood with his back to the camera and Mondo stood next to him looking uncomfortable. Opposite Kenji was a third man who was making an obscene hand gesture at the camera. Whatever was going on, the man must have wanted to chase Kelly away.

"Do you know who that is?" I indicated the third man in the conversation.

"His name is Derrick Tanaka. I think the other one is Joe Taylor."

"Joe Taylor? Where have we heard that name before?" I asked.

"He's the one they said didn't show up for work," Chance said. "What were they doing, Kelly?"

"I dunno. They split up right after I took the photo. Kenji walked off with the Taylor guy."

"Would you send me a copy of that one, too?" Chance asked.

It went that way for another thirty minutes. With the exception of the photo taken at the City Council meeting, I didn't much see the point, but since we were in information-gathering mode—and this was on Chance's dime—I was willing to let him take the lead. We were nearing the end of our hour, and we still hadn't gotten any indications of who might have wanted to harm Kenji. It seemed Kelly was perfectly happy showing her photos to someone else and naming names or saying, 'I don't know.'

"This has all been helpful, Kelly. We really appreciate your time, but I wonder if you might give us your impressions?"

"Impressions? Of what? The project? The people? I'm a photographer, not a shrink."

"We're not asking you to psychoanalyze them. You've seen them multiple times. And you've caught some of them in very candid moments. We're exploring the theory that Kenji didn't disappear willingly. Which of these people should we talk to?"

"You think someone murdered him?" she scoffed.

"Nobody said anything about murder," Chance cautioned. "McKenna's just saying that someone might be trying to derail Kinohi Village."

Kelly screwed up her face and shook her head. "What? By killing the man behind the project? Serious? There are plenty of people who think this project should stop, but they're not running around killing people."

It appeared our working relationship with Kelly was based on us having cash and being appreciative of her photography skills and nothing more. She was acting like a spoiled brat, and I'd had enough. "You can drop the sarcasm. You've been taking pictures. You've seen these people in action. All we're asking for is a little help. Now, are you going to cooperate or what?"

Kelly chewed on her lower lip for a few seconds, then let out a little huff. "Whatever. The person who knows more about Kenji is Celeste Campbell. She's a reporter who's been working on the story. I've sent her some of my photos, and she's agreed to use them. She's done a lot of digging into Kenji's background. If anybody's going to know who he was in contact with, it'll be her."

Okay, I was impressed. Celeste was a regular on our evening news station. "Do you have her contact information? It'll save us some time."

Letting out an exasperated sigh, Kelly pulled out a piece of paper and wrote down the name and number. "That's all I know. I can't tell you anything else. And don't tell her I sent you. I don't want to be involved."

"Involved in what?" I pressed.

Her eyes darted towards the front door. She chewed on her lip again. "You have to go now. There's nothing else I can tell you."

As she let us out the door, I wondered about Kelly's words. Had she truly meant she knew nothing else that would be of value? Or was she hiding secrets of her own? If we discovered she was lying, we'd be back. And take another look at Kelly Atkinson.

12

AT THIS PARTICULAR POINT IN time, my life didn't feel like mine. I'd always been a loner, yet I would soon be married. I was riding in a red Ferrari, a car that cost more than I could ever afford. And I had developed friendships I never would have expected. I turned sideways in the plush leather seat. Chance was eying one of the high-end stores that drew shoppers from around the globe. I felt a warm glow deep inside.

"Thanks for adopting me, Chance."

He did a double take, which was quickly followed by a furrowing of his brow. "Adopting you? I don't understand."

"When you rented the apartment from me and I ran your credit check, I couldn't figure out why you'd want to slum with us at the Sunsetter Apartments."

"First off, McKenna, those apartments are far from a slum. You've got prime beach location, killer sunsets, and it's quiet."

"But you could have lived anywhere. There's lots of other places with those same attributes."

The light changed, Chance eased his foot down on the gas, and we inched forward about a half block before coming to another stop. "The truth is, I was trying to change my life when I rented from you. I'd always run with the rich crowd, and all it got me was trouble. When I talked to you, and you told me you'd been a skip tracer, I was fascinated. Then, when I got to know you, it was like, he's a really good guy. And I could learn a lot from him. In some ways, I wish my dad was more like you."

The warm glow in my chest swelled to envelop my entire body, but compliments were not something I dealt with easily and my natural inclination was to change the subject. "Lots of people shopping today."

Chance gave me another quizzical look, then said, "My dad was always working. You're more caring. Compassionate. I'll bet you had some doctors or nurses in your family."

That hadn't been the case for my parents, who'd both worked low wage jobs. Further back, I had no idea. And then there was the letter I'd received from a man claiming to be my half-brother. Was there another side of the family? It wasn't a question I was prepared to deal with right now.

I cleared my throat. "I don't know what I had in my family. It doesn't really matter, anyway."

"What's going on with you, McKenna?"

"Nothing. Just thinking about my priorities. That's all."

"You're sounding like a man who thinks his life is over. You've got a wedding coming up. Snap out of it."

Traffic came to another stop near the Duke Kahanamoku statue. To avoid any further admonitions, I watched an old couple, he in a wheelchair, she pushing, as they made their way through the maze of pedestrians. When they reached the base of the statue, they stopped. She took off her lei and he handed her his, then she placed both over one of Duke's arms. Some tour guides told visitors that if they left their lei on the statue, they would be sure to return to Hawaii. It seemed like a silly gesture, but it was a sign of hope, something that, for now, seemed in short supply.

"I…I haven't told Benni this, but when I was a kid, about the only relative my parents ever talked about was a grandfather who…suffered from dementia."

Chance regarded me for what felt like forever, but it was really only until the light turned green. He touched the gas and said, "Neither of your parents suffered from it. Right?"

"I really don't know. They split up when I was in my twenties. Dad went off for a safari in Africa and we never heard from him again. Mom moved to Ireland and we just gradually drifted apart. She died of pneumonia twenty years ago. Either one of them could have been affected and I wouldn't even know."

"I'm sorry. No brothers? Sisters?"

My spine stiffened. Did I tell him? "I didn't even have any friends on the mainland. Always the loner. That was me."

"Wow. You were a sad case, weren't you? No wonder you left. My situation wasn't nearly that desperate."

"The difference is, you came here to live a dream. You were running towards something; I was running away."

Chance went silent, seeming to let my words sink in, then asked, "Running away from what, McKenna?"

With the exception of Benni and her brother, I'd never told another soul why I moved to Hawaii. Was I about to break my silence with Chance, too? I should trust him. After all, we'd saved each others lives on more than one occasion. Pulling in a deep breath, I said, "I was running from what I'd become. And from the memories of a bad relationship. Now, can we leave my life history behind? I'm moving forward, not looking back."

Chance's phone buzzed. He checked the display, raised his eyebrows, then wrapped his fingers around the wheel. "Lexie's already at your place. She and Benni are having a glass of wine."

"Let's hope it's just one." I chuckled. "Maybe you better step on it."

"You're a riot, McKenna. Do you think that's what Kenji's doing? Trying to leave his past behind?"

"Maybe, but deep down? I'm worried about the guy. From everything we've heard, nothing has indicated that he might have just lost it. In my opinion, he either had a complete breakdown—something I consider very unlikely at this stage, or he's come to some sort of harm."

"I'm worried that you're right." Chance eased his foot off the gas to slow for the Sunsetter Apartment entrance. "You need to be careful with this guy you're meeting tonight. How about if I go in with you and sit at the end of the bar or in a booth?"

"I'll keep that in mind. We can talk strategy over dinner."

Chance's phone buzzed again. His eyes widened at the image on his screen. "We'd better hurry. Lexie just sent me a photo of an empty wine glass."

"Let's go." I turned and double-timed it across the parking lot with Chance right behind me.

The sounds of women laughing greeted us as we approached the front door. When I entered, Benni was just reaching for a bottle of Chardonnay on the coffee table.

"We're here! Step away from the bottle, ma'am."

Benni and Lexie glanced at me, then at each other. They rolled their eyes, and, in unison, muttered, "Party pooper." They both burst into laughter.

81

"Hey, babe." Chance strode forward, bent over, and kissed Lexie.

Sitting up straight and giving me a mock glare, Benni said, "Well, McKenna? Don't I get a 'hey, babe'? Or are you going to be a grump in addition to being a party pooper?"

Adopting my best John Wayne swagger, I made my way across the room, and lowered my voice. "Hey, hot stuff."

Benni rolled her eyes. "That was awful," she said between giggles.

Not one to be easily deterred, I followed Chance's lead. When the kiss finished, Benni fingered my cheek. "Okay, tell you what. I'll take that greeting anytime. Just skip the…."

"John Wayne," I offered.

"Sorry, but it's more like Scooby Doo."

I endured a few more minutes of humiliation as we closed up the apartment and made our way to Benni's car. Benni handed her keys to Chance. "Here. You've been volunteered."

"Shotgun," I called out.

"Boys," Benni said and laughed.

Lexie gave her a high-five.

The drive was a major success in my opinion—no stress, no humiliation. Dinner was at a restaurant owned and operated by one of Benni's cousins. It was basically a hole in the wall, but the food was excellent and, in my case, gluten-free. On the way to the meeting, we drove by a man pushing an overflowing shopping cart in which he'd stuffed a sleeping bag, a raggedy duffle bag, and loose pieces of clothing.

"You think that's everything he owns?" I asked as the man disappeared from my side mirror.

Glancing back, Chance said, "I don't know. I need an answer, McKenna. Do you want me to go in with you? I'm sure I can stay out of sight."

"No. I'll go in alone. If I were setting up a meeting like this, I'd show up early."

"Control the situation."

"Exactly. Then again, maybe this guy's not that smart."

Chance gave me a self-satisfied grin. "There is no greater danger than underestimating your opponent."

I raised my eyebrows, surprised that he was quoting one of my favorite sources. "It sounds like you've been reading *The Art of War*."

"You recommended it, so I picked up a copy. Pretty smart dude for a three-thousand-year-old Chinese general." Chance made the next turn and pointed ahead about a half block. "There it is. The Airport Tavern. Lovely. It's a bigger dive than I thought it would be."

With its white paint, red trim, and lime green faux awning, the place scored a ten for cheesiness. The parking lot was a further testament to the place's lack of appeal—it was empty. This was a bar, of course, so maybe it would start hopping after nine or ten.

"We can wait in the parking lot if you want," Chance said.

"I'll be okay," I said confidently, then transferred the hundred-dollar bill from my wallet to my pocket. Stepping out of the car set my nerves on edge, though. And as Chance drove away, my confidence felt much like my version of John Wayne. A bad imitation.

13

THE POLISHED SURFACE OF THE Airport Tavern's bar, clearly the most expensive piece of furniture in the place, was dull in spots from too many spilled drinks and lack of maintenance. Wall art was nonexistent with the exception of alcohol advertisements. What was impressive was their selection of liquor. At least, it was impressive to a cheapskate like me who never hung out in bars. My motto had always been, why pay for something by the glass when you can get a bottle at the grocery store?

The bartender, a young hipster—mid-twenties, hair tied up in a man-bun, red checkered shirt with the sleeves rolled up—held a glass containing an amber liquid as he watched the large-screen TV hanging over the bar. Mr. Hipster had tattoos, which I was sure he classified as body art, on all visible skin surfaces.

There were no other customers in the place, so I acknowledged the guy by flashing him a shaka sign. He returned the gesture, put down his glass, and picked up a white bar towel.

I walked the length of the bar, noting that no two stools were alike, and took the last one.

"What'll it be, brah?"

Water? Not in this place. I wouldn't trust anything that came from a tap in this dive. I ordered a glass of house red, hoping the alcohol would kill anything that wasn't supposed to be in the glass. Mr. Hipster gave me a raised eyebrow, at which point I shot back a quick, "I have celiac disease. No beer."

He contemplated me for a second, then picked up a glass from beneath the counter. After finding a bottle and pouring, he set the glass in front of me. "Happy Hour. Two-fifty."

I handed him three ones and told him to keep the change. He didn't appear thrilled by the size of the tip and drifted away. The wine had a bit of a bite to it, but it wasn't terrible. While I sipped, I texted Chance. *Bar empty.*

Mr. Hipster returned to where he'd been when I walked in, picked up his glass, and made his way back to me. "Got a cousin with that condition."

"I've had it for awhile." I watched him over the rim of my glass, wishing he would back off, suspecting he wouldn't.

"Hey, you see those homeless dudes on your way in? We had a couple of them set up camp last week. Had to call HPD and have them taken away. Tough situation. You know, brah?"

Apparently, this guy wasn't going anywhere. "Nobody was hanging around out front when I came in, but I agree that Hawaii's got a huge problem. What do you think of Kinohi Village?"

"Good project. I'm hoping it'll help some of these people get off the streets."

For some reason, I felt relief knowing that Mr. Hipster might be sympathetic to the cause if my mystery man started getting hostile. The bartender gazed up at the TV and let out a heavy sigh. Cocking his head toward the screen, he asked, "You hear about this?"

A picture of Kenji Ito filled the screen, but soon cut to Celeste Campbell, the same reporter Kelly Atkinson had mentioned. Celeste, a pretty Asian woman, stood in an open field looking windblown, but determined. She alternately pointed at a mound of dirt behind her and pushed strands of her blonde-highlighted hair away from her face when the trade winds gusted. When the camera panned to the distant background, my blood ran cold. Those buildings were part of Kinohi Village.

"What happened?" I asked hoarsely.

"Dude's been missing since yesterday. About an hour ago he turned up dead."

I set my glass on the counter, my desire for anything alcoholic suddenly gone. On the screen, Celeste's mouth moved, but I couldn't focus on the words. Instead, my thoughts were on Kenji. His daughter. The project. No matter how I tried, I couldn't force away my visions of doom.

Celeste droned on about how much uncertainty Kenji's death might bring to the project. Suddenly, our efforts to find out who had it in for Kenji felt even more important. I rested my elbow on the bar and buried my forehead in my hand.

"How did he die?" I croaked.

"You ain't looking so good, brah. You okay?"

"Kenji Ito was a friend of the family." It wasn't a complete lie, more like…truth fudge. "Do they know what happened?"

"Celeste said HPD is investigating. Somebody murdered him."

My mind raced with all the standard questions. Who? What? Why? When? Especially when. Was that why he'd missed Sue's meeting? "What else did she say?" I pressed.

"There might be some kinda corruption going on, you know? Maybe the FBI gonna be brought in. Don't sound good for the project."

My phone pinged with a message from Chance. *Someone coming. Text back if not your guy.* I wasn't sure how to respond, or if I even should. Benni was in the car with Chance. I closed my eyes and shook my head. Poor Benni. She was going to take this hard. And what about Sue? My thoughts stopped abruptly when a man I recognized walked in. He was around forty and had close-cropped dark hair. He wore a T-shirt with some sort of weird abstract design across the front. It was Derrick Tanaka, the worker Kelly had captured in one of her photos.

Tanaka stopped just inside the door, gave the room a once over and, apparently satisfied, entered. Something about him made me think he was a surfer. Whether it was his easy gait or the skin weathered by the sun, I wasn't sure. Maybe it was just that he looked like he'd grown up here. He allowed himself to give the bar a final once-over before he locked his eyes on mine.

"Seems like you have another customer."

"Huh. Imagine that." The bartender approached the new arrival. "Beer?"

Tanaka held up a finger and fixed me with a steely gaze. "You McKenna?"

Nodding once, I gestured at the stool next to mine. As he took a seat, he sneered at my glass of wine and I realized what a mismatch this was. Right now, I totally regretted refusing Chance's offer to be here as backup. This guy might have a paunch, but he was stocky. He had to outweigh me by...a lot.

And he had a good twenty years on me. Only an idiot would have come in here alone.

The bartender returned with the beer and gave me a raised eyebrow as he slid the drink in front of Tanaka. Money changed hands. Mr. Hipster left.

Though I had no desire for the wine, I took a healthy swallow. It was game on. Time to give this guy a little truth-litmus test. "You have a name?"

He shoved his face close enough for me to be overpowered by the stench of stale cigarettes. Okay, there were two things that made my skin crawl. An overzealous tattoo artist, and this guy in my face.

"You don't need it. You wanted to know about Kenji Ito. Find a guy named Joe Taylor."

Ah, the other man in Kelly's photo. Obviously, Tanaka thought he had the advantage. I'd let him keep that impression for now. "You gave me that name on the phone."

"And you were gonna bring a hundred bucks."

I reached into my pocket, pulled out the hundred-dollar bill, and held it up. Inwardly, I felt a small flush of satisfaction when Tanaka fixated on it. I'd seen Chance do this before, and I had to admit, there was a certain perverse satisfaction in watching someone else jump through hoops for money. "You said you knew why Kenji fired Taylor. You get this when I get the information."

"He was a worker on the project. Don't know all the details." He stopped and his eyes widened when they wandered to the bill I still held in my hand.

"Seriously? You expect me to pay you a hundred bucks for that?"

His jaw tightened. He took a long pull from his beer. "Kenji fired him for being drunk on the job. It was all bogus."

"So how do I find this Joe Taylor?"

"That wasn't the deal. I told you why Joe got fired. You want to know how to find him, that's gonna cost you more."

The front door opened. Voices drifted in. Women's voices. Benni's. Lexie's. With Chance following them. My confidence surged like a wave at high tide. I must have smiled because Tanaka was immediately on alert.

"What's going on here? You were supposed to come alone."

"I did. But my friends must have gotten tired of waiting in the car. Just like I'm tired of you. What you've given me is a poor excuse for information. It's nothing other than a weak attempt to extort money for nothing."

Chance slipped behind Tanaka. Laid a hand on his shoulder. Applied some kind of pressure with his thumb. The man's eyes widened, he gritted his teeth, and sucked in a breath. When he could breathe again, it sounded like a dog panting on a hot day.

"I wouldn't try to move." Chance released the pressure, but kept his hand in place. "That's called the brachial plexus. And it's a very painful spot. Now, the man asked you a question. Do you know the answer or was he right and this was just a shakedown?"

"Okay, okay. What do you want to know?"

Chance glanced at me. "Your show, McKenna."

Okay. Litmus test, redux. "What's your name?"

He hesitated, Chance applied pressure, and the man blurted, "Derrick Tanaka."

"Now we're getting somewhere," I said.

14

BENNI AND LEXIE PARKED THEMSELVES at the far end of the bar, which was just inside the entrance. Strategically, it was a brilliant move. They could keep Mr. Hipster engaged while Chance and I 'chatted' with our reluctant informant. If I wasn't sure Tanaka was a total dirtbag, I might have even felt sorry for him. He had, after all, already endured a fair amount of pain. Either that or he was a master at grotesque facial contortions.

Now that Tanaka had a better understanding of his predicament, I figured it was time to expedite matters. "Let's be clear, Derrick. We're not going to stiff you out of Mr. Franklin, but you need to be more forthcoming with your answers or my friend here is going to apply a little pressure to that broken plexi-whatever on your shoulder."

"Brachial plexus, McKenna." Chance sighed. "And damage to those nerves can cause paralysis in the arm."

Tanaka tried to turn his neck toward Chance, but stopped suddenly and groaned through gritted teeth.

"Sorry," Chance said. "You really shouldn't move so quickly when somebody's doing this to you."

At the far end of the bar, Benni and Lexie laughed at something Mr. Hipster said. Since delivering their two glasses of wine, he seemed determined to keep them entertained. Right now, he had his elbows planted on the bar and was gazing at Lexie. Obviously, the guy was totally smitten. Thank goodness they were ignoring the TV. I turned my attention back to Tanaka.

"Let's talk about how you learned Joe Taylor was fired. Are you a friend of his?"

"No. We worked together."

I narrowed my gaze. "At Kinohi Village?"

"Yeah. We were on the same crew."

Good. At least he wasn't lying. "Was Joe Taylor drinking?"

"He didn't drink nothing on the job," Derrick sneered.

"Nice way to dodge the question. Let's try this a different way. Was he drunk on the job?"

This time, Tanaka hesitated. I didn't need a verbal response; I could see the truth by the fear in his eyes.

"So how often did he show up drunk for work?"

Derrick cut his eyes in Chance's direction. "Maybe once. Twice."

"If he was showing up drunk, then why do you say Kenji fired him for no good reason?"

Once again, Tanaka hesitated.

Chance sighed. "Really? Why won't you just answer the man and get this over with?"

"If I tell you, you gotta promise not to use my name."

The wave of euphoria that had washed over me when Chance walked in suddenly turned to dread. "Who are you afraid of?" I demanded.

91

Tanaka didn't answer. And that's when things went downhill. Okay, it was more of a plummet. Chance applied more pressure. Tanaka cried out. The bartender charged our way yelling at us to leave his customer alone. Chance had to let go—and our source of information slithered off his chair to a spot several feet away. Well, rats.

Mr. Hipster, suddenly the protective proprietor, eyed Tanaka. "You okay, brah?"

"My arm…" he whimpered.

"Out!" The bartender pulled out his phone and held it up. I'm calling 9-1-1 if you two don't leave right now." He glared first at Chance, then me.

Chance raised his hands and started to back away. He was reaching for his wallet when I decided to give Tanaka one more try.

"Tell me what you're afraid of. Maybe we can help you."

He laughed derisively, then sneered, "You got no idea what bone you're chewing on." He turned and scurried out the door.

Not one to be easily deterred, Chance flashed an officialesque badge. I'd seen it before; it was his Phillip Marlowe Online Detective Agency private-investigator-in-training badge. Basically, it was a student ID.

Chance pocketed his wallet before Mr. Hipster got a good look at it. "We're investigating the disappearance of Kenji Ito."

The bartender did a double take, then pointed at the TV. "You mean that dude?"

Benni, Lexie, and Chance all looked up at the big screen. Celeste had changed her position. She now stood some distance in front of an area swarming with police and surrounded by crime scene tape. I recognized the procedures and a detective I'd met on a previous murder investigation.

A wave of nausea flooded my veins as Benni's jaw fell and her eyes misted over. Benni's hand went to her heart, then her mouth. Her shoulders began to shake and she wiped her cheeks with her fingers. Lexie put her arm around Benni's shoulders, but also seemed fixated by the news.

On the screen, Celeste was introducing the woman who had found Kenji's body. My jaw dropped when I saw her. It was Kelly Atkinson.

"I've been documenting this project since the beginning," Kelly said. "I came out here to take some photos. That's something I do almost every day."

"Now, she gets talkative," I grumbled.

"Perfect opportunity for an on-air commercial," Chance added.

Wisely, Celeste pulled back the mic.

"Good girl," I said. "She knows how to control an interview."

"How did you find the body?" Celeste moved the mic closer to Kelly.

Pointing at the dirt mound now surrounded by crime scene tape, Kelly said, "The backhoe over there caught my attention. Then I noticed the ground looked like it had been dug up or something. You know, it wasn't packed down like everything else. I went over to check it out. I saw a shoe kinda buried. That seemed totally weird, so I took a picture of it. Then I realized the shoe was on a foot."

"Is that when you called the police?"

"For sure. I was totally freaked out, so I dialed 9-1-1."

Kelly started to say something else, but Celeste pulled the mic away again. "To all outward appearances, this is a senseless killing. Kenji Ito was a noted philanthropist. He was a man devoted to his family. But there have been recent allegations about irregularities surrounding the project. It appears the real Kenji Ito was not the same man we all saw from the outside. Is this a case of an innocent man wrongly accused? Or, does this murder point out that there was something to those allegations? HPD will certainly be trying to find out. Celeste Campbell reporting from Kinohi Village."

Her obvious attempt to smear Kenji's name outraged me. "Who does she think she is? Judge and jury?"

The bartender seemed to have forgotten all about throwing us out. He was still watching the screen, shaking his head. He muttered, "Can't trust nobody these days. They all got an agenda. I always thought that dude was trying to help people, but he might've been just as crooked as all them politicians."

"That's what we're going to find out." Chance regarded me. "Right, McKenna?"

At the other end of the bar, Benni was in a full meltdown. Whether I wanted to find Kenji's killer or not was pretty much irrelevant. Benni would want that killer brought to justice. She'd also want Kenji's good name restored. In such a high-profile case, HPD would eventually find the killer. But while they were working the leads and making no comment, reporters like Celeste Campbell could continue to drag Kenji's name through the mud to boost their ratings. We'd already spent a day digging into Kenji's life. We'd found plenty of allegations, but no proof. Well, somebody had to come to the man's defense.

There was no way I could even consider letting Benni down. But even deeper than that, I had another reason to do this. It was her comment from last night—*your baggage is my baggage*—that rang in my head. Sitting in this stupid dive bar that smelled of stale beer and sweat, I was forced to face reality. My time as a loner was over. I now fully shared in Benni's life and that meant

I wanted to clear Kenji's name, too. If that meant finding his killer, so be it.

I looked Chance in the eye, my jaw set, my determination locked and loaded. "You bet we are."

Mr. Hipster gawped at us like we were from outer space. "How are you gonna do that?"

"We'll start by finding that clown you stopped us from interviewing," I snapped. It irritated me that we even had to backtrack. But, thanks to the good Samaritan bartender, that's what we needed to do.

"We'll catch up to him tomorrow, McKenna."

I grimaced. "I know. Tomorrow we can pay him a little visit at work. I just hope he's there and hasn't gone underground."

"He'll be there," Chance said, then opened his wallet and looked at the bartender. "How much do I owe you?"

"Five bucks for the two glasses of wine."

Benni's eyes were rimmed in red and her face was now smudged with mascara. My heart broke at the grief she must be feeling, so while Chance plopped down a ten and told Mr. Hipster to keep the change, I went to Benni. She wrapped her arms around my neck and her voice cracked as she spoke.

"Who would kill him?"

"I don't know, but Chance and I will get to the bottom of this."

"What? Why? Let HPD handle it."

"They'll work the murder. But they're not going to do anything to save Kenji's reputation." I snuck a peek at the bartender and sighed. The court of public opinion was in session. "If we don't do this, everything Kenji worked for could be jeopardized."

Tears misted Benni's eyes as she watched me for the longest time. I waited, in some ways hoping she'd tell me to back off, all the while knowing I'd never get my wish.

Finally, she whispered, "Be careful."

A pall of silence fell over our little group as we stepped through the front door into the night.

15

NOT UNTIL AFTER I MOVED to Hawaii did I come to love the feel of sand between my toes, especially in the evening when the grains still held the warmth of day. Tonight was no different. The first stars twinkled against a gradient sky that began with a bright yellow band on the horizon and slowly blended into deepening shades of blue and black.

Benni walked next to me, her hand clasping mine. We'd been silent since our walk began. Whether she chose to tell me how she felt about Kenji's death or not was less important than the fact that we had this time to distance ourselves from the tragedy of the day.

The number of people on the beach increased as we approached one of the nearby beach condominium complexes. Lovers strolled hand-in-hand. Kids romped in the lazy surf at the shore. Artificial lighting, feeling both garish and intrusive, cast the slowly moving surf into iridescent white bands that crawled toward shore.

Benni's hand squeezed mine and she stopped. Her brow furrowed in the harsh lighting. "Can we go back? I can't deal with all this."

"Of course."

We did an about-face and drifted down to the waterline. Wavelets washed over our feet, making little rippling sounds before coming to a stop and retreating. Benni bent down to pick up a small stone polished by years of wave action. She stroked its surface a few times, smiled weakly, then returned it to the sand.

"I'm sorry," I said. "You really cared about him, didn't you?"

"I care about all my clients, but Kenji was special because I've known him for so long. I can't believe he's gone. Why? It's so…"

"Senseless?"

"That seems so cliché. But, maybe that's the only way to describe it. I was friends with Sue in elementary school."

"You were friends with half the island in elementary school," I countered.

The corners of her lips curled up and her tone lightened as she spoke. "No. I was related to half the island. But friends? Maybe a quarter."

"It's nice to see you smile. Especially here under the…well, there's no moon, but there are a few stars."

"Condo security lighting. Loud parties."

I kissed her, then pulled her close. "You are down, aren't you?"

We resumed our stroll. It wasn't until we'd gone several steps that Benni responded.

"There's so much hatred in the world. In school, Mrs. Nakamura tried to teach us how to be tolerant."

"Why do I have the feeling this gets back to living with aloha?"

"It's like yin and yang. It's all connected. She always told us we should try to understand, not judge."

"I thought your dad didn't like haoles. How'd he deal with his daughter coming home with all these inclusionary ideas?"

"He was very resistant. I never did convince him there was a better way."

"You know, Mrs. Nakamura's got good intentions, but..." I stopped, shook my head, and said, "Never mind."

Benni cocked her head to one side and scrutinized my face. "What? Did Auntie do something?"

How did I tell her about the old lady's meddling? The brochure. The full-court press for a big wedding. The self-doubts I now had. "She came to the apartment this afternoon. After you talked to her."

"Was she upset?"

I took a deep breath. The steel blue and yellow along the horizon had almost disappeared and was now only a thin band of deep mauve. Above, more stars filled the sky. "She had a wedding brochure with her."

"Oh my God." Benni dropped her head and laughed. "Let me guess, she wanted you to arrange a large wedding."

"That's exactly it. And if that's what you want, I'm okay with it. I mean, I'd be happy with it. It's your big day and I want it to be perfect for you."

"It's our big day," she said pointedly. "There's something you should realize about Auntie. I love her dearly, but she's fixated on what she missed. Think about it, her mother was a picture bride from Japan. She married on the dock in a mass ceremony with all the other brides from the boat. And when Auntie married, her family couldn't afford anything extravagant. "

"You're saying I should ignore what she's telling me?"

"No. I'm asking what kind of wedding would make you happy? I'm interested in what you want. It's the same question you're asking me, but in reverse. And you've been very noncommittal about this so far."

The trade winds whispered in my ear. Wishing I understood their meaning, I pointed at the horizon. "Did you know the moon, which was a waning crescent tonight, set at 5:08 p.m.?"

"I have no idea how you know the exact time, but it sounds to me like you're using one of your skip tracing secrets on me."

I chuckled. "Number nine, actually—when you're cornered, create a distraction. But I wasn't doing it intentionally." The ribbon of mauve along the horizon was almost gone now, leaving behind only a black canvas on which someone had scattered a handful of glitter. "What I want," I mused. "Good question."

"Do you even know?"

The truth was, I hadn't given much thought to my preferences. I'd been so focused on making the day special for Benni that… "I think I lost sight of myself," I blurted. "And maybe…I want something small so we don't get buried in debt before we get started."

"That's a practical decision."

"Ouch. You want me to think with my heart."

"You're getting closer. What I really want is for you to share what's in your heart. Are you yearning for an extravagant service with a hundred guests? Or do you want to keep it small and intimate?"

"I know I want to be with you. I want to be the best that I can be for you. Those things are the most important to me. Why am I the one taking all the heat? What do you want?"

"I want you to not get hurt by some deranged killer."

"Ah, number nine again."

A tiny wavelet lapped at our feet and Benni smiled. "It wasn't intentional."

The Sunsetter Apartments came into view and we continued along the beach, our feet slapping against wet sand, Benni's steps in time with mine. We stopped to let the water splash over our toes. "This," I said. "I want this. The sand. The surf. The trade winds. Our closest friends. Even your grumpy old dad if he'll come. And you, most of all, I want to spend my day and the rest of my life with you."

"You're saying to keep things small?"

"Absolutely. Your turn."

"The same. It's what I've said all along."

And she had. I just hadn't been listening. "I'm giving the brochure to Chance. Maybe Mrs. Nakamura will get her big wedding yet."

But even as one weight lifted, I felt a new one taking its place. As I'd found out before, investigating a murder was dangerous business. If Benni still wanted me to clear Kenji's name, all I could promise was to avoid danger when and where I could. That wouldn't make her feel better, so maybe the answer she needed was something else altogether.

"I was watching you in the bar when you first heard the news about Kenji."

Any trace of a smile she might have had disappeared. Her voice faltered. "That was such a terrible moment."

"It was. But it was also a turning point for me." I described how I'd realized I was no longer alone and how our lives were now intertwined. When I finished, I said, "From now on, when I do something, I'll be thinking about how it affects us, not just me."

She kissed me on the cheek and whispered, "I love you."

"I love you, too."

Then, she bit her upper lip and looked over her shoulder at the apartment. Our apartment. "There's something else you should realize. While I respected and loved Kenji, I would rather have his killer go free than see you come to harm."

"Letting someone get away with murder isn't an option."

"Nor is losing you. I'm serious, McKenna. Be careful, and if it gets dangerous, turn what you have over to the police." Her smile returned, and she quickly added, "You are not getting out of this marriage, so don't even think about dying on me."

"Promise," I said as we started toward the lānai. All the time wishing the burden of finding a killer didn't weigh so heavily on my shoulders.

16

THE CEILING FAN BLADES MOVED in an endless, almost-silent blur. Set to low, the fan created the gentlest breeze that brushed my skin with it's cool caress. With my arms over the top of a lightweight blanket, I listened to the shushed murmur of Benni's breathing. The numbers on my bedside clock read 10:47.

Each time I started to drop off to sleep, another scrap of information about Kenji Ito intruded on my thoughts. So many contradictions. He was a good family man—but maybe not. He cared about his employees—or did he? He'd disappeared voluntarily—or was murdered before he could even make it to his daughter's big presentation. None of it made sense. Not even Kelly's version of how she found the body.

Kelly Atkinson's description seemed reasonable enough until Benni and I did some channel surfing to see what the other stations were saying. We discovered Celeste Campbell had scooped them all. It was certainly possible Celeste was in the neighborhood when the 9-1-1 call went out. In fact, if I believed in the unicorn called coincidence, I'd go for that option. The problem was, I didn't believe in unicorns. What I did believe in was the treachery of man—or in this case, woman.

I slipped out of bed, pulled on a pair of shorts and a tee shirt, then crept out of the room and closed the door behind me. Setting up my laptop on the dining table, I began a search for Kelly Atkinson. It hadn't occurred to me until the constant circling of the fan blades had almost sent me into a trance, but she'd mentioned a quote-unquote gig that had kept her afloat when someone stole her equipment. What I wanted to know was if that job was her work at Kinohi Village. Was she, or wasn't she, being paid by someone to be there?

My first virtual stop was Kelly's website. It had a beautiful design. Soothing colors. Easy-to-read text. This was a first-class job. The main element on the home page was an impressive slide show of photos that included a sunrise at Makapu'u Beach, another of the sun setting behind the Honolulu Harbor, and one truly spectacular shot from Haleakalā. Kelly's work was stellar—these were the kinds of pictures people paid real money for—and there were so many amazing shots that I temporarily forgot what I was hoping to find.

On the products page I found all of those shots from the home page and many more for sale. Delving further, I found a section for astrophotography and another for what Kelly called 'project documentation.' Basically, these were more photos from her one and only project to be documented—some Chance and I had already seen. There was no client list. Nothing to indicate she was being paid. I had nothing more than I'd had before spending thirty minutes on a wild goose chase, and that ticked me off.

I might be at a dead end with Kelly for now, but my determination to question her motive—was it altruism or greed?—burned in my gut. A long time ago, I'd learned that if one path was closed off, you tried another. It was time to find out how Celeste had scooped all the other news channels.

Like Kelly, Celeste also had a website. Immediately under the banner and to the right of the page was a bio photo. It had obviously been taken by a professional. Out of curiosity, I checked the credit. Read the name. Read it again.

"No way," I whispered. But there it was, clear as could be. Kelly Atkinson was credited with taking the photo. And she'd been very clear that she didn't like doing studio work. "What are you two up to?" I said aloud.

The instant the words popped out of my mouth, I clamped my jaw shut. So far, I hadn't woken Benni. But if I started talking to myself, I would for sure. Making a zipping motion with my fingers across my closed lips, I went back to work.

In the top menu, the first item was Celeste's bio. It was well-written and, not surprisingly, engaging. Apparently, even as a young girl Celeste had wanted to be a journalist. She began preparing for her dream job in third grade when she used her grandmother's wooden spoon as a microphone to conduct interviews. The bio skipped from those early days to 2010, the year she began working for the Honolulu Star-Advertiser.

To be truthful, I had no idea how old Celeste was, but I'd place her in her late thirties to early forties. If I was correct, she hadn't gotten into her dream job until she was around thirty-years-old. Assuming she left high school when she was eighteen, her bio was missing at least twelve years. Where had she been for more than a decade?

The other oddity was that Celeste didn't mention any education or career preparation for her time at the Star-Advertiser. It was possible she'd had to work her way up the ladder. Admittedly, starting at the bottom wasn't exactly brag worthy, but it could show her perseverance. She'd covered everything from sports to feature stories during her six years at the Star-Advertiser, but after surviving two rounds of layoffs, had been caught in the third. She'd made the transition to TV news and had quickly shown herself capable of handling breaking news. It was an impressive—and speedy—recovery. Very impressive, and now that I was in cynical mode, I felt like I was being asked to believe in unicorns again.

I'd dealt with plenty of debtors caught up in downsizings on the mainland. In those cases, I'd been the bad guy. The one who had to tell them they were going to lose their car or their home if they didn't find a new source of income. What that meant was Celeste's story was nothing new to me, or to the hundreds of employees laid off at O'ahu Publications when the business ran into its worst nightmare—an amorphous giant called the Internet.

I could just imagine the terror jobseekers felt every time the company announced a new round of layoffs. From office clerks to seasoned reporters to editors, they were all dumped into a market restricted by geography and economics. Tourism ran Hawaii, so all those laid-off news people must have found few local opportunities. Few could have continued in journalism if they didn't want to relocate. And yet, Celeste had pulled it off.

The next page I checked on Celeste's website was called *In The News*. It was filled with links to news stories Celeste had either written or covered as part of a team. The longer I scrolled through the list, the more my vision blurred. Finally, sleep felt like it was closing in, but I wasn't ready to stop. A few entries in the list contained Kenji's name or the company's name. It appeared that Celeste had a preoccupation with Kenji, and most recently, Kinohi Village.

Using earbuds, I watched the video clips, which included coverage of almost every meeting for the project from its inception. By the time I'd seen three of those clips, I'd seen enough. Her stories were either those of a hard-nosed journalist determined to keep the players honest, or she had an ax to grind.

The bartender at the Airport Tavern had spoken of Celeste as though he knew her. I'd bet he knew her the same way as all the other people who watched the nightly news. She was the reporter on the scene. The one who was charged with conveying the truth. But, whose truth?

Given her platform, how many people had Celeste turned against Kenji Ito? Was Kelly Atkinson one of those? Maybe that was their connection. Kelly's gig. There were just too many coincidences involving Celeste and Kelly for my taste.

Celeste being on the scene to cover Kenji's murder didn't bother me at all. She was a reporter and that was her job. What bothered me was her being first by such a significant margin. And that she'd gotten what appeared to be an exclusive interview with the person who discovered the body. Someone who obviously would have relished exposure on multiple networks, but had settled for one.

My eyelids felt like someone had poured wet cement over them. Exhaustion was taking it's toll on my ability to think clearly. Tomorrow morning I'd share my findings with Chance. Together, we could review what we'd learned about both Celeste and Kelly.

I closed the lid of my laptop, went to the lānai screen door, and slid it open. Stepping outside, I took in a breath of fresh air.

The ocean had calmed. The waves were soft and quiet. Though barely visible in the darkness, I made out the silhouette of someone walking along the beach. Suddenly, whoever was down there turned and walked purposefully in my direction.

17

AT EIGHT MINUTES BEFORE THE stroke of midnight I slipped out the screen door and crossed the grass to the sand. The figure I'd seen by the water walked toward me. Male. Tall. Easy gait. He raised an arm and waved. I waved back. As we closed the distance, I recognized Chance.

Once we were within talking distance, I said, "What are you doing out here? You're too young to have trouble sleeping."

He shrugged and kicked at the sand. "Lexie's at her place tonight. I've been out here for about an hour. I saw you working and considered joining you, but I figured it might wake up Benni."

"Thanks for that. I'm sure she appreciates it." With the exception of us, the beach was deserted. "You know, I haven't been out here this late in a long time. I forgot how beautiful it is. And, of course, now I'm not sleepy."

"I sometimes come out here to unwind." Chance gazed at the sky as he spoke, his voice distant, almost as though he were speaking to the stars. "So much of what we heard today sounds bogus."

"I know. One of them being the time of death. If it's true that Kenji wouldn't have missed Sue's presentation, that means he must have been killed sometime yesterday."

Chance checked his watch and sighed. "You're almost right, McKenna. It's after midnight, so today's Wednesday."

"Okay, wise guy. I think someone killed him Monday afternoon. At least that would explain why he missed the meeting."

A strong breeze gusted, almost as if it wanted to join the conversation. Chance seemed to be pondering some dark thought. "Yeah, Monday. HPD will nail that down for certain, but you know what also doesn't make sense? That whole thing with Derrick Tanaka. He never did say how he got your number, and he was so afraid of talking. Somebody's got to have him under their thumb."

I hated to admit it, but I'd been so bothered by the minutiae of the day that I'd skipped over the Tanaka incident altogether—and he was one of the day's glaring inconsistencies. "You're right. He might be worried that he's next."

"So why come to us at all? The guy could have laid low, never said a word, and had no worries. And yet, he volunteers to become a snitch."

"A snitch who doesn't want to talk."

"Totally. That's a guy who's either seriously deranged or needs money desperately."

"There's another option, you know. What if he's working for someone? He got into an argument with his boss and decided to rat him out. He got to the bar and realized what a bad idea it was, chickened out, and ran at the first opportunity."

"That's a lot of suppositions from someone who doesn't believe in coincidence," Chance said.

"It is, but there's no coincidence. It's all based on good old-fashioned greed and McKenna's Skip Tracing Secret #9."

"That's the one about creating distractions, right?"

"Very good, grasshopper."

Chance snickered. "Sometimes, I just think you make up this crap to mess with my head."

"No way. This one came from one of my first skips. Each time I got close, something happened. The last time, I'd traced the guy to San Francisco. I got to the house, peeked in the garage, and saw the car. Thought I had him for sure, so I called a tow truck. I had the driver park in the driveway so my guy couldn't get away."

"So you got the car. Doesn't sound like there was much of a distraction going on."

"That's where you're wrong. I went to the door and knocked, but my skip wouldn't answer. In the meantime, my driver got a call from his dispatcher saying his truck had nicked a car while making a turn a few blocks back. The owner of the car was going to file hit-and-run charges if the driver didn't show up in about two minutes."

"So your tow driver left you alone?"

"Right. And there wasn't much I could do without him. I wasn't about to let some dirtbag get the better of me, so I decided to park in the driveway. While I was crossing the street to get my car, the garage door opened and my skip drove away."

Chance eyed me for a few seconds, then smirked. "I'm never sure when you're telling me the truth and when you're making it up as you go along. So does this little fable have a happy ending?"

"Eventually, but that's a whole different story." I cleared my throat, determined not to tell him the rest. "Now, I want to know what's been going on with you."

"Nothing to worry about."

"That won't work on me. Not here. Not now. It's after midnight, Chance. I'm tired and I want sleep, but I also want to know why you've been so detached lately. I have another prospective tenant meeting tomorrow at noon, and I…"

"Lexie wants kids," Chance blurted.

"What?"

"You know, keiki. Maybe it's you and Benni getting married —I don't know. A couple weeks ago she just said it during dinner. I didn't know what to say."

"I may not be much of a marriage expert, but I think there's a simple answer to this question. Do you love her?"

"I'm crazy about her, but it's not that—it's me. I don't think I'd be a good dad."

The urge to burst into laughter nearly overpowered me. Fortunately, I held it in and was able to maintain a straight face. "I don't think any first-time dad is ready."

"I'm too immature. I like my free time. I want to do some philanthropic work. I…what if I get killed on the job?"

This time, I couldn't stop the urge. "What job? Private investigator? I haven't checked mortality rates, but I'd bet most of those guys live to a ripe old age. Unless they drink themselves to death."

"I'm being serious, McKenna. I'm worried. We've been in a couple of pretty shaky situations. Kind of like your skip. When people get desperate…at least you recovered your car."

I sighed and shook my head. "Actually, I didn't."

"But you said the story had a happy ending."

"It all worked out."

Chance crossed his arms over his chest and craned his neck forward. "Tell me what happened. Now."

I didn't want to relive ancient history, but it appeared Chance had found a diversion from dealing with my questions about him and wasn't about to let this go. "Fine. This was before cell phones. I followed the guy for a little while, but lost him. I stopped at a phone booth and called the office. They said my guy had called in and I could pick up the car. The keys were in it. He left it on Highway 1. Gave me the exact mile marker and everything."

"Sounds like a pretty good deal to me."

"Here's the bad part. When I got to where he said the car was located, there were cops all over. I told one of the cops who I was and he said he'd show me the car. He took me to the edge of the road and pointed down the side of the cliff. There was my car. On the rocks. Totaled. The guy had left the keys in it alright, but he hadn't set the emergency brake and he'd left it in neutral."

It took a few seconds for Chance to respond. "You've got to be kidding me."

"Nope. Like I said, there was a happy ending. The insurance paid off the loan on the car. So there you have it—McKenna's Skip Tracing Secret #9. Now, I'm beat. It's been a long day and I need some sleep."

Gazing at the shoreline, Chance seemed lost in thought. I was about to tell him I'd see him in the morning when he crossed his arms over his chest and faced me. "Do you really think I'd be a good dad? What if I wasn't? What if Lexie and I broke up? I'd never want to do what Missy's husband did and abandon a child."

"That's not your style, buddy. You're too responsible…and you've got plenty of money just in case you do get flaky."

"Right now. But maybe Missy was right. Maybe we're all only one step away from disaster."

18

ON WEDNESDAY MORNING, CHANCE AND I headed back to Kinohi Village. Because our intention was to bypass Julie the Gatekeeper, we'd coordinated a plan with Benni. For now, we were parked about a block from the entrance in a spot where the nearest shade was a pipe dream. At least I'd planned for this possibility and worn the cheap version of a Panama hat. It not only gave my skin some shelter from the sun, but also let my scalp breathe through the woven material. Chance had gone with his new favorite baseball cap—gray and blue with a surfing stick figure on the front.

"You're sure she's going to be leaving?" Chance asked.

"Positive. Benni said that Sue scheduled a ten o'clock meeting to go over the business continuation plan. As the senior person on the site, Julie was required to be there."

"How do we know she hasn't already left? We could be sitting here all morning."

"Benni will text me when Julie shows up." A few seconds later, my phone pinged with the message I'd been waiting for. "Talk about perfect timing. Julie just walked in. She must not have come to the job site at all…"

The Ferrari roared to life and cut me off mid sentence, but I wasn't about to complain. The moving air felt wonderful. The heat was also taking its toll on the picketers. There were fewer here today than on our last visit. Comparatively speaking, we zipped through their line with no trouble at all.

Chance parked in front of the office. "Hardhats, anyone?"

"Sure. At least we can say we tried."

Entering the trailer, which we expected to be empty, turned into a life's most embarrassing moment. Missy was there—and she was nursing her baby.

"Sorry!" Chance blurted and started to retreat.

Missy laughed, laid a small towel over the baby's head, and waved us into the room. "It's okay. After four kids, I don't worry about being interrupted during feeding time. It's just part of life, yah?"

Standing behind Chance, I patted his shoulder and tried to sound reassuring. "See what you're in for, buddy? Someday Lexie will be doing that same thing."

He blanched, which made both Missy and me chuckle.

"My husband was the same way with our first. You'll adjust."

"He's new to the whole idea of keiki," I said.

"Like you're an expert?" Chance shot back.

"Not worried about it. My swimmers are all dead. Yours, on the other hand, are ready to dive into the channel and…"

"Enough!" Chance rolled his eyes. "McKenna, sometimes I wonder why I put up with you."

A few years ago, he might not have. But since then, I'd changed a lot. "I'm a lot more fun that I used to be." I turned my attention to Missy. "We actually came in here for a couple of hardhats. Can you help us out?"

Missy checked a nearby desk calendar, frowned, then shook her head. "I don't see an appointment for you. I'm sorry, but Julie had a meeting. Was she expecting you?"

"We were just in the neighborhood." The lie rolled off my tongue without hesitation.

The baby's head lolled slightly under the towel, which must have been the signal that feeding time was over and nap time was on. Missy repositioned her shirt and put the towel on the desk. "Julie's pretty strict."

"Too strict?" I asked, then quickly added, "This is all related to Kenji's murder."

Missy's expression fell, and her lower lip quivered. "I don't have time to watch the news, but everybody's talking about it. Who would want to kill him?"

"That's what we're trying to find out," Chance said. "Do you suppose you could help us?"

"How?"

Talk about a green light. I caught Chance's attention and motioned toward Missy with my eyes.

"You could begin by telling us about Derrick Tanaka and Joe Taylor," he said.

"Oh, those two." Missy's upper lip curled in disgust. "Where do I even start?"

"How about with Joe Taylor? Was he fired for being drunk on the job?"

"And why Derrick Tanaka would know about it," I added. My comment was met by a mild visual poke in the ribs from

117

Chance. Got it. Wait your turn. Only one interrogator allowed at a time.

"All I've heard are rumors," she said. "Julie never said why Kenji fired Joe, but the coconut wireless says it wasn't a legit firing. As for Derrick, he's got his nose in everything. He's a troublemaker."

Chance rested one hip on the desk and hunched forward slightly to make his presence less imposing. "What kind of trouble does he cause?"

"He's always stirring the pot, yah? Usually, if there's a rumor, he's the one who started it. It's almost like he deliberately wants this project to fail." She paused, then added, "I wish they'd have fired him instead of Joe. At least he never got people all riled up."

Chance might have a black belt in karate, but I had mine in reading people. A subtle change in Missy's demeanor led me to believe she was willing to tell us more. I stayed far enough away from Chance to be sure he couldn't jab or kick me. "What do you mean, instead of Joe?"

She bit her lip, then looked down at her baby, who was now sleeping peacefully. "Joe's had a lot of problems."

"What kind of problems?" Chance asked.

"He was kind of direct. And he could be super critical of how people did their jobs."

"So Derrick didn't like him?"

"They didn't get along."

"Derrick told us they were friends," Chance said.

"So not true," Missy said with a snort. "A couple days before Joe got fired, he called out Derrick for badmouthing Kenji. They kinda got into it. Julie said she had to give Joe a warning. That's about all I know."

Chance acknowledged Missy's help with a reassuring smile and a head nod. "No worries. Can you tell us where Derrick is now?"

Missy pointed out the window. "Somewhere out there. I don't keep track of the workers. I've got enough problems with the tenants. One of them called me first thing, all worked up and worried about what's going to happen to the project. That was the first time I heard about Kenji."

The clock on the wall reminded me we might not have a lot of time. We didn't know how long the meeting with Sue would last, and we definitely wanted to be out of here before Julie got back. "Tell you what, Missy. We need to talk to Tanaka, but I'd like to leave you one of my cards. If you think of anything else, just give me a call."

Chance also gave her one of his. She pocketed both. "I'll grab two hard hats. Good luck out there."

Outside the office, the sounds of construction again assaulted our ears. A trencher dug holes for an irrigation line. The rap-rap-rap of electric hammers alternated with the high-pitched whine of drills. A couple of houses away, Mondo and Freddie were building a wooden lānai in the middle of several homes. We meandered through the area, nonchalantly waving to anyone who glanced our way. With no sign of Derrick Tanaka on the outside of the homes, we started searching inside. We found him on our third try. He had his back to us. I gave Chance a thumbs up and he moved in.

Chance tapped Tanaka's shoulder. Tanaka spun on his heel, his jaw dropped, and he immediately searched for an exit route. He had none.

"What do you guys want?" he stammered.

"Answers." Chance moved closer, planted his thumb near that magic spot he'd been using last night, and stared intently at Tanaka.

Right now, the poor man looked like he was about ready to pee his pants. That was fine by me. In fact, it was perfection in a bottle for our purposes. "Why don't we continue our conversation from last night? Do you like working here, Derrick?"

"Yeah. Why?"

"Because most guys who are happy with their jobs don't go around badmouthing their bosses," I said. "And most bosses don't like hearing that kind of thing has been happening on the job. Am I right, Chance?"

"Totally."

Tanaka's attention wavered between Chance and me. Finally, he must have decided the only way he'd get rid of the guy who could physically hurt him was to play nice with the one who was asking questions. "I don't like what I'm having to do, brah. I got a wife and three keiki. I needed some extra money to make ends meet. You know?"

"Keep talking." Chance's tone leveled off, but he still maintained his grip on Tanaka's shoulder.

"Graham's the dude to talk to."

"Tynsdale?" I blurted. "I thought he was just a protestor?"

"No way, brah. All those losers out front? He organized 'em all. He got me into this thing, too. Dude's a genius about this kinda stuff. Knows all the buttons he can push to make people do what he wants."

Chance and I exchanged a look that I interpreted to mean something like we'd both run out of patience with this clown.

What was he trying to pull now? "What buttons of yours did he push? Was it enough to make you commit murder?"

"I didn't kill nobody."

"Then what did you do?" I snapped.

"I was supposed to spread rumors. Graham told me what to say. I knew the guys that would fall for it. Repeat it. You know? Pretty soon, nobody knows where it started and everybody thinks it's true."

Chance stepped to within a few inches of Tanaka and gritted his teeth. "I am so tired of you. What rumors did you spread?"

"The last one was about Joe Taylor and him being fired for no good reason. A couple days before Joe got fired, me and him kinda got into it. Julie gave him a warning 'cause I got a couple of the guys to say he started things. The morning he got fired, I went to Julie and told her Joe threatened me. She fired him and since she couldn't say nothing about it, I told everyone they claimed he was drinking and it wasn't true."

Finally, I understood the role Tanaka played. "You're a real piece of work, Derrick."

Tanaka hung his head, then peered at me. "I needed the money, brah."

At last, a shred of truth.

19

WE FINISHED WITH TANAKA AND returned our hardhats to the office. Missy was talking on the phone when we walked in. She waved, we returned the greeting, and then a soft cooing came from the floor near her feet where the baby was playing happily with a colorful toy.

"If only life were so easy," I said.

Missy finished her phone call, bent down, and jabbered in baby talk. "I know. Life was so easy when I was little. I had no idea how poor we were, but we were happy. Did you find Derrick?"

"We did," Chance said. "He confessed that he set Joe up to be fired. And that he's the one who started the rumor Joe wasn't really drunk."

"That man. What's his problem?"

"We're not entirely sure," I said.

Chance inched by me, uncertainty on his face.

"Go ahead," Missy chuckled. "She won't break."

Chance swallowed, then knelt next to the carseat and held his finger out. Five tiny fingers clasped onto what was apparently interpreted as a new toy. Chance's eyes widened and he sucked in a breath. The next thing I knew, he was talking baby talk. Oh boy, unless I was mistaken, he'd just fallen head-over-heels in love with the idea of kids.

Ignoring playtime, I said, "Tanaka gave us a couple of ideas, but we have to do some digging to see how much of what he said is true."

Chance had a stupid grin on his face when he looked at Missy. "She's adorable." He immediately started talking again in a strange tongue I'd never mastered.

With my partner out of commission due to baby-brain, I decided to charge ahead on my own. "If you don't mind my asking, have you ever seen Graham Tynsdale and Tanaka together?"

Missy's eyebrows went up. "Those two? Why? Is there a connection?"

Rats. This girl was way too curious for me to be lobbing out careless questions. "Again, we don't know. Have you ever seen them together?"

"Never. The protestors can't set foot on the property, and if a worker went out there, everybody would know."

"That's helpful." And it was, because she'd not only answered the direct question, but another one—just how devious might Graham Tynsdale and Derrick Tanaka be?

Unfortunately, my ride was still enthralled by the game of grab-the-big-pinky, which I was beginning to suspect he'd be happy to play for the rest of the day. Talk about a comedown. I'd arrived in a smoking-hot red Ferrari. And now I might have to take public transit home?

"Uh, Chance?"

"What, McKenna?" Not even a hint of interest.

Thank God I had a monthly bus pass. "We should be going. We still have…um…people to see."

"Right."

"Chance! Snap out of it. We're trying to find a killer, not an adoption candidate."

He shook his head and stood. "Sorry. I got a little distracted."

"It happens a lot," Missy said with a sly smile. She lifted her chin and indicated the construction area. "You should see some of these guys. They might act all macho, but she turns them into big marshmallows."

I grabbed Chance's shirtsleeve and tugged. "Come on. We need to get you out of here before the spell becomes permanent."

We thanked Missy for her time. On the way out the door, Chance gave the little bundle of joy a final wave. That was the final straw. Once I got Chance alone, I was conducting my own little intervention.

As the office door closed behind us, I said, "What's going on with you, buddy? Last night you were freaked out about the idea of kids and today your brain turned to mush when that little girl grabbed your finger."

"You saw?" He beamed at me, a stupid-me grin pasted on his face. "Wasn't she awesome?"

"In the car, kid. You need a baby-brain antidote. The Ferrari should do it."

Chance kept glancing back at the office. As a result, he stumbled—twice—getting into the car. Once in, he started the engine, adjusted the rearview mirror, then gave me a sheepish grin. "I'm thinking about getting rid of the Ferrari."

"Maybe it's best if you wait. You know what they say—don't make any life-changing decisions immediately after trauma."

"I haven't suffered a trauma, McKenna. What are you talking about?"

"Trust me on this. That little girl cast an evil spell on you. If it doesn't wear off in twenty-four hours, Benni's got a cousin who knows a witch doctor. We can fly him in if we have to."

Chance muttered under his breath as he shoved the car into gear. The trip out of the project went smoothly. Graham Tynsdale was still not in sight, but if the man was working for someone trying to bring down this project, we'd find out. Guaranteed.

As we neared Kelly Atkinson's place, I noticed that the stupid grin Chance had been wearing since his baby encounter was still there. I suspected he really would sell the Ferrari, marry Lexie, and start a family. I was happy for him, but feared it could be the end of our partnership—or, at a minimum, his lease. After all, who wanted to raise a baby in a one-bedroom apartment?

We scored the same parking place as on our first visit to Kelly's—last spot before the fire hydrant and right next to the concrete pony wall with untamed weeds on the other side. Classy, huh?

As we crossed the street, I said, "Let's go straight up to the studio."

Chance studied the second-floor unit. "I hope she's in. Why didn't you want to call first?"

"We need the element of surprise." I slipped open the gate and cringed. "This thing needs some TLC. So much for surprise." I waited for Chance to close the gate, then we climbed the stairs.

On the way up, Chance asked, "McKenna? Does Benni really have a cousin who knows a witch doctor?"

"No. I made that up. Besides, I think you just answered your big question from last night. You'll be a great dad. Why would I want to get in the way of that?"

"Thanks," Chance said absently, then gestured at the door. "Go for it. I'm right behind you. If she's with a client and doesn't want to be disturbed, she can take it out on you." He paused, chuckled, then added, "I'll catch you if you fall backwards."

"I might have to take back my compliment." But it was nice to see Chance's sense of humor returning. There was not a doubt in my mind that if something truly dangerous did happen, he'd step in to help me. So, without any compunctions about what might be on the other side of the door, I knocked.

After a few seconds with no answer, I harrumphed. "Maybe she didn't hear me. I'll try again."

"What are you waiting for? Knock, already," Chance chuckled.

I did. Louder, this time. Then a third time.

"We surprised her, alright," Chance said.

"You didn't think she'd be here, did you?" I grumbled.

"She's a photographer who shoots outdoors. This early in the day, I'd expect her to be out taking pictures so she can come back this afternoon and process them."

"Okay, you got me. She must be busier than I thought."

"Let's check with the girl in the main house. Maybe she knows something."

"We can do that, but you're taking the lead on that one."

"No worries. I'll just turn on the charm." He flipped his hand nonchalantly and headed down the stairs.

We exited the gate, turned left, and made another left at the corner. This time, I followed him up the stairs. The main door was again open. With the trades to our backs, the breeze kept up a steady flow through the screen door. This time, at least, it was silent inside the house.

I tapped Chance on the shoulder just before he knocked. "By the way. If something bad happens there's no way I can catch you." I pointed behind me. "Bad back."

"Gotcha." Chance turned and knocked.

The same platinum blonde we'd spoken to yesterday eventually appeared on the other side of the screen door. When she saw us, she approached warily. "What?"

"We're here to see Kelly, but she doesn't appear to be in," Chance said calmly.

"She left last night."

It felt like a thunderclap had gone off in my head. Talk about déjà vu. How many times had I heard that line in my career? "Do you know where we can find her?"

The girl dabbed at her cheek with a wadded-up tissue. "No. I don't. I'm calling the police if you two don't leave right now." She pulled a phone from her back pocket and held it up. "You don't scare me."

Chance pulled out his PI-in-training ID and held it up against the screen door. "We're investigating the death of Kenji Ito. Because Kelly found the body, we wanted to see if she could recollect anything she didn't tell the police."

She eyed us suspiciously at first, then reached into her front pocket and pulled out a business card. Glancing from the card to Chance's ID, she took a deep breath and unlatched the door. "Kel left me your card. I'm worried something's happened to her."

"Do you think it has?" Chance asked.

She shook her head, pushed open the door, and gestured for us to enter. She wore leggings, an oversized tee, and had about an inch of dark roots showing. Not being one who followed the celebs closely, I wasn't sure if that was still in style or a fad on it's way out. Either way, it was a look that seemed to work for her. If I were to pass her on the street, I'd assume she was a carefree, hip, twenty-something. But here? Now? No way. This girl was worried.

She latched the screen door and led us into the living room, where she stood with one leg stretched in front of her and her arms crossed. I recognized the defensive body posture, but even more than that, there were signs of an underlying fear—the tugging on a few strands of hair, wrapping them around her finger, and chewing on her lower lip. And this time, it wasn't because she'd fallen in love with Chance.

"What's your name?" I asked.

"Barbara."

"Do you think you're in danger, Barbara?" I asked.

"I…I don't know. Kel didn't say anything like that in her note."

"She left a note?"

Barbara nodded absently. "Could she be in danger?"

"Let's hope not. Did she give you any indication of what she was running from?"

A shaking of the head. A hard swallow. "Could this be related to that guy's murder?"

What did we say at this point? The only thing we knew for sure was that Kelly found the body, reported it to the news, came home, then left. You didn't have to be a math whiz to add two and two and come up with an answer that led to Kelly being in over her head.

20

A DELIVERY TRUCK ROARED BY, shattering the otherwise quiet atmosphere inside the home. Barbara flinched, gripped her arms around herself, and shot a nervous glance at the front door.

"Do you have a key to Kelly's studio?" Chance asked.

"No."

"I know we're strangers to you, but if Kelly's on the run, she might need help," I said. "She told you that you could trust us? Right?"

Barbara hesitated, but then nodded. "Sorry, this is all so weird. The studio's always been her workspace. I don't go in unless she's there. Kel's always said that just because she works from home doesn't mean we should treat her photography business any differently than if she had a real studio."

"Have you known her long?" I asked.

"Ten years."

My pulse picked up. Ten years? She must know Kelly better than anyone. "So you two are good friends?"

She held up her left hand. Showed us the wedding ring on her finger. "We were married in 2013."

Oh. Now I got it. The apartment over the garage really was just a studio. I scanned the room. There was a definite feminine influence, a subtle choice of colors and accessories that made the place welcoming and elegant all at the same time.

"You have a lovely home. Have you lived here long?"

"My parents owned it. I grew up here and never thought I'd want to stay, but after I met Kel." She smiled, hugged herself again as though she were cold, and said, "Things change."

Chance seemed to pick up my intention and focused on a large print of Honolulu Harbor. It was a photograph that had been printed on canvas in three sections. Benni had dragged me into a few local art galleries, where I'd been introduced to the concept of a triptych. In this case, the image wrapped around the edges of each section to add a sense of depth.

I admired the image and pointed at it. "Lovely piece."

"Kel's work. She must have spent a hundred hours at the harbor watching sunsets to get that." The tension in Barbara's face relaxed as she talked. "She's got others throughout the house. My favorite is over there."

She pointed at a wall with another sunrise over the ocean. In this one, 'The Mokes,' a pair of islets off Oahu's coast, were bathed in the morning sun. It was one of Oahu's most photographed spots, and Kelly had framed the scene under the graceful arc of a palm frond.

"Magnificent." The real question was, how did we get off the subject of Kelly's work and on the subject of her disappearance?

"We heard she spent a lot of time at Kinohi Village," Chance said.

Barbara visibly tightened up again, pulling her arms in. It was as though she wanted to curl up into a ball.

"It's okay if you're not comfortable talking about this." Giving Chance a minor dose of stink eye, I added, "We might need to give her some space."

"No. It's okay. It's just…the whole thing's so frightening. After Kelly saw some news story on the TV about this project coming up for a big vote with the City Council, she decided to go. She said it sounded like there was a lot of controversy and if she got the right photos she might be able to get more exposure. Kel's always been hungry for recognition."

"Did you see the news story, too?"

"No. I was working. She told me about it the next day. That's when I told her she shouldn't waste her time on it."

"Why's that?" I asked.

"There's always controversy on these big projects. I figured she was just blowing things out of proportion. Kel's one of those people who's brilliant artistically, but doesn't always show a lot of common sense."

"Are you the opposite?"

"I'm an ER nurse. I have to be practical."

"Right. So you two were attracted to each other because you were so different?"

"Kelly appreciates my practicality; I adore her creativity. She said I should exercise my right brain, so I've been trying to learn the piano. It's a huge challenge."

"Ah, you're the one we heard yesterday."

A deep flush radiated into Barbara's cheeks, but she seemed to relax again. "That's embarrassing."

It was, but I wasn't about to criticize. "So Kelly was looking for a way to boost her business?"

"Totally. She said if her photos and her name were attached to a big news story, the right people might see her work."

Chance's gaze narrowed. "A news story? Did she want to be an investigative reporter?"

"Oh, God no." Barbara put her hand over her heart and laughed. "Kelly almost flunked high-school English. She said she talked to some reporter who'd been at the City Council meeting. Celeste something-or-other. Sorry, I don't remember the last name."

"Her last name is Campbell. She's the one who interviewed Kelly after she discovered Kenji's body."

Barbara made a face. "Oh, God. She discovered the body? I wish I'd have known."

"So Kelly didn't tell you about it? She was interviewed on camera."

"No. I picked up a shift last night. The last time I saw Kel was yesterday afternoon. I've been trying to reach her all day, but she hasn't answered her cell. She's been kinda moody lately, so I've been worried sick." She wiped her cheek with her fingers.

Off to the side, I spotted a box of tissues and signaled Chance by cutting my eyes toward it. He caught my signal, picked up the box, and held it out. "I'm sorry for what you're having to go through."

"Thank you," Barbara murmured as she plucked out a tissue and choked back a sob. "I called the hospital and talked to one of the ER nurses. She said she'd call if…if Kelly came through. You know, if something happened to her."

"Nice to have those kinds of connections," I said.

"Some benefit. At least we're married so they can talk to me if the worst happens."

"Let's not go there yet, okay?"

Barbara grimaced, but didn't say a word.

"Would you mind sharing the note?" I asked.

She reached into her back pocket and pulled out a folded piece of paper, which she handed to me.

I've stumbled onto something big and have to disappear. Don't know when I'll be back. Love you, K. PS You can trust this guy.

As I reread the words, my mind buzzed with questions like what could be so serious that Kelly would abandon her life here? Or why would she place so much trust in Chance based on a single meeting? The only answer that made sense was that her disappearance was related to Kenji's murder and she was desperate.

"Has she ever taken off before? Maybe for a weekend— whatever?"

"We always tell each other where we're going. In fact, we usually use an app that lets us see exactly where the other one is."

"Have you tried the app?" Chance asked, hope painted on his face.

"I did that right after I called and got voicemail. It doesn't make any sense because the last location for the phone was along the canal around eight last night. There's been nothing since."

As the saying goes, déjà vu—all over again. Someone disappears. Their phone is dead. They're either afraid of someone hurting them or are running from the law—or they're already dead.

"Would you mind showing me a few of her things?" I asked.

"Like what?" Barbara's eyes widened and she shot a sideways glance at Chance, who was now thoroughly engaged with his phone.

"I used to be a skip tracer. That means I had to find people for a living. Sometimes, it's the littlest things that can provide a clue. Things you take for granted might actually be able to lead us to her."

"I don't know. This is all so weird."

Barbara's arms tightened over her chest again and I suspected I'd hit a little too close to home. Whatever angle Chance was working might be our only hope. The silence lasted only a few seconds.

"Well, good news," he said with a grim smile. "There have been no reports of drownings in the canal. It could be she disposed of the phone to avoid being traced. About the only way I can see her doing that is to toss it into some deep water."

"Of course," I said. "The canal. The phone might not die immediately, but it wouldn't last long. Which means, we're back to the question of what would freak her out so much she'd feel the need to leave everything behind?"

I could only think of one thing. And I wasn't about to verbalize it in front of Barbara.

21

AT THE MENTION OF KELLY ditching her cell, Barbara returned to panic mode. Desperate to find her spouse, she wanted to rehash the same questions and answers, fears and doubts. It was perfectly understandable, and while I was confident that I could find Kelly if I spent enough time at it, that wasn't going to happen right away. Most likely, the fastest way to bring her home safely was to put Kenji's killer away.

As we returned to Chance's car, I reminded him of the meeting with my next prospective tenant. She was coming on her lunch hour, so with any luck she'd be employed, personable, and ready to rent.

"Now? Seriously, McKenna?" Chance's voice rose. "How does renting an apartment fit in with solving a murder?"

"Chillax, buddy. It won't take long. I have a good feeling about this one. Remember, I'm supposed to be an apartment manager, which means I should manage the apartments once in a while."

Chance dropped down into the driver's seat and started the engine. "Okay, I get it. Day job. Obligations. Anyway, I'll track down Celeste Campbell. If Kelly was working with her, she must know something. She might even have some sort of reliable background on Kenji."

"Sounds like a plan. Now we both have work to do." I wanted to put a good spin on this, but the reality was I'd never gotten over my primal instinct—the thrill of the hunt. It was a drug I found myself craving at times. And, let's face it, managing an apartment complex was not even on the same playing field.

We arrived at the Sunsetter parking lot with about ten minutes to spare. I had time to get inside, open up to let in some fresh air, and try to make myself presentable. As I said, I was expecting good things from this lady and wanted to make the right impression myself. The meeting was at noon, but at five minutes before, my phone rang with a call from Sue Ito.

Now what did I do? Take the call? Send her to voicemail? Rats. I pressed the green button on the display to answer. "Hey, Sue. I'm glad you called, but I only have a few minutes. I have a meeting coming up."

"It's okay, McKenna. We can talk afterwards."

"Thanks. I'll call you when I'm done."

"I wanted to tell you about my meeting with Benni and Julie."

What part of 'I'll call you' didn't she understand? I made small circles with my fingers as if that might speed up the conversation. "Sure, no problem."

"I have a clue for you, too. Something that will really help. Bye."

The line went dead just as a woman called to me from the front door. What the heck? Who did that? Dropped a bombshell and then hung up?

"Hello, Mr. McKenna!"

I didn't recognize the voice.

"We had a noon appointment!"

I groaned. Right now, I felt like I was being slapped in the face with my own words. I had an apartment to manage. Time to suck it up and do my job. Besides, I liked the sound of this woman's voice. Cheerful. Nothing like Spy Man.

"Be right there." I slipped the phone in its holster and headed to the front door.

The woman standing on the opposite side of the screen had a very professional appearance. Lightweight red blazer over a gray dress. Her necklace, with its red gemstone and colorful beads, looked expensive. Hair, well-coiffed. Middle-aged. My inner apartment-manager spirits soared. A stable tenant with a steady income. Hallelujah.

"Aloha," I said in my most chipper tone. A little too chipper, actually. I sounded like an excited chimpanzee. "You must be Lisa Proulx."

"I am. I hope this time is convenient for you. It's so hard to get away from work during the day."

"The timing is perfection. Where do you work?" I asked as I opened the screen door.

She took a couple of steps back and said, "Bank of Hawaii. Investment services."

A banker. She fit the image. Conservative hair. Makeup. Wall Street, Hawaiian style, all the way. Excellent. I held out my hand and took a step forward.

"Sorry." She backed up. "I like to keep personal space."

"Oh. Sure. No problem."

I offered to show her the apartment. She agreed, so I led the way and she followed. Along the way I went into some of the advantages of the Sunsetter Apartments—beach access, close to town, plenty of places to walk. At the apartment door, I stopped and turned, and did a quick double take. She was wearing a mask. My heart sank.

"Um…why are you wearing that?"

"I wear it in close quarters. There are so many germs in the air. And there are some nasty bugs around. I can't afford to get sick."

"Sure. I get it. You want to stay healthy."

"Absolutely. Now, has the apartment been sanitized?"

"Yes. It's been thoroughly cleaned. The tenant was very good and did an excellent job."

"So it wasn't done professionally?"

"No, but I inspected it myself before I agreed it was ready."

"I see." She scanned the interior of the unit as she reached into her purse and pulled out a pair of nitrile gloves.

My euphoria was slowly turning into foreboding. What was coming next? Was this lady some sort of hypochondriac? Or worse—some sort of apartment cop I'd never heard of? "Have you been sick lately?"

"I never get sick," she said matter-of-factly, then pulled a pack of cleansing wipes from her purse, extracted one, and wiped down the doorknob and closed the door. With the wipe still in hand, she went to the microwave and cleaned the handle. She opened the door, checked the inside, then the top of the appliance. "Hmmm…appears clean," she murmured.

Still hoping to turn this situation around, I went to the front window, adding a key selling point as I walked. "You get a lovely breeze in this unit thanks to the trade winds."

"Stop!" Lisa barked. "What are you doing? Don't open that. You'll let in all the dust. If someone who is sick is walking by, there's no telling what they might pass on."

Forget foreboding, we were headed for a crash landing with no survivors. Disaster City. She didn't belong in an ocean front apartment complex, she belonged in a sealed high-rise. Someplace with sterilized walls, furniture, and appliances.

"I see." Cautiously, I added, "Maybe this isn't the best housing solution for you."

"What exactly are you saying?" she snapped. "Are you refusing to rent to me because I'm concerned about staying healthy?"

Yikes. What was she? One of the bank's lawyers? It was time to pull out another of McKenna's Skip Tracing Secrets. Number 1—be flexible and go with the flow—would do nicely. "That's not what I'm saying at all. I couldn't be more concerned about your health. In fact, there are some very unhealthy things about living near the ocean, you know?"

She stopped, peered at me, and said, "Really? Like what?"

"Well, for starters, people who go to the beach shouldn't walk on the concrete with bare feet." Okay, so it sounded stupid to me, but Lisa was definitely hooked.

"They do that? That's unsanitary. They should be fined."

"I agree," I said. "But you know how litigious people get these days. They want to fight every single regulation, even the ones that are for their own good. All it takes is one violator and that walkway out there is host to all kinds of disease. There's no way to stop it, either. I'm sure you know how busy HPD is.

139

They're not going to drop everything to rush out and issue a citation for walking barefoot in public. Besides, what good does it do to be tied up in court fighting with your neighbor about whether he can saunter around with no shoes when you might be dying from God knows what?"

Lisa cast nervous glances around the apartment, her eyes like a pair of lasers in search of dirt, disease, pestilence. But even more than her eyes, the skin on her forehead gave her away. There are plenty of cliches about people turning green, but I never actually believed someone's skin could take on the color of a dried out lime—until now.

"Would you open the door, please?" Lisa croaked.

"Of course." I did as she asked, stepped aside, and gave her backside a little wave as she hurried toward her car. When her footsteps had faded, I locked up the apartment.

"Well? How'd it go?" Chance asked as he approached, his expression eager.

"She's…uh…thinking it over."

"When's she move in?"

I hesitated, briefly considered telling him the truth and giving him the details, but decided it was best to keep this one to myself. "She's got other options to consider first. It doesn't matter, I've got another one to contact. Whichever one is the best, that's the one I'll pick." Assuming there actually was a good one. I caught my flash of cynicism and gave myself a mental red card. Benni was right, I should try to live with more aloha in my life. A positive outlook, that's what I needed.

"I'm sure one of these possibles will make an excellent tenant. By the way, Sue called just before this lady showed up. She said she's got a clue. Come on. I'll bet she knows something that will break this case wide open."

"I'll grab my laptop and meet you there." Chance flipped me a shaka sign and headed for his apartment.

As I returned to mine, I congratulated myself on becoming more positive. I was turning into a regular living-with-aloha expert.

22

WHEN I ENTERED MY APARTMENT, I took a deep breath. The stuffiness that had hung in the air before had lifted. The open windows, including the lānai slider, had allowed the trades to do their thing and refresh the entire unit. The truth was, living in a sealed apartment might work for someone like Lisa Proulx, but it was definitely not my thing.

I dialed Sue's number and she answered on the first ring. She seemed to have forgotten her earlier bombshell, so I reminded her.

"Oh, yah," she said. "Before I get to that, I also wanted to let you know I talked to Julie. She was kinda concerned about you and Chance being at the construction site without her around."

I felt a flush of anxiety. Was she going to tell us to stay away? There was one way to stop that option in its tracks. "We may need to go back. Some of those workers have given us a completely different picture than the one Julie gave us."

"Oh? What did they say?" Her tone had changed—moving slightly from eagerness to caution.

"What we have so far is not really concrete."

"McKenna, I'm not a child. Tell me what they said. He was my father."

Hmmm...this was a side of Sue I hadn't seen before—the crabby side. She sounded more like a petulant child than a grown-up to me. Would rational work? If it didn't, this could quickly turn into something resembling two siblings squabbling over a favorite toy. "I'd really rather get some corroboration before I start repeating what could be false rumors."

"I'm the one who asked you to find my dad. I'm the one who has to run the company now. I should know what's going on. Are you going to tell me or not?"

Hmmm...'not' seemed like not an option. "Okay, but you have to think about this as a process. It's like panning for gold. You have to go through a lot of detritus before you get to the nuggets."

"I get that," she said deliberately.

"According to the people we talked to, Kenji could be quite ruthless."

"That's not true!"

"Sue, it doesn't matter whether it's true or not. It all comes down to why someone killed your dad. He could have been the nicest man in the world, but if someone didn't like him, they might badmouth him. And if they hated him enough, they might even commit murder."

"You're saying you don't believe these people then? Who are they?"

I silently cursed myself for letting this conversation go so far. "No. I will not let you go down that path. That's exactly the sort

143

of thing someone who hated your dad would see as vindication of their claims. You have to let Chance and me talk to people, find what they think is the dirt, and then use that to trap the killer."

There was a long pause, then Sue said, "Do you really think that will work?"

"It's the only avenue we have. Please, let us figure this out for you."

"Okay. I suppose I have to trust you."

I mouthed a silent thank you to the heavens that we'd finally returned to an adult conversation.

"But, here's something you should know about my dad. He was the kindest, most caring man in the world. He went out of his way to hire people who just needed a helping hand. I don't understand how they could turn on him like that."

"That's what we want to find out." Eager to end this conversation and get on to one more productive, I said, "You have a clue for me?"

"Yes. My dad was friends with one of the detectives at HPD. I talked to him and he told me what my dad had on him when they found the body."

"Were you expecting them to find something in particular?"

"What do you mean?"

Great. Crabby Sue was back. This was another possible disaster in the making. "I was just surprised you were able to deal with such a difficult task so soon after the murder."

"Oh. Sure. Okay. Well, one of the things my dad always carried on him was his wallet."

Not exactly earth-shattering news. "That's pretty normal."

"It was custom made of wood and resin. It was a pretty blue, kind of like the ocean, and a tan that was kind of like wet sand. It was worth a lot of money."

Custom made? The follies of the rich. "I'm sure the police will get it back to you once they locate it."

"That's the thing. It wasn't on him when they found the body. Someone stole it. He always carried cash and credit cards. Do you think this could have been a robbery?"

I could just see the headlines—Homeless Man Steals Wallet of Benefactor Before Killing Him. Closing my eyes, I took a deep breath and went with my gut. "I don't think it was a robbery. The police will explore that possibility, but I'm more inclined to wonder what was in the wallet that could make it worth killing a man."

"Excuse me?"

The screen door opened and Chance poked his head inside the apartment. I motioned for him to enter.

"Other than the cash and credit cards, do you know what else your dad kept in the wallet?"

She paused. Why? It was a simple question. She either knew or she didn't—unless she was hiding something.

"No."

It had taken a long time to get to that one word. Long enough that I had to wonder about her truthfulness. I hated it when the person you were trying to help lied to you. While it wasn't an everyday occurrence, it did happen in real life. But Benni had convinced me Sue was not one of those people who could lie and feel no remorse, so I bet on Sue's conscience winning out and stayed silent.

Chance mouthed, "What's she doing?"

I motioned for him to be patient with a raised finger and waited patiently until Sue broke her silence.

"That's not true. My dad carried a computer memory card with him. He called it his insurance."

"What kind of insurance? Please, this could really help."

"I don't know. He never told me what was on the card. He only said that if something happened to him, it would explain everything."

"Did you tell this to the police?"

"No."

"Why?"

"Because I'm not sure what's on that card is entirely legal."

Holy crap. Don't tell me we had a whole new motive for murder. Had Kenji been blackmailing someone?

"I have to go McKenna. A couple of men with badges just walked in." The line went dead.

Without waiting for him to ask, I recapped the conversation for Chance. He began firing off questions I didn't know the answers to. Did I think Kenji was killed over the contents of the wallet? Could it have been illegal? A second set of books?

"I don't know, I don't know, and I don't know. That's about all I know."

"That's not much, McKenna. In fact, it's a big fat nothing."

"Exactly. What's strange is that she was so eager to tell me about this missing wallet, but the minute I asked why it was important, she got defensive."

Chance sat back on the sofa, crossed his arms over his chest, and stretched his legs in front of him. "As I see it, she's either covering up or feels guilty over not knowing what was in it."

146

"The thing about a robbery-gone-bad scenario is that except for those protestors, nobody out there would have dared commit that kind of crime."

"How do you figure?" Chance asked.

"Think about what Mondo and Freddie told us. Those guys are dependent on their jobs to support their families. Whether they liked Kenji or not, they wouldn't want things to change. And the tenants? Killing Kenji would only make it harder for them to realize their dream of getting off the street."

Shifting forward, Chance sat with his elbows on his knees. "So we're back to Kenji might have been blackmailing someone. Considering what Barbara told us about Kelly disappearing, this could be bigger than we ever thought."

"Right." I swallowed hard. The assumptions had come quick and easy. Almost too easy. But, if they were true, it would explain Kelly's disappearance. And Derrick Tanaka's reluctance to talk.

23

DURING MY SKIP TRACING DAYS, my hunches had almost always panned out. That's why, at least right now, I thought our best bet was to focus on the other person who had dropped off the scene. "We need to find Joe Taylor," I said.

Chance did a double take. "Why? You think he was being blackmailed by Kenji? Or that he was the blackmailer?"

"I don't know what he is. He might be nothing, but he could be a key to everything that's happened. He was fired, and a few days later someone murdered Kenji."

"So Taylor gets fired on Friday, then comes back on Monday and kills the man responsible? Seems like a stretch. Why wouldn't he just do it at the time he was getting canned? And why leave a backhoe out there to draw attention to the spot where he buried the body?"

"Unless he was interrupted. It's possible he was using the backhoe when Kelly showed up. That would explain why he got sloppy and left a shoe sticking out of the ground." I heaved a heavy sigh. Nothing made sense. "I feel like a dog chasing its tail. We're right back to the original question when we started."

"Agreed," Chance said. "Why did Kenji miss Sue's presentation if he was alive? No matter what anyone says, I can't imagine him standing up his daughter like that."

"What I can imagine is someone who's driven to make her mark professionally calling Celeste Campbell instead of the cops. Kelly could have done it to cement a working relationship. Maybe she thought she could control the situation and then realized she couldn't."

"You're sounding like that crazy guy who wanted to rent the apartment. You said he was big on conspiracy theories, right?"

Actually, I didn't know if Mr. Smith would have known a conspiracy from a sandwich, but the more I ran the sequence of events through my head, the more I kept coming up with the same solution. We could be dealing with a huge coverup. And that meant we could be walking into a very dangerous situation. Maybe even the same one that had caused Kelly to disappear.

Twenty minutes later we were entering the Outrigger Hotel on Waikiki Beach. Money flows like water on this strip of Kalākaua Avenue where high-end shopping is the standard. The discriminating shopper can pick up anything from a Coach handbag to a pair of Jimmy Choo shoes to a Tesla. The official motto for this part of Waikiki should be, *You got money? We got you covered.*

"I love this place," I said as we approached the receptionist at Duke's Waikiki.

Chance laughed quietly. "You love it when I'm paying."

"That's not entirely true. They have a gluten-free menu. Excellent food. Great service. The sand and the beach are just footsteps away, so the view doesn't get much better. However, the food does taste pretty darned good when you're footing the bill."

We told the receptionist, a pretty girl with glossy black hair and a killer tan, that we were meeting friends and gave her their names. She smiled, made a note of some sort, and told us to follow her. We wended our way through the maze of tables and chairs in the bar, which were occupied by what felt like equal proportions of diners and drinkers. Once through the crowd, we were led to a mostly empty section adjacent to the outdoor patio. Far from the commotion of the bar, we still had a perfect view that included sand and surf.

Benni and Lexie sat at a table bordering the outdoor patio, each with a glass of white wine before them.

I kissed Benni, then took my seat next to her. "You two scored one of the best tables in the place. My money says your cousin got you this table."

"You don't bet," Benni countered.

"A sure thing isn't really a bet. Well?"

"Okay. She's the manager and she happened to see us walk in."

"Pays to be related to half the island." I looked across the table at Chance. "Honolulu might be a big city, but it can also be a small town. Remember that, buddy."

"Don't you forget it either, McKenna," Lexie said pointedly. "You're about to become part of a very big family."

The conversation briefly turned to family news. Lexie's fashion-blogger sister was negotiating a big deal with an island clothes designer. Benni's brother Alexander and his wife were expecting—again. Chance and I were the only ones with nothing to share.

Halfway through her wine, Benni said, "You called me, McKenna. What did you want to talk about?"

"We need a little help."

Benni smirked, rolled her eyes, then raised her wineglass and winked at me. "You two need a lot of help."

Lexie, of course, got a huge kick out of that and the two of them exchanged a high five. Personally, I still thought any attempt at bribery was going to backfire, so why not let Chance take the heat? I regarded him from across the table.

"It's your question. You ask."

All of a sudden, Chance's confidence wavered. The guy who hadn't broken a sweat forcing Derrick Tanaka to pay was nervous as could be. "What the heck? Right, McKenna?" When I didn't answer, he cleared his throat and continued. "Benni, you want Kenji's killer brought to justice. Right?"

"Of course."

"And you're willing to help us if we need it. Right?"

Benni rolled her eyes and heaved a dramatic sigh. "Get to the point, Chance."

"Yeah, babe. This isn't like you. What's up?"

"We're trying to find Joe Taylor," Chance said.

Benni and Lexie exchanged a look of confusion. "Who's he?" Benni asked.

"A former employee of Ito Development. He was fired on July 6, the Friday before Kenji went missing. We're not sure, but we think he might know something about what happened."

Lexie sucked in a breath; her brown eyes widened. "Do you think he's the killer?"

That was the same reaction I'd expected Benni to have, but hers was completely different. She was frowning and gazing at her wineglass as though something about this whole discussion concerned her.

"We're still trying to sort that out," I said. "Taylor is kind of a...a wildcard. Benni, you seem to be bothered by something. Does the name Joe Taylor mean anything to you?"

She shook her head. "Oh. No. Not the name. The date. I've been going over the books and there's the strangest entry for that date. Kenji withdrew five-thousand dollars that day. It's nowhere to be found."

I had a flashback to Sue's comments about the wallet. Her reluctance to tell me what could have been in it. "That's a lot of money for anyone to use as petty cash."

"Kenji wouldn't do that. He was a meticulous record keeper and insisted that if the business were ever audited, he wanted thorough records. He documented everything."

"And yet, you're saying this entry's not documented. Very... strange, wouldn't you say?"

"Yah. I thought it was when I saw the entry."

"Were there any others like it?" Chance asked.

"None that I've seen."

"You know," Lexie said. "When I was little, my dad was always telling me and my sisters stories about the old days. There was a lot of corruption back then. Maybe that's what Kenji was caught up in." She screwed up her cheeks and cringed. "Sorry, Benni. It's just a thought."

"This project has gone smoothly," Chance added. "Maybe it's been too smooth."

"Look you guys, I've known Kenji for a long time. I'm telling you, there has to be another explanation."

It was the perfect opportunity, and I wasn't about to let it pass. "That's why we need to find Taylor. If he knows something, we'll crack him like a walnut."

The reactions ranged from a simple rolling of the eyes on Benni's part to outright laughter on Lexie's. Chance was somewhere in the middle—he buried his forehead in his hand and watched the tabletop.

"Okay, maybe not the best choice of metaphors, but we could get him to talk. We just need to find him." Raising my eyebrows expectantly, I said, "So if we had an address…"

"I get it. You want me to snoop around the payroll records."

"Snoop has such a negative connotation," I said. "Let's call it investigating, okay?"

"Call it what you want, McKenna, but you're lucky because Sue really wants to find out who killed her dad. There's no doubt about that." Benni paused and then sighed. "The problem is she also wants to protect his reputation. There's so much coming at her right now that she's not sure what she should do."

"In my opinion, the best way to protect his memory is to know what skeletons were in the closet."

"McKenna's right," Chance said. "I've screwed up enough in my life to understand that you can't hide what you've done forever, but you can control the narrative if you're willing to deal with it head on. The best way she can help her dad's reputation is to know the good and the bad. Assuming there even is any bad."

"That's what we can hopefully find out from this Taylor guy. Plus, since Kenji fired him, maybe we can tie Taylor back to the killing."

Benni grimaced and seemed to disconnect from the conversation. Around us, tables had been filling up with diners.

Chatter about the menu and the atmosphere mixed with server greetings and exchanges created a lighthearted experience at the other tables, but at ours, we all remained silent while Benni processed our request.

24

IN THE END, BENNI AGREED to get us the address for Joe Taylor. Of course, given that no good deed goes unpunished, Benni performed the good deed while Chance and I drew the punishment. We were stuck in the middle of rush hour traffic and our destination was on the opposite side of Honolulu in Waianae.

When Chance made the turn onto Ala Akau Street, my suspicions were confirmed. This was the low-rent district. No view. No ocean. No single family homes in this neighborhood. Just apartments packed into dense clusters. I'd chased many a skip in developments like these and knew their insides well— basic appliances, small rooms, lots of noisy neighbors. There were elementary, middle, and high schools not far away. All of it was perfect for families on a tight budget.

These families didn't live here because they wanted luxury. They needed cheap rents that would hopefully enable them to put food on the table, pay the utilities, and maybe have a tiny amount left over for Christmas and birthday presents.

Joe Taylor was in the second building on the street. It was ugly by any standard, painted a brownish mustard color with brown trim and no distinguishing architecture. I'd seen some drab color combinations in my life, but this one took the cake.

The parking lot was dotted with only a few cars. An old beat-up white Chevy in the first space had it's hood up and all four doors open.

"You think he's issuing an invite to steal it?" I asked.

"No self-respecting car thief would bother," Chance shot back.

"That's what I was thinking. Our guy's place should be in this building. Let's hope he's home."

The parking was close to the apartment entrances, but we were both stunned when the entrance actually led to a lānai where a table and chairs shared space with a couple of kids' bikes that hadn't been new in twenty years.

"Weird design," I said as I let Chance take the lead and knock on the front door.

A petite woman with bronze skin and her hair pulled back in a loose chignon answered the door. She carried an infant on her hip and eyed us suspiciously. "What do you want?"

"Is Joe home?" The way the words flowed from Chance's mouth, I almost believed we were old friends.

"He not here. Had a meeting."

"Oh," Chance said, nodding enthusiastically. "Is that the one at…um…"

"Pōkaʻī Bay Beach Park," the woman snapped impatiently. "This one getting fussy." She slammed the door in our faces.

When Chance turned around I said, "Nice work. You played that like a pro."

Chance rolled his eyes and shook his head. "Now what?"

"We go to the park, of course."

Five minutes later, we were sitting in the parking lot at Pōka'ī Bay Beach Park. It was pretty typical—swaying palms, gorgeous ocean, struggling grass. There was still plenty of open parking, so here we sat, trying to figure out which of these local guys was Joe Taylor.

"She said he was at a meeting," Chance said. "Who holds a meeting at the park?"

"AA, buddy. They hold regular meetings in parks on the island. I'll bet you anything our friend Joe is an alcoholic."

"How do you know that?"

"He was fired for being drunk on the job."

"No, I mean, how did you know about the meeting?"

"Oh. I looked it up."

Chance frowned at me, then asked, "Why?"

Uh-oh. I'd said too much. It was time to backtrack unless I wanted to make this very personal. "I was curious. That's all. Just one of those esoteric pieces of information I found interesting."

"Okay. I'll go with that. But there's got to be fifty people here milling around. This is like trying to find a needle in a haystack."

"I don't think it's going to be difficult at all. You see that guy sitting over there at the picnic table?"

"You think that's him?"

"No. But I'll bet he knows our guy. Let's go."

Before Chance could question me further, I was out of the car and striding across the asphalt. Halfway to the table, Chance finally caught up. "Why do you think he can help us?"

"Because…he's got a clipboard." I waved to the man, then called to him. "Hey, how you doing?"

"Staying strong, brah. You're new. What's your name?"

"I'm McKenna. This is my associate, Chance Logan. We were told Joe Taylor would be here. Have you seen him?"

The man tossed a careless glance over his shoulder and turned back to me. "He just went to the restroom. He's coming now." He turned back to Taylor and called out, "Hey, Joe. These two wanna talk to you."

A frown creased Taylor's forehead as he scrutinized us. "Who are you guys?"

Chance stepped forward. Introduced himself and me, then explained that we were investigating Kenji Ito's death.

Taylor's shoulders fell when he heard Kenji's name and he hung his head. "He was a good man. You know."

It wasn't the type of response I'd expected. Not from the man Kenji fired. "Do you know a man named Graham Tynsdale?"

"Who?" Taylor scrunched up his face and craned his neck forward.

His reaction was so quick and genuine that I felt sure he'd never met the man leading the protests. "This might get kind of personal. Can we talk privately?"

Taylor shook his head. "No need. This is my brother-in-law, Dwayne. He knows all my problems. I ain't got nothing to hide."

I wasn't so sure he'd feel the same once he heard the questions we had. "We want to talk about the day you were fired. You sure you don't want to change your mind?"

Both men laughed. "Believe me, I heard it all," Dwayne said.

"That's right. What he didn't hear from me, he got from my wife. What do you want to know?"

Chance and I exchanged a shrug. I pointed at him, indicating I'd let him take the lead.

"Why were you let go?" Chance asked.

"Kenji heard I was showing up drunk."

"Were you?"

"Yeah. Legally, I was."

"And you didn't think that was a problem?"

"I thought I could get away with it."

"Did you also think you could get away with killing Kenji?"

Dwayne stood abruptly and faced Chance. Anger etched on his face. "What you trying to pull? He didn't kill nobody."

Joe raised his hand to calm his brother-in-law. "It's okay, Dwayne. First I heard of Kenji being dead was on the news. Believe me, brah, I'm the last one who wanted something bad to happen to him."

Chance appeared skeptical, which was exactly how I felt. "Why?" I blurted.

Joe squinted at me and shook his head. "Why what?"

"The man fired you. I'd think you'd be happy to see him dead."

"What's that fancy word that new guy uses, Dwayne?"

"Ironic," Dwayne said with a wry smile.

"Oh yeah. You thinking I wanted Kenji dead is ironic. He saved me from myself."

"How did he do that?" Chance asked.

Dwayne's eyes flicked in the direction of the parking lot. "We got more people coming. I gotta start a meeting." He gave Joe a friendly backslap on the shoulder with his fingers. "And I don't think you want everyone knowing all your business."

A man and a woman approached from the parking lot. They'd arrived in separate cars, but were now chatting. She was showing him something on her phone. Off to our left, there was an unoccupied picnic table in the shade. It was far enough away that we wouldn't be heard unless someone, namely Joe, started yelling.

"Why don't we use that table?" I asked.

"It all gonna be coming out anyway." Joe's shoulders slumped as he walked. It was like a huge weight was pressing them down. When he got to the table, he turned to face us and leaned against it.

"So how did Kenji save you from yourself?" I asked.

"My dad and Kenji went to school together, brah. After I got married, my dad got me a job with Kenji. He taught me everything from how to run heavy equipment to doing finish work on cabinets. When things got lean, I had to work for other guys for a while, but I been with him for ten years now."

"Heavy equipment? Do you know how to operate a backhoe?"

"Of course. Kenji taught me."

Which meant he would have known how to bury the body. "If everything was so wonderful between you two, then why'd he fire you? Why not just give you time off to get your life together?"

Joe choked out a strangled laugh. "He did. Kenji was always good to me. He paid me five-thousand bucks so I could pay the rent and feed my family. He didn't want my family to suffer 'cause of my stupidity. He said if I got sober for three months, he'd give me my job back. Don't you see, brah? We had a deal. And now that he's dead, I ain't got no job to go back to. I'm gonna lose everything."

25

TAYLOR BURIED HIS FACE IN his hands and let out a sob. "Who's gonna hire a middle-aged drunk? Eh, brah?"

Even though I'd never been an alcoholic, I felt a strange kinship with this man. I understood his pain. It was exactly why I'd moved to Hawaii. I'd never expected anyone to hire me. For me, though, life had worked out. I laid a consoling hand on his shoulder. "You'll rise above this. You just have to be strong."

The man's eyes seemed to search mine for some sort of reassurance. "You think so?"

"Draw strength from your family." Back at Dwayne's table, the group had grown to seven individuals. All working hard to turn their lives around. "And from them. It's what Kenji wanted you to do, right? Don't let him down."

Joe nodded numbly and watched another person join the group. "I should be getting back. You got any more questions?"

"Just one," Chance said. "Did Kenji say anything that would have indicated someone wanted to kill him?"

"No, brah. He did say there were dark forces trying to stop the project. But he didn't say nothing about somebody wanting to kill him."

"Dark forces?" I asked. "Really? That's what he said?"

"Yah. He didn't tell me what they were." Joe grimaced, then watched the table where Dwayne had started the meeting.

"You should join them," I said. "Mahalo for your help."

Chance and I stood in silence gazing out at the ocean waves. "Our suspect list is dwindling, McKenna."

"Suspect list? We don't have one."

"You're right. We're screwed."

I sensed the depression in Chance's tone. From his downturned mouth to his hands stuffed in his pockets, it all screamed, things were not going well. "We still have Graham Tynsdale," I said. "Maybe we should focus on him."

"Maybe. We thought we'd get somewhere by following the money, but it only landed us here at an AA meeting with a guy who couldn't possibly want to hurt Kenji."

A sailboat in the distance bobbed on the ocean's surface. Whoever was on that boat had to be having a grand time. Far better than we were. "You're right. We wanted to follow the money. But we've only researched one transaction. I wonder if Benni's turned up anything new. I'll call her right now."

In some ways, calling Benni felt like an act of desperation. It hadn't even been two hours since she'd given us Joe's address—and now we needed her help again. Unfortunately, I got her voicemail. Unsure what to say, I hung up without leaving a message.

"What happened?" Chance asked.

"It went to voicemail."

"Like, right to voicemail, or after a few rings? If it went straight there, she might not want to talk to you."

"Chance! It's no big deal. I'll see her tonight. Speaking of which, we're going to be in the middle of rush hour—again. Let's get this drive over with."

It was five-thirty by the time we reached the Sunsetter Apartments and we were both exhausted. Chance, because the traffic had been atrocious; and me, because I was secretly feeling the same way Chance had been after our talk with Taylor. I just hadn't wanted to say anything for fear of bringing down my friend.

Benni was already home, and when I walked in, she told me I had a message from a Kimberley Klinger. It was about the apartment, and after listening to the message, I thought my luck might be changing. "Good. I need a better option than either of the ones I've got. She said she could be here tomorrow at ten. I'll call her back and confirm."

I returned Kimberley's call, got her voicemail, and left a message that we could meet at the time she requested. After hanging up, I said, "Let's hope she shows. I've never had so much trouble renting a stupid apartment."

Benni gave me a consoling smile. "You poor thing. Tough day?"

"Joe Taylor."

"Don't tell me you didn't find him."

"We found him. That was the easy part thanks to your help. We also solved the mystery of the missing five-thousand-dollars."

"That's great! I knew you'd figure it out." She crossed the room, kissed me, and said, "Well?"

"The money went to Joe Taylor for living expenses. It was kind of a severance pay package."

"Excuse me?" Benni craned her neck forward and frowned. "Kenji fired the man. Why would he give him that kind of money?"

"Because Taylor's worked for Kenji for ten years. His father and Kenji were longtime friends. It's one of those convoluted, twisty island relationship stories. And because they go way back, Kenji told Joe he'd rehire him when he got sober."

Benni took my hand and led me to the kitchen, picked up a glass of wine, and handed me one of my own. "Does this mean you've changed your mind about Kenji, then? Has this proven to you he wasn't up to no good?"

"Certainly not with that five grand. It also means we've lost a suspect."

"What about that protestor you and Chance were so hot about? What happened to him?"

"We asked Taylor about him. He doesn't know him. This Tynsdale is kind of a ghost. For all I know he's off railing against some other cause. Kelly Atkinson told us she'd seen him protesting in various places."

Benni rested one hip against the counter and sipped from her glass. "What about her? She disappeared. Yah?"

"According to her partner she panicked and said she had to leave town. We think she must have seen something and is afraid the killer will come after her next." There was a faraway look in Benni's eyes, and I wondered what she was thinking. "We can use any help we can get."

After a short hesitation, she said, "What if she's afraid of something else?"

"Like what?"

"Being caught? What if she's the one who killed Kenji?" Benni stopped, shook her head, then added, "Never mind, it's a stupid idea."

"Maybe not. Chance and I thought the same thing for a while, but Kelly just seems way too ditzy to be a killer. Her partner says she doesn't have a lot of common sense. Does that sound like the kind of person who would kill someone, then bury them with a backhoe?"

"Don't be fooled by a pretty face, McKenna. Besides, Celeste Campbell just announced on the news that Kenji was killed by a blow to the head. Apparently, the police still don't have the murder weapon."

"Which could be almost anything on a construction site." I sighed.

"Maybe your ditzy photographer isn't such a bad option."

"She was the first one on the scene, so there's no question she had the opportunity, maybe the means, too."

"And you said it kind of sounded like she had it in for him." Benni regarded me over the top of her glass.

"How'd she bury the body? She's just...your size."

"There was a backhoe nearby. Yah?"

Right. The backhoe. I took a sip from my glass, walked over to the dining table, and plopped down into the chair. "So she argues with Kenji, whacks him over the head, and then grabs a backhoe to bury him. When the job's done, she calls Celeste and has her come out so they can report it. Wow. That's quite a theory. And it all depends on them having an argument over... something. What would be big enough to cause her to commit murder?"

"Maybe he caught her in the act of doing something to sabotage the project and she panicked."

165

My back stiffened as I considered the possibility. "Right. There was some sabotage out there. There's too many ifs in that theory for me, but it is possible she knows who the killer is."

"So you think maybe she saw it happen?"

"That seems more likely to me," I said confidently.

"Then why didn't he kill her, too? If you're going to commit murder, why leave a witness behind?"

"You wouldn't. Unless the witness is also your alibi. We're considering all possibilities and she's as likely as anyone else. Except for Joe Taylor, maybe. Can we talk about something else for a while? I need time to clear my head."

Benni smiled and flipped her hair back. "Since you mentioned it. There is this little thing we're planning called a wedding. Can we talk about it?"

"Sure. Where's the brochure Mrs. Nakamura left?"

"Over by the phone."

I started to get up, but Benni stopped me by wagging her finger at me. "We don't need the brochure to talk."

"Oh. Okay." So much for just choosing Package A or Package B. I had a feeling this was now going to get much more complex. There had been a lot of add-ons in the brochure. "So you've already decided which option and add-ons you want?"

"No. I told you. I'm not interested in a big wedding."

Her sincere tone stopped me. Could Mrs. Nakamura be wrong? It didn't seem possible. "But Mrs. Nakamura said all girls want a big wedding. That's not true?"

"Really? You believe that?"

"I'm not a woman. How do I know what you guys want?"

Benni huffed, then smirked at me. "You could try listening."

Uh…okay. She had me there. Now that I thought about it, I had been listening, I just hadn't been believing. "Before Mrs.

Nakamura stuck her nose in this, we'd decided on a small service. But I always kind of felt like you were saying that to make me feel better. Because of my…financial situation."

"You thought I'd settle for a pity wedding because you're not rich?"

I swallowed hard. "When you put it that way it sounds…"

"Ridiculous?"

"Like I was being a complete idiot. I get it. You told me what you wanted, and when it wasn't what I expected, I doubted your word. Then, I let myself be convinced I was right and you were wrong. I'm sorry. I never should have let myself have so many self-doubts."

"Don't worry about it." She kissed me and smiled when she pulled away. "You just have to trust that when I tell you I want something, I'm not doing it to make you happy."

There were so many directions I could take this conversation right now—most of them bad. But I could see that now, so maybe I was getting smarter in the relationship department. That, and living with aloha. I was actually turning into a better person.

"You know what I'd like?" I asked.

"What?"

"Another glass of wine, some dinner, and then a chance to just relax with you without any tenant calls, discussion of murder, or anything else."

"Does that mean you don't want to talk about the wedding?"

"Actually, that would be an excellent subject for us to discuss and resolve while we're relaxing."

26

I AWOKE THURSDAY MORNING AFTER a restless night. The conundrums that kept me awake ranged from serious to ridiculous—had Kenji been dead for two days or three? How exactly was Kelly Atkinson involved in this whole mess? And was I ever going to rent that stupid apartment? As the saying goes, what I had to do was soldier on. I had landlord duties to attend to, and while Chance and I had complained about our dwindling suspect pool, I'd concluded overnight that it might be far larger than we thought.

Chance grumbled when I told him we couldn't do anything until after my tenant meeting, but he then headed out to hit the ocean surf. While he did his thing, I did mine and took another dive into the relationship between Kelly and Celeste. As Chance and I had seen at Kelly's studio, she'd taken her first photos of the project the night of the City Council meeting. Most of Celeste's early stories focused on financial donations made by organizations, trusts, and individuals. The accompanying photos, which were always taken by a staff photographer, included check presentations, volunteers, and the solar microgrid that would eventually power the village.

For someone who'd complained about a lack of money, Kelly had spent an inordinate amount of time taking photos of a project that had no artistic or monetary value. And since she'd disappeared with some BS story about stumbling onto something big, I was extremely suspicious. The more I thought about it, the more I realized Benni might have been correct—Kelly didn't deserve the benefit of the doubt I'd been giving her. She had to be up to her neck in this—the question was, how?

In an article about the purchase of the land, one not written by Celeste Campbell, a new name surfaced—China Gaardner. Apparently, while Kenji was negotiating to secure the land for the homeless project, China had been trying to broker a deal for a large commercial development of the parcel. The process had turned into a hotly contested battle between two factions—those who felt we needed another upscale live/work development and those who saw value in helping the homeless. The whole thing sounded vaguely familiar, but I couldn't recall why.

Out in the ocean, Chance was doing the smart thing, getting his focus by doing something he loved. Unlike when he'd first arrived in Hawaii, he now had some good surfing skills and could ride almost any wave our little beach threw at him. He wasn't ready for the Banzai Pipeline with its killer waves, but he could hit most other beaches and make a respectable showing.

I stood to get more coffee, looked down at my laptop screen, and realized what was bothering me. According to Julie, Kenji had considered hiring an investigator to find out who Graham Tynsdale worked for. What if it was China? So who was she? I did a search for her and came up with a website for Island Project

Real Estate Management. On the About page, there was information about China, but no one else. She was, apparently, the entire company.

Her bio went into more personal details than I'd have expected. It included the fact that she was the only daughter of Japanese and Filipino parents, had two children of her own, and had gone to the University of Hawaii. Based on the lighting, background, and composition, I assumed her photo had been taken in a studio by a professional. Her long straight hair had been heavily, but tastefully, highlighted. To be sure I wasn't overlooking the obvious, I checked the photo credit. It wasn't Kelly Atkinson.

I had to admit, by the time I'd finished with China's bio, I'd formed a definite positive opinion about her. She was a dynamic, take-charge woman. That image was further reinforced by her website—someone had done a masterful job of making her small company appear large. Between the fact that the company had been in business for ten years and that I could call for 'project appropriate references,' I was convinced China Gaardner could handle any commercial project from beginning to end.

I returned to the article where I'd originally read about China. Reread it. That led me to another story in the *Star-Advertiser* from the day after the City Council approved Kinohi Village. According to the article, things had gotten very heated during the meeting. China had even made accusations of corruption on the City Council. Why hadn't Kelly mentioned that?

It had been a long time since 1977 when the mayor of Honolulu was indicted on charges of bribery. Those charges had eventually been dropped, but apparently people like China still relied on the memory as a way to raise questions about city government.

In addition to her project management activities, China was also a realtor and would have made a few percent in commissions off that land deal. She had the best of both worlds. The project management work she did could consume a huge number of billable hours, which meant that for her company, there was a lot of money on the table. How much? A hundred thousand? Two? Three? On top of that, her clients had lost out on millions in potential profits over the course of the project.

No wonder China had raised a stink. I could also see how when her private project failed in favor of the public one, Kenji was the one man to blame. I scratched out a note on a piece of paper—*talk to China Gaardner*. At the very least, I'd like to know who her clients were. She might not be willing to tell, but it was worth a try.

I continued my search until nearly ten, by which time my eyes were crossing and I was wondering if my Internet searches had been jinxed. At two minutes to ten, someone knocked on the door. Finally, it was tenant time.

Kimberley Klinger reminded me of a high school basketball player—tall, rail thin, and someone I most assuredly had to look up to. Mentally, the craning my neck part didn't bother me, but physically, it might just give me—well, a pain in the neck.

During introductions, Kimberley explained she was a maritime engineer. Never having met one of those before, I was curious and asked what she did and if she traveled much.

"I'm part of a team. We maintain the onboard equipment. And yes, I do travel, but I want an apartment as a home base. I've just been transferred here from Long Beach."

"Sounds perfect," I said as I unlocked the door and stepped inside. "It's small, but that's pretty standard here. This unit has a galley kitchen—there's a dishwasher, garbage disposal…the fridge is also included."

"I see." She turned away from the kitchen and walked into the living room.

Hurrying around the kitchen counter, I led the way to the bedroom and bath. "As you can see, there's a good amount of room in here and the bath has a standup shower." I smiled. "Sink and toilet are included, also."

Kimberley crossed her arms over her chest and stared down at me. "We need to talk."

Holy cow. She'd made up her mind already? But from the look on her face, it might not be in a good way.

27

KIMBERLEY STOOD OVER ME, HER air of disdain coming through loud and clear. This was a whole different person. A new vibe. It almost felt like this meeting had turned into a fierce negotiation. The thought of interviewing another tenant had no appeal, so my best course of action was to adopt the persona of Mr. Cooperative.

"What would you like to talk about? I can see you've got something on your mind. I'm sure we can work it out."

"The place needs work."

That caught me off guard. The unit was old, but in excellent condition. "What's wrong?"

"There's no handheld shower head."

Ah, leave it to an engineer to notice the small details. "Easy fix. Consider it done."

"The countertop tile. It's atrocious. It reminds me of an eighties time warp."

I'd say one thing for this woman. She was decisive. Maybe that was part of her engineering background. She was right about those white four-by-four tiles. They were original. "Personally, I agree with you. But when I priced the cost of a replacement, the owner had a fit. We used the pale gray grout sealer to make it a little more modern."

"It will never do. It has to be replaced. Granite or quartz. Those are the only two acceptable solutions."

"Uh, Kimberley. I think you're forgetting that this is a rental, not a condo you're purchasing."

"If you want me to be a tenant, you'll do what I say."

Okay, there was a difference between decisive and bossy. A big one. Especially when she hadn't even put down money. "There is one way I might be able to get what you want, but we'd have to be signing a multiyear lease. How long were you planning on staying?"

"I hate moving. I doubt that I'd move for several years."

"Let me talk to the owner. If we're signing a multi-year lease, he might make an accommodation."

Kimberley nodded curtly and started walking toward the kitchen. As she walked away, she said, "Excellent."

I breathed a sigh of relief, thinking that might be the end of her list, but I was wrong.

"Now, I'm also going to need new appliances in the kitchen. These aren't showing visible signs of corrosion, but the salt in the air rusts equipment from the inside out. They'll be useless in no time. They have to go."

"Believe me, I know how hard the salt and humidity are on things. I'm the one who gets called every time an appliance fails. You won't have to worry. When they go, we'll replace them."

"That's unacceptable. I need them replaced before I move in. I don't want to come back after being gone for several weeks and find out my refrigerator died. And then there's the layout. I know it would be difficult to rearrange things, but I do detest galley kitchens. There's almost no counter space to work with. And while you're making more space, I'd like to have a built-in breakfast bar added."

A breakfast bar? I didn't have one of those. None of the units did. Even Chance, who could buy the entire complex if he wanted, hadn't asked for a breakfast bar. That's when I realized this was never going to end. Kimberley Klinger was one of those tenants who wanted everything her way and expected someone else to pay for it.

"You know what, Kimberley? I think you should be considering a place to buy. That way, you can customize until your heart's content. Now, if you'll excuse me, I have another appointment."

"What do you think you're doing? You can't just brush me off like that."

"Actually, I can. You're a prospective tenant. The operative word there being prospective."

She planted her hands on her hips in an obvious attempt to intimidate me. "I took time off work to come here!"

"You chose the time." And enough was enough. Rather than letting her drag this out and turn it into a whining session, it was time to cut my losses. I stood a little straighter, zeroed in on her oh-so-prominent nose hairs, and said, "We're done here. I need you to leave so I can lock up."

Kimberley spun on her heel and marched out the front door. When she was gone, I gave the unit a final once-over. It did have a dated appearance. But it was clean, had a fresh coat of paint, and the tile floors had been replaced a couple of years ago. I sighed as I locked the door behind me. On my walk back to my apartment, I passed Mrs. Nakamura. We exchanged greetings, and, in her own not-so-subtle way, she asked the obvious.

"You were showing the available apartment?"

"Yes, but I don't think she's going to work out. Expectations, and all that."

"Yours? Or hers?"

"Hers."

"Ah." Mrs. Nakamura dipped her chin knowingly, then said, "As you would be so fond of saying, Mr. McKenna. Champagne taste on a beer budget." She cackled as she walked away.

Right about then I was ready to let Mrs. Nakamura do any additional tenant interviews. The old lady was sharp as ever. From what I'd heard she ruled her fourth-grade classes with an iron fist. I'd love to see what would happen when the demanding engineer came up against the immovable will of an old schoolteacher. There was no doubt in my mind whose ship would sink.

I pulled out my phone and checked the time. I'd wasted twenty minutes with Killjoy Kimberley. It was time to get back to Chance and move along on the investigation. I went to his apartment, knocked, and waited until he called for me to come in —which only took a few seconds. He was standing in the kitchen, his hands on the counter, his head tilted to one side.

"What's up?" I asked.

"I was just thinking how this apartment would benefit from new granite and a fallaway countertop on the other side." He paused, then continued. "You know, kind of like a breakfast bar."

I glared at him. "You were listening."

He scrunched up his face. "You did have the windows open. And her voice...carried."

"If I hear the words 'breakfast bar' again, I might have to start eviction proceedings. Now, while you were out surfing, I was working on the case. I came across a woman named China Gaardner." I explained what I'd discovered and we agreed it would be good to have some background before we went barging into her office. Chance volunteered to call Lexie and have her talk to her dad, who had been there the night of the Kinohi Village vote. If anyone was going to remember China's protest, it would be Councilman Ashbrook.

While Chance dialed, I paced. It irritated me that Kimberley's voice had, as Chance put it, carried. Anyone who was home might have heard that conversation. Now that I'd had a few minutes to think about it, I had a ready response—are you willing to put up with several months of no kitchen while the contractors come and go? The islands were like that—it could take a month to change a light fixture.

"You're pacing, McKenna." Chance gave me a smug smile.

The scowl I returned only amused him more.

"I'm on hold. Lexie's home and is checking with her dad."

"Let's hope he doesn't decide you're a bad influence on his daughter."

"He's already decided that, but Lexie, her sister, and her mother, all told him the decision on who she married was hers. I believe their words were—then you can say no if he ever proposes to you." Chance held up his finger, then told Lexie he was putting the phone on speaker.

"Hey, McKenna."

Lexie's lilt filled the room and lifted my heart. I'd grown to love the way the locals stretched out some syllables and elevated their pitch at the end of a sentence. "Hey, Lexie. Tell me you've got something good for us."

"I don't know how helpful it's going to be, but my dad does remember China Gaardner. He says she fought the project every step of the way because of the cost to the City."

"How much money are we talking about, babe?" Chance asked.

"Millions. Potentially. Between the direct costs and the lost tax revenues."

"That's an interesting argument," I said. "Do you think she was really watching out for the City's interests? Or was that just a politically correct way of saying she and her client were losing out?"

"My dad and a couple of the others felt that's exactly what she was doing. They also felt that Kenji's solution to getting people housing was going to save money in the long run. Their feeling was that if they didn't try this, it could cost them a lot more in the future."

"Anything else?" I asked.

"Actually, this is the best part. My dad said he might have been more open to China's argument if she hadn't confronted him before the meeting. She told him there was a sizable coalition building that felt my dad was unfit for the council. She said his vote against the project would prove all the naysayers wrong and would ensure his reelection."

"She threatened him?"

"She called it a polite heads-up. That made my dad super angry and they really got into it."

"Was Kenji at that meeting?"

"Of course, it was the night his project was going up for a final vote."

I drummed my fingers on the tabletop, not sure this was even worth our time.

"What are you thinking?" Chance asked.

"I'm thinking that unless we can find out who China Gaardner's clients are, we could be wasting our time."

"I don't know if this will help, but my dad said he heard China talking on her phone before the meeting. It sounded like she was reporting in to someone else."

Chance grinned. "Her client, that's definitely who we want to connect with."

"Agreed. Now we just have to figure out how to get a name."

28

THE OFFICE FOR ISLAND REAL Estate & Project Management was on the twelfth floor of the Finance Factor Center in Honolulu's central business district. Built in the 70s, the construction was old-school with far more concrete than glass and far fewer floors than its more modern counterparts.

When the elevator chimed, we exited and Chance went to the directional sign on the wall. Standing with his back to me, he pointed to his left. "That way." When he turned around, he frowned. "McKenna? You're not looking too good. What's going on?"

While it was still only morning, I was beginning to feel as though I'd put in a full day of hard labor. "Let's just say Kenji's murder is starting to get me down. Let's go."

We walked along the hallway, our slippahs tapping against the bottoms of our feet, but making almost no sound on the padded carpet. After his third furtive glance in my direction, I'd had enough.

"Will you stop looking at me?" I snapped.

"You sure you're okay?"

"I just haven't been sleeping much. It's catching up to me. When I get home, I'm catching a nap."

Chance gave me a quick thumbs up and said, "Right after this."

The office carpeting, a soothing gray, was an extension of what was in the hallway. The paint was a standard contractor off-white with a couple of teal accent walls thrown in to add interest. Elegant island-print lithographs, spaced evenly between the windows, gave the space a welcoming feel. Up here on the twelfth floor, I'd expected a grand view, but the only thing visible out the office window was the skyscraper on the opposite side of the street.

A young woman with high cheekbones and a fair complexion sat behind a desk just inside the entrance. With sleek hair pulled back in a ponytail, she reminded me of a teenager trying to pass for someone older. I figured this was another opportunity for Chance to turn on the charm, so I hung out behind him.

"Hi. My name is Chance Logan. You are?"

"Brittany." The girl flushed and her green eyes widened. She reached up and pulled on her ponytail, positioning it over her shoulder.

There were certain advantages to working with someone who was tall, fair, and devilishly handsome. One was that people, not just women either, took an immediate liking to him. Whoever said looks didn't matter obviously hadn't met Chance Logan. Given the receptionist's immediate infatuation, I saw no point in doing much more than acting as his shadow. I had no need to think. I could just watch the magic happen and enjoy the show.

"We were hoping to catch a few minutes with China," Chance said casually.

Brittany rolled her eyes. "Oh. I'll check."

"What's wrong?" Chance asked.

She shook her head and rolled her eyes again. "She's been in a mood lately. Do you have an appointment?"

Chance planted his hands on the desktop and wrinkled his nose. "Brittany? Do I really need one?"

A conspiratorial grin formed on the girl's lips and she whispered, "I don't think so. Wait here."

"I'd rather surprise her. You understand, right?" Chance followed that up with a quirking of his eyebrows and another movie-star smile.

Brittany flushed again, then bit her lower lip and whispered, "Oh. Okay."

"You're the best," Chance said.

She started to say something as we walked past her desk, but I cut her off with a quick, "I'm with him."

The poor girl turned about three shades of red, then put her head down and started tapping on her keyboard.

China's office was backed by another of those teal accent walls on which she'd hung several framed documents. The boss lady sat at her desk and, if I'd had any doubts about her business being lucrative before, they were dispelled when we walked through the door. Though she was older than in her photo, China had all the right touches in all the right places. Blonde highlights. Expensive blouse—probably silk. Nails perfectly manicured. This woman had expensive taste and knew how to wear it.

When China saw us, she closed the folder in front of her and stood. Chance approached with his hand extended. He introduced himself, told her we were doing background research on Kinohi

Village, and buttered her up by saying he'd heard she was an excellent resource on the subject. She held out her hand, but when Chance took hers, she winced.

"Looks like that hurts," I said.

"I slipped in yoga class this morning." She rubbed her wrist subconsciously, then asked, "What are you trying to find out?"

"We've heard there might have been some...irregularities... on the project," Chance said.

China sat a little straighter and regarded Chance closely. She gestured at the chairs in front of her desk. "Have a seat."

Suddenly, it appeared we'd gone from being unwelcome and potentially hostile intruders to possible allies in the Kenji wars. I couldn't wait to see her reaction when she found out the real reason we were here. While Chance did his thing and BS'd his way into China's confidence, I spent my time checking out the office.

The only personal effect on the desk was a photograph of the boss lady, a man, and two boys. The frame was an intricately carved koa wood—a type I'd priced just once. The phrase, 'out of my league' ought to cover it. Her coffee mug was stenciled with 'World's Best Mom.' The boys, who appeared to be in their teens, knelt in front. The man had his arm around China's shoulders. At least in pictures, China had a good home life. And a very comfortable one.

In the corner next to a two-drawer filing cabinet, there was a gym bag with an Aloha Yoga logo on the side. When I turned my attention back to the conversation, China's elbows rested on the desk and she was leaning forward. Apparently, she must have asked what kinds of things we'd heard because Chance lowered his voice as if he were sharing a secret.

"Misuse of government funds," he said.

China steepled her fingers and gazed at Chance, then me. "What did you hear?"

"We're still trying to sort out all the details," Chance said with a nonchalant flip of his hand.

"It's not every day people just march into my office with information like this. You're not reporters of any kind?"

"No, we're not. Has the press been hounding you?"

"Inquiries are a natural part of my job."

Listening to these two was like watching a fencing match. Thrust, parry. Do it again. China's abilities to give non-answers were top notch, which would make her good at her job. Chance, however, seemed to be enjoying the challenging opponent. He countered with a casual, but direct, reply.

"I'll bet after you blew the whistle on what was really happening at Kinohi Village, you got a lot of inquiries."

"More than usual," she admitted, then turned her attention to me. "You're awfully quiet."

"Oh, sorry. I didn't want to interrupt." I gestured at her hand. "That's got to slow you down in yoga. Yah?"

She seemed surprised by my interest in her physical injury. If she only knew my real purpose, which was to distract her and, hopefully, encourage her to drop her guard.

She curled her fingers together, then spread them out. "It should be better in a few days."

"How long have you been a yogi?" Chance asked.

Yogi? As in Berra? Or the cartoon character? Apparently, neither. China seemed pleased that we'd switched subjects and that one of us spoke the lingo.

"I started, maybe, five years ago. Normally, I take a class before work." She raised her eyebrows and beamed at Chance. "Do you practice?"

When Chance said he did, she turned her attention to me.

"Never tried it." I paused, then added, "At least it won't stop you from showing properties. And at least it wasn't serious. Not like what happened to Kenji Ito."

I'd expected a reaction at the mention of Kenji's name, but there was nothing. I hadn't discussed this strategy with Chance, but it seemed the only way we'd get answers from China was to put her in a box with only one way out.

"Were you bothered by his death?" I asked.

China's genuine smile from the yoga discussion quickly faded. "What are you implying?"

"He's not implying anything," Chance said quickly. "Are you, McKenna?"

"Well, actually, I was wondering when Ms. Gaardner last saw Kenji."

"The last time I saw him was at the City Council meeting."

I was pretty sure that was a lie. A good one, but a lie nonetheless. "Was that the meeting where you claimed the process was rigged?"

China's eyes widened and she was now staring daggers at me. "I don't think I like your tone. And again, it seems you're insinuating something. What are you getting at?"

"You stand to gain a great deal if Kinohi Village goes under."

China slammed her palms on the desktop and stood. "You two are cops. You're here about his murder. I had nothing to do with it. And we have nothing further to talk about."

"That's not exactly correct," I said. "The land would go back up for sale and you could resurrect your deal on the property. The one you were brokering for an anonymous third party."

"Get out," China said sternly. "Or I'll call security."

185

Chance reached into his back pocket and pulled out his wallet. I suppressed a smile, knowing what was coming next. He did exactly as I thought he might. He opened his wallet, flashed his PI-in-training ID with the shiny little badge, then stuffed the wallet back in his pocket. It all happened so fast China couldn't possibly have read it.

"I didn't want to do it this way," he said, then cut his eyes in my direction. "Unfortunately, my partner's left me no choice. We can talk about this here or…well, you know where."

"I didn't do anything!"

"Have you heard of conspiracy, Ms. Gaardner?" I asked.

"You're going to charge me with conspiracy? To commit murder? I'm calling my lawyer!" She reached for the phone and started to dial.

"You really want to make this official?" Chance asked.

"That's right," I said. "Everything is very quiet right now. You get your lawyer. We kick this up the ladder. The press finds out. Ugly."

"I hate to think of what your clients would say," Chance added.

China shot a few more daggers my way, but she did put down the phone. "I have a nondisclosure agreement with all my clients."

"I'm sure there are points we can cover that are outside the scope of your NDA," Chance said.

"What do you want to know?"

"Where were you Tuesday afternoon?"

"Here. Working. Brittany and I were working on a project."

"And what about Monday afternoon?"

She let out a huff, picked up her phone, and tapped the screen a few times. "Showing properties."

"Who were you showing properties to?"

Nice, I thought. Chance hadn't fallen for the BS answer.

China hesitated and ground her teeth. "I was working with someone from West Construction. The company is considering several properties. I can't discuss the particulars because of my NDA. They don't like word of their future projects to get out before they're firmed up. Once property owners hear it's them, they want to jack up the price."

"We'll need to confirm that," I said.

"If you go to them, I'll get fired."

"Oh, right." I pretended to think for a moment, but I knew exactly what question I wanted to ask next. For now, China Gaardner was feeling the heat. And that was just fine by me.

29

WATCHING CHINA GAARDNER, I FELT a strong sense of satisfaction. We'd boxed her into a place where she either had to answer our questions or force us to take her to jail. Leaving off the fact that we couldn't really cart her off to the pokey, it seemed like a pretty good trap. Especially since she didn't know we were bluffing.

"Who was your client for the Kinohi Village deal?" Chance asked.

China's perfect complexion paled. She folded her hands in front of her. Opened her mouth as if she were going to say something. And stopped. Finally, swallowing hard, she said, "I can't tell you who my client was for the Kinohi Village project. That's all there is to it. I told you, I have an NDA and if I break it, I'll be ruined."

Well, crap. And we didn't have one of those cool *Mission Impossible* fake jails we could throw her in either.

"You do realize you might be facing charges," Chance said.

There was really very little point in doing this, but I had to play along, even if it was a waste of time. "Murder, conspiracy. The DA will probably find others."

"I'll talk to my lawyer," China said adamantly.

Double crap. We really were screwed now. I stood, let out an exaggerated huff, and said, "Your choice. Let's go, Chance."

"Don't leave town," Chance said as we walked out of the office.

In the elevator, I snickered as I punched the button for the lobby. "Don't leave town. Good one."

Leaning against the back wall, he laughed. "I've always wanted to say that. It was one of my lines in the movie, but I got fired before we shot the scene."

"This is the movie where you got drunk and stole the helicopter?"

"I didn't really steal it."

"Right. You just borrowed it without permission and crashed it on the set."

"Exactly."

The elevator came to a stop, the doors opened, and the people waiting stood aside as we exited. On the way out the front door, I stopped, exaggerated a sigh, and said, "Sometimes you have to fly by the seat of your pants."

"You know, McKenna. If I didn't like you so much, I might be tempted to kill you right now."

Holy cow. Why hadn't I thought of that? "That's actually brilliant. We've been locked on all these people who hated Kenji, but what if his killer was a friend of his?"

Chance's eyes widened. "Or a business contact."

"You know what, I have a sudden urge to visit Aloha Yoga."

"I thought you were exhausted."

"Actually, I'm pretty charged up right now."

"Okay. But you want to take up yoga? Now?"

"No." I pointed in the direction of China's office. "The boss lady had an Aloha Yoga bag in the corner. I'll bet that's the studio she goes to."

"Now who's the brilliant one?" Chance quirked his head toward the car, which was parked about a block away. "What are we waiting for? Let's go."

Aloha Yoga was located on the second floor of a commercial building in Kaimuki. This was a popular area for several reasons—it was easy access from Waikiki and other beaches, wasn't that far from the University of Hawaii, and had some great restaurants.

Though the building wasn't much to brag about, the inside of the studio was tastefully done. Lots of soft blues and greens. A display filled with items like blocks, straps, and a rolled-up mat. The girl at the front desk was blonde, bubbly, and immediately began her welcome spiel. I figured I was safe, but Chance might easily be sold on a deluxe spa package for Lexie.

When the receptionist finished, I said, "We're here to talk to the instructor who teaches the early morning class."

"Which one? The first is at six. There's another every hour until noon."

"Let's try the six o'clock class," Chance said. "One of your students is China Gaardner. We'd like to talk to her instructor."

The girl tapped on a keyboard, checked the screen, then straightened up. "You're right. China's in the six a.m. You'll want to talk to Phyllis. She's in back." She gestured around a partition that blocked the view from the outside.

We went in the direction she'd indicated. I was surprised at how large the place was, and by the fact that there were a bunch of women all bent over in a downward V formation with their hands at the front of their mats and their feet at the back. A poke in the ribs snapped me out of the mind numbing daze I'd slipped into.

"It's called downward facing dog," Chance whispered.

"Oh. Kind of looks like it…I guess."

A woman who was apart from the others was lying face down on a mat, her left leg stretched out behind her, her right crossed under her chest. My first thought was that she'd broken something and we should call an ambulance, but then she lifted herself up into the same doggie position the class was still in and walked her hands to the back of the mat.

"Welcome to Aloha Yoga. Can I help you?" She had the darkest green hair I'd seen in ages and green eyes that coordinated with her hair. She also had the island lilt. Friendly. Inviting. And almost, but not quite, enough to make me want to take a class.

"My name's McKenna. This is my associate Chance Logan. We understand you were the instructor for the class in which China Gaardner hurt her hand."

"Excuse me?" Phyllis's green eyes flashed. "She's saying that happened here?"

"It's possible I misunderstood her, but I do believe she said it was this morning."

Phyllis shook her head. "No way. She did not do that in class. She was injured when she walked in Tuesday morning. I told her she shouldn't put pressure on it. She blew me off and tried anyway, then had to skip a lot of the poses."

"Tuesday?" I gaped at her. "Are you sure?"

"Positive. She came in Tuesday morning with her hand all bandaged up. She must have learned her lesson because she wasn't in yesterday or today." Seeming to realize she'd been talking about one of her students, she quickly asked, "Who are you anyway?"

"China may have information pertinent to an investigation we're conducting," Chance said smoothly.

Phyllis's eyes widened. "An investigation? You mean, like, police investigation?"

"What other kind is there?" Chance asked.

I had to admire his phrasing—honest and misleading all at the same time. I also admired how he was slouching just a bit so he wouldn't tower over our subject so much.

"We need to keep this confidential," Chance said as he regarded Phyllis.

"Of course. Wow. Is China a suspect?"

"At this stage, we're simply compiling information."

Phyllis's mouth rounded. "Oh. I see. What did you want to know?"

"You said China had the injury when she came in. Did she tell you how it happened?" Chance asked.

"No. I have too many clients in that early morning class to spend much time chitchatting. And, to be honest, China has never been one to socialize. There is one gal who gets along with her, but she goes to work right after we finish."

"Would you mind giving us her contact information?" I asked.

"Ewww." Phyllis winced. "I don't know how Naomi would take that. Why don't I call her for you?"

How was that going to go over? "Don't you think she'll get suspicious when you start asking questions?"

Phyllis laughed. "Not really. I'll just tell her I'm being nosy, that's all. Naomi and I get along really well."

"When can you call her?" I asked.

She pulled a phone out of her pocket. "How about right now?"

Chance gave her a thumbs up, and we stepped aside to give her some faux privacy. Soft music played in the background, but the room was quiet enough for us to easily overhear this side of the conversation.

"Hey, Naomi. Phyllis. Got a question for you."

"You think this will get back to China?" I whispered.

"Let's hope not." Chance turned his attention back to the conversation.

"Just me, being a busybody. What's up with China? Did she tell you how she got hurt?" After a pause, she continued, "Thanks. See you tomorrow."

Phyllis pocketed her phone and shook her head. "Naomi said she asked how it happened and China told her she fell in the shower. That's gotta be bogus."

"Why's that?" I asked.

"Seems weird, that's all. China can hold a tree pose with the best of them."

I had no more desire to learn a tree pose than I did that get-down doggie move.

"So she has excellent balance," Chance said.

Not being one to be left out, I added, "Good point."

Phyllis laughed and patted her shoulder with one hand as she grinned at me. "You have no idea what a tree pose is, do you?"

Something evil in me stirred. I chuckled and pointed at Chance. "I'm clueless, but this guy…show us, buddy."

He smirked at me. Stepping out of his slippahs, he raised his right leg to his left inner thigh and stretched his hands above his head.

"Good form." Phyllis clapped lightly. "Nice job."

Crap. I hated feeling like an idiot.

30

ON OUR WAY OUT OF Aloha Yoga, I felt none of the anticipation I had on the way in. Chance appeared to sense my change in attitude and we both remained quiet until we reached the Ferrari, which was parked on a side street about a block away.

"McKenna, I'm sorry about the yoga thing. I didn't mean to make you feel bad."

"You mean stupid."

"Come on. A lot of people don't know anything about yoga. Besides, it's not something you'd want to do anyway. Right?"

"I don't think so."

"So why are you so bothered by it? Are you getting tired again?"

I closed my door and watched glumly as a woman wearing black yoga pants and a tank top walked into the building. Why was I bothered? "Actually, I'm not tired and what's bugging me has nothing to do with yoga. I'm starting to feel the pressure of

195

the wedding. And of not being able to rent that stupid apartment."

Chance fired up the engine and put the car into gear. "Come on. I'll buy you lunch. You'll think more clearly when your stomach's not growling so loud."

"You don't have to do that. We need to regroup on this whole China Gaardner thing."

"I have an even better idea." Chance checked his mirror, signaled, and pulled into traffic. A confident smile spread across his face. "I know what'll make you feel better. We're going on a good old-fashioned stake out."

I had to admit, the idea had a certain appeal—provided we were focusing on someone worthwhile. "Who are we staking out?"

"China Gaardner. If she came to class with an injured hand on Tuesday morning, our original time of death timetable might have been correct. Think about it. She could have met with Kenji, whacked him on the head, then buried the body."

"So she hurt her hand when she whacked him on the head? Come on, Chance. It's a nice theory, but what about the backhoe?"

Chance shook his head and sighed. "I don't know yet, but we'll figure it out."

"Is that the question you're hoping to answer with this little escapade?"

"No. I want to know who her mystery client is."

I did my best not to sound stupid again. "How the heck are we going to do that?"

Chance explained his plan as he drove. Personally, I thought it was nuts. Then again, I was getting a free lunch, and we'd gotten away with some pretty crazy stuff, so what the heck?

Street parking was tricky, but we found a spot in the shade a few blocks from the Finance Factor Center. We didn't think China knew what kind of car Chance drove, but why take the risk? When he offered to run down to a nearby sandwich shop that had gluten-free options, I took him up on the offer.

While Chance made the sandwich run, I took the elevator to the twelfth floor. My assignment was to find a spot where we could watch China's office door without being caught. No small task considering that most office buildings don't provide hidey-holes for spies.

My left out of the elevator took me past China's door, allowing me to peek inside as I passed. Brittany was at her desk, thoroughly engrossed by her computer. I slipped into the men's rest room and texted Chance after using the facilities. His reply said he was on his way back with lunch. I ventured further down the hallway. It turned left, and eventually dead-ended. With my hopes rapidly sinking, I retraced my steps.

After passing China's door again, I wandered down the hall to a room where a man in a subdued-print shirt was waiting for a Keurig coffee maker to finish it's cycle. I stopped and backed up. It was a small break room. Perfect.

The man picked up his mug and turned around. He saw me, smiled, and said hello. He didn't appear the least bit suspicious when I explained that I was here for a meeting and needed a place to have lunch. I asked if there were any restrictions on who could use the room. He told me to help myself and wished me a good day.

I waited until he was halfway down the hall before I did any further poking around. There was a mini-kitchen, complete with a sink and a refrigerator. Comfortable chairs and a table. What more could we ask for? I sent Chance another text, this time telling him to come to the twelfth floor and turn right as he came out of the elevator. About two minutes later, the elevator chimed and Chance appeared carrying two paper bags, one in each hand.

"You found us a spot?" Chance asked.

I gestured at the break room, then towards China's office.

He checked out my find, then stood next to me, a wide grin on his face. "You scored, McKenna. You scored big time."

"Thanks. I thought it was pretty good."

He handed me a bag marked with the letters GF. "Here. You go first. I'll keep watch."

"Good, I'm starved. Stakeouts always did make me hungry."

While Chance stood guard, I grabbed a cup of water and sat at the table. My sandwich was a standard turkey and Swiss on a gluten-free roll. When I saw the bag of gluten-free jalapeño chips, I moaned. "Oh, one of my favorites."

Chance laughed and flashed me a thumbs-up. "I know. Take your time. I think we're going to be here for awhile."

After taking one bite of my turkey and swiss, I decided this sandwich was definitely gourmet. I savored every morsel, enjoying the opportunity to simply chill out with my thoughts. By the time I finished, it was twelve-forty-five.

True to his word, Chance was still keeping guard, but his upbeat demeanor had tarnished a bit. "Maybe this was a bad idea," he said. "I was just sure they'd both go to lunch by now."

I stood, tossed my trash in the wastebasket, and we changed places. "Sit down, eat, and if nothing happens within half an hour, we'll strategize."

Fifteen minutes later, other than Chance having finished his sandwich and chips, our situation hadn't changed. The door down the hall was still open and that meant this little stakeout might turn into a fake out.

Chance stood next to me, casually resting one shoulder against the wall. "How are the wedding plans going?"

"Don't ask."

"Mrs. Nakamura?"

"Her little visit has me so confused. Benni and I had agreed on a small wedding, then the old lady butted in and convinced me Benni was agreeing with me because it was all we could afford. Then, Benni said she really did want a small wedding and I shouldn't be listening to Mrs. Nakamura. But Benni's got a big family. I don't want them mad at me."

"Wow. You sure know how to complicate things. Benni's not the type to go along if that's not what she wants. If she says she wants small, you should believe her."

"I know."

"Wait. That's what's bothering you, isn't it? She has a lot of people she can invite and you don't."

"Aren't these two ever going to lunch?" I grumbled.

"You're dodging the question."

"And you're interfering. Like Mrs. Nakamura."

"If you need relatives, I can loan you a few. You can have my Aunt Flo. She's a real piece of work."

"So's my brother," I snapped.

Chance pulled himself away from the wall and stood straighter, staring at me all the while. "Brother? I thought you were an only child."

Crap. I'd let the cat out of the bag. I sighed, pulled out my wallet, and extracted the letter. "Read that."

Slowly, Chance unfolded the paper. The crease of his brows deepened as he read out loud. "Dear Wilson—This will come as a most awkward surprise, but I believe we are half-brothers. As you can see from the enclosed sketch of our family tree, you and

199

I have the same father. Please call me if you would like to know more about my branch of the family." Chance stopped, his eyes grew wide, and he stammered, "Are you kidding me?"

"Afraid not." Down the hall, China's office door was still open. I might as well deal with this now. "You're the only person I've shown this to."

"You haven't told Benni?"

"No. I don't think she'd be very happy to learn about Stephen McKenna."

"How long have you had that letter?"

"A couple of weeks. I did some research on him when I got it. He has six kids, two ex-wives, and an ex-girlfriend. He also had a little altercation with the law."

"How little?"

"He's a convicted felon."

"What?" Chance exploded.

"He was locked up in a high-security penitentiary until last year."

Chance took a steadying breath, folded the letter, and handed it back to me. "So you've got a brother who's an ex-con. Big deal. Anything else about him that you know?"

I flipped my hand to one side nonchalantly. "He's an alcoholic."

"Is that the reason you knew about the AA meetings?"

Down the hall, Brittany exited the office and closed the door behind her. I breathed a sigh of relief, thankful we'd be getting off the subject of me and that I could avoid answering Chance's question. I stepped out of Brittany's line of sight and pulled Chance with me.

"We just got our opening. Brittany's going to lunch."

Chance pulled out his lock picks, then put one hand on my shoulder. "You don't have to go in with me. You can stay here and be my lookout."

"Meh. There's already one felon in the family. Let's go."

31

CHANCE KNELT IN FRONT OF China's office door, lock picks in hand, and set to work while I paced behind him. The longer it took for him to open the lock, the more my confidence eroded. As his fingers struggled with the little metal tools, I became convinced we'd never get in.

"You need more practice with those things," I said.

"Shhh…I'm trying to focus."

"I wonder if the cops can charge you with almost-breaking-and-entering?"

"Shut up, McKenna." Chance contorted his face into a mask of concentration.

I watched the elevator indicator. If that bell dinged… "What if China shows up?"

"Then she'll call the cops and we'll be the ones in jail." Chance said as he twisted the picks and the door opened.

"Well, I'll be. You did it. Great job. Do you suppose they have gluten-free in prison?"

Chance rolled his eyes as he slipped into the office. I followed, closing the door behind us. The empty room was deathly quiet.

"Hello? China?" Chance waited, then said, "Let's leave the door unlocked. We can always say we found it that way."

Sure. Why not? We could also say we were rifling filing cabinets just to pass the time. "Did you want to start in the boss lady's office?"

"Absolutely. If we don't find anything, we can try out here." He reached into his back pocket, pulled out two pairs of nitrile gloves, and handed one pair to me.

"You've thought this all the way through. I'm impressed." And terrified. Standing outside China's office door felt like my last opportunity to turn back. "A prison record is not the kind of wedding present I wanted to give Benni. You'll have to find us a good lawyer."

"Maybe you could ask your brother? I'm sure he knows one."

"Nah," I said. "The guy was in the federal pen. His lawyer couldn't have been that good."

"Right," Chance said as he went through the open door and stood behind China's desk. I followed him in and surveyed the room, realizing my defense mechanisms were running full throttle. I also realized the Aloha Yoga bag was missing.

"Boss lady must be gone for the day. Her bag's gone."

"Let's hope," Chance said as he sat.

While Chance literally riffled China's drawers, I turned to the filing cabinet, grabbed the handle, and pulled. It was locked. "You have any keys in that top drawer?"

Chance checked, pulled out a small keyring, and tossed it to me. The first one I tried turned easily in the lock. To my surprise, with the exception of about a dozen file folders, the top drawer was empty. The files were labeled with names—most likely those of clients. I'd come back to those after I ran through the other drawers.

The second drawer contained a gray cashmere sweater that had been folded up and a pair of fluffy slippers.

"This desk is a waste of time," Chance said.

I turned away from the cabinet to see what Chance was doing. He was leaning back in China's chair, his hands casually clasped behind his head. "You know, McKenna, you really should talk to Benni."

"About what? Arranging for bail if we get caught in here?"

"No. The letter. You've been carrying it around for a couple weeks, so it has to be bothering you. She'll want to know about it. And this new family of yours."

I turned back to the file cabinet. I'd been so close to doing exactly that, but then I'd chickened out. My jaw tightened as I absently flipped through the files in the top drawer again. He was right. I'd been making excuses since the day the letter arrived. Maybe it was a mistake. Or a scam. Or…or…or…it was classic me. Tonight. I cleared my throat.

"Based on what's in this file drawer, I'd say China doesn't have that many clients. I count fourteen. Most of them have a nondisclosure agreement signed by both parties. I'll take a photo of each one. Maybe it will lead us to the anonymous client."

"You suppose there's any relationship to Graham Tynsdale?" Chance asked absently.

"I don't see his name here." The desk phone bleeped. The noise shattered the silence—and my nerves. I pushed the drawer in and turned back to the desk, where Chance was bent over one of the bottom drawers wearing a somber expression.

"This isn't getting us anywhere," he said.

Quite frankly, I couldn't agree more. "Maybe she keeps her business on her laptop."

"Maybe," Chance murmured. He turned his attention to the ceiling. "Or in the cloud."

"Brittany's desk had a computer. I'll check that. Let's hope she hoards more than the boss lady." I went around the corner and sat at Brittany's desk. The computer, of course, was password protected. I did a quick search of the desktop and top drawer. Apparently, the girl was not one of those people who wrote her password on a piece of paper and left it near the computer. Too bad. Without that, it would be impossible to gain the access we needed.

I did a check of the trash and came up with nothing useful. The same with the paper recycling can, which was next to a paper shredder. Out of curiosity, I checked the shredder bin. It was half full. The only thing we were going to get out of this little adventure would be a list of names. Whatever business China Gaardner did, we weren't about to find it via this method.

Out in the hall, the elevator bell dinged. I jerked to attention and watched the door. "Chance! Somebody might be coming." I grabbed one of the chairs in front of Brittany's desk and sat.

Chance came and stood in the doorway of China's personal office. "I found something," he said.

It seemed impossible to me that he could be so cool when we were about to get busted for breaking-and-entering. I bit my lower lip and waited, praying we didn't hear the sound of a key in the door lock.

"Nobody's coming, McKenna. It takes, like, ten seconds to get from the elevator to the door. Chillax, you're too jumpy."

"We need to get out of here. Either one of them could be back any minute."

"Almost done. But, first, you have to see this." He gestured for me to join him with a crooking of his finger.

"What's so important?" I griped as I followed.

Chance stood in the doorway pointing at the HVAC vent. "Do you see it?"

"See what? All I see is duct work."

"Look closer. Inside."

I peered at the vent, thought I saw something unusual, then moved closer. Only when I was directly underneath, could I make out the body of a webcam. "Holy cow."

"Yeah," Chance said. "Holy cow. Let's go."

We walked past Brittany's desk and stood at the door. "Best way to handle this is to act like we've done nothing wrong," I said, trying, but failing, to cover the tremor in my voice.

"Just open the door, would you?"

"You can do the honors."

Chance shook his head and grabbed the doorknob. He turned it and stepped into an empty hallway. We removed our gloves as we walked nonchalantly to the elevator, punched the button, and waited. A few seconds later, the elevator arrived. Our luck held; the car was empty. I pressed my back against the wall and breathed a sigh of relief when the doors slid closed.

"So somebody's got China's office under surveillance?" I asked.

"It would appear so. That was definitely a webcam."

"Great. So whoever is watching caught us on video. Let's hope it wasn't the cops."

"Even if it was, I don't think they're going to do anything about it."

"Unless there's a complaint."

"True. But we left everything the way we found it. Besides, I don't think it's the cops."

The doors opened and we made our way to the street. Brittany was coming toward us, happily chatting with an older woman. Neither seemed to be paying attention to what was happening around them, but I wasn't taking any risks and did a quick one-eighty.

I tugged on Chance's sleeve. "This way. Talk about timing. We made it out just in time."

Chance nudged me with his elbow. "Told you it would be no problem."

The look on Chance's face betrayed his inner anxiety. There were a lot of things I could say, but I decided to let him have his moment of bravado. "Why do you think somebody is spying on China?"

"Tanaka must have been telling the truth. This has to be bigger than we ever thought. Kelly Atkinson went on camera to report Kenji's murder. Later that night, she disappeared. And what about the murder? The killer used a backhoe to bury the body. Most people would have no idea how to operate that kind of machinery."

The light turned green. While dodging the oncoming passersby in the crosswalk, Chance went left and I went right. When we met on the other side of the street, I said, "Are you thinking the murder was a professional hit?"

"You have to admit, it's a possibility."

"It seems like a stretch. If The Company was still around, I'd agree with you."

"The Company? Do you mean the CIA?"

"No. The yakuza. But they're largely a thing of the past. They don't have the total control over the island like they used to."

"Who said the killer had to be part of a gang? I'm talking about someone who has a lot to lose and decided the easiest way to deal with a problem was to get rid of it. What if Kenji just knew too much?"

A chill coursed the length of my spine despite the eight-two degree temperature. Swallowing hard, I said, "That would track with why Kenji told Sue he kept some sort of insurance in his wallet. And if Kelly found out, she either ran to save herself..."

"Or she's been dealt with and nobody's found the body."

I looked around nervously.

"What's the matter? You forget something?" Chance asked.

"No. I'm just trying to figure out if we're next."

32

CHANCE DRUMMED HIS FINGERS ON the steering wheel while I scrolled through the photos I'd taken in China's office. Admittedly, pictures of nondisclosure agreements would normally rank high on the boredom scale, but given the stakes—finding China's anonymous client or not—I wasn't the least bit bored.

"Anything useful?" Chance asked.

"I have names for fourteen clients and, as China told us, she's got nondisclosure agreements with all of them. Everything's signed and dated, but they don't tell us who's an active client."

A gentle breeze drifted through. I turned my face into it and let it ruffle my hair.

"China mentioned that she was showing properties to someone from West Construction. Were they in there?" Chance asked.

I showed him the photo of the agreement. "Signed by Tommy West, himself. What are you thinking?"

209

"Let's give it a try. At a minimum, we can determine if she was lying about her alibi."

"You're assuming we're right about Monday."

"Assuming."

While I continued to peruse photos, hoping desperately for something, anything, that might help us, Chance got directions to West Construction from the GPS. "Uh, McKenna? We're not going to need the car to get there."

"Really? Where are their offices?"

"Back where we came from. The only difference is West Construction is on the sixteenth floor."

I turned off my phone, stuffed it in my pocket, and got out of the car. Closing my eyes, I relished the soft breeze and let it caress my skin. Chance had his way of unwinding, but this was my mind, body, and soul rejuvenation. The trades were a part of Hawaii's life blood, and they'd certainly become part of mine, for without them I could never bear the heat and humidity.

We trekked back to the Finance Factor Center and once again passed through the elegant lobby. I didn't mind the return trip because it gave me another opportunity to admire the gleaming green-and-white tiles and elegant wood trim. For a forty-plus-year-old building, this one was in excellent shape. This time, we had company in the elevator, so we all played the ignore-each-other game and watched our phones or the floor indicator as we made our short journey.

I'd always assumed that renting one of the top floors in a downtown skyscraper carried with it a certain air of respectability. That assumption was confirmed when the elevator doors opened at the sixteenth floor. West Construction & Engineering was etched into the double glass doors. Already, this was way more impressive than Island Real Estate. Unlike China's office with its plebeian lock and key, this office was guarded by an electronic card key system and surveillance cameras. At least from outward appearances, the big money was in developing real estate, not selling it.

An elegant counter fronted to the entrance. Behind the counter sat a petite brunette with long, straight hair. When the glass doors closed behind us, it was like entering a cone of silence where even the air deadened any sound. Our footfalls disappeared in the thick carpeting, leaving behind only the clip-clopping of our slippahs against the bottoms of our feet.

The brunette smiled at us. Began with the routine. Who were we here to see? Did we have an appointment? Oh, I'm so sorry, you'll need to call and make arrangements. Apparently, Amanda —that was the name engraved on the nameplate—had taken the same receptionist classes as Brittany. The difference was, Amanda must have excelled because she seemed immune to Chance's charm.

After about a minute, I was convinced we were not going to pass without the use of physical force. Chance must have come to the same conclusion, so he decided to try a different tactic— the old 'Lefty sent me' line. In this case, he substituted China's name.

Amanda wasn't buying it. Her steely gaze didn't waver. In fact, the condescending smile she gave him said, 'nice try, rookie.' Even as a bystander, I felt like I'd just witnessed a gawky high-school freshman strike out trying to pick up the prom queen. Despite the total shutdown, her response was silky smooth. "I'm sorry, but you'll need an appointment to see anyone."

Chance wasn't used to dealing with women who were immune to his charms and seemed taken aback. While he tried to regroup, I made the mistake of peering past Amanda.

"Don't even think about it," she snapped, all pretense now gone.

What was she going to do? Tase me?

A man with neatly trimmed white hair and a salt-and-pepper beard approached the desk from a long hallway. He carried a manila file folder, smiled to acknowledge us, then dropped the folder into a basket on the corner of the desk and turned to walk away.

"Mr. West!" Chance blurted.

The man did an about-face and regarded us. Chance held out his hand to introduce himself. When he said his name, recognition dawned on West's face.

"You're Lexie Ashbrook's fiancé."

"That's right."

West stepped forward, shook hands with Chance, then winked at his receptionist. "It's okay, Amanda. This is Councilman Jack Ashbrook's someday-to-be son-in-law."

"Sorry, Mr West. I had no idea."

"No worries." West gave us both a sly grin. "Amanda's my protector. You have no idea how many people want to pitch me projects or ask for a job. Anyway, what can I do for you?"

"This is my friend, McKenna. We wondered if you might have a few minutes to chat?"

"Sure," West said casually. "Amanda, would you call my two-fifteen? I'll be a few minutes late."

Amanda flashed her boss a pleasant smile and said she'd take care of it right away. West told us to follow him and led us down the hallway, his muted-print Hawaiian shirt flowing as though it had been tailored of expensive silk. Judging by everything else in this place, it probably had.

The walls, a soothing gray, were dotted every few feet by an artist's rendition of a West Construction & Engineering project— a not-so-subtle visual reminder that this company had worked on some prestigious Honolulu construction jobs. As if to emphasize the importance of their work, cameras watched our every move. This place was like Fort Knox, but with better interior decorating.

"You've been involved with all these projects, Mr. West?" I said.

He stopped, turned, and faced me. "Please, call me Tommy. My father started the company, so we've had a lot of years to build our reputation. We also know how to bid jobs properly. Word about that gets around."

I shook my head slightly. "I don't understand."

"Some guys have a reputation for not including everything in their bids. They get a client hooked on a cheap bid, then have to start raising the price with change orders. We don't play that game. Put the work in up front and it saves you money later on— that's my motto."

Having been recently stuck with one of those guys for a small job at the Sunsetter Apartments, I had an appreciation for the philosophy. "Good way to do business. So you have a lot of jobs going at once?"

"They're at varying stages of progress. Anywhere from bidding to finish work. Never have all your eggs in one basket. That's my motto."

Not wanting to get us thrown out, I resisted the urge to ask how many mottos he had. Then again, I had a bunch of skip tracing secrets. Who was I to judge?

"When's the last time you saw Councilman Ashbrook?" Chance asked.

"A few weeks ago. We played golf. That's when he told me you and Lexie were getting serious—at least, in his opinion."

Chance smiled politely. "There's nothing definite yet. Do you see him often?"

"Not as much lately. I should call him and set up a tee time. Do you play?"

"I never had the patience. My dad was very disappointed when I didn't take to the game."

"Doesn't matter how good you are if you enjoy it. What about you, McKenna?"

"I never had the time. Or the money."

"It does take a lot of patience and time, especially in the beginning." Tommy cocked his head toward the end of the hall. "My office is this way."

We followed him into a large room filled with matching Koa wood furniture. There was a massive desk with an intricately carved front, a round conference table with four chairs, a credenza littered with trophies, a bookcase on which there were several photos, and two visitor chairs. Even with all the furniture, this office felt larger than my living room. Honolulu stretched into the distance through the windows behind the desk. Apparently, as the boss, Tommy had chosen the office with the good view, not the side with the view of another skyscraper.

The trophies on the credenza were a mix of business and golf awards. The little brass golfers in mid swing atop their koa wood bases were obvious testaments to Tommy's abilities. Even a newbie like me could tell he wasn't just another divot digger out there killing perfectly good grass.

Tommy went to the table and pulled out a chair. "Please, have a seat. What brings you here?"

"I'm sure you knew Kenji Ito," Chance said.

The comment must have taken Tommy by surprise because his dark eyebrows went up and his brow furrowed. "We go way back. What's this about?"

"We're looking into his death."

"Ah. So this is a professional call." Tommy smiled and rested his elbows on the table. "I heard that you were working on your private investigator's license."

"We've been asked by the family to see what we can find out."

"Aren't the police investigating?"

"We're approaching this from a different angle."

I kept my mouth shut, hoping Chance's BS was sufficiently vague that Tommy wouldn't worry about whether we were stepping on any official toes. Whether he was buying the line or not, I couldn't tell.

"You said you'd known Kenji for a long time." Chance said. "When did you meet?"

"We started out working for my dad at the same time. In those days, we had to do every job you can think of." He stopped, chuckled, then added, "Simpler times. There are days when I kind of miss them."

"Had you seen him lately?" Chance asked.

"Kenji? No. As our companies grew, we became more like rivals." Tommy paused and cocked his head toward the reception area. "Out front, I heard you mention China's name. What's this got to do with her?"

"She told us she was working with someone from West Construction on Monday afternoon. Were you aware that she was showing properties to someone in your company?"

Tommy scratched his head and made a face. "Is that what she told you? The truth is I've known China for several years. That woman knows how to work a deal like nobody else. She's made us both a ton of money."

"But?" Chance coaxed.

"This is a little awkward. She hasn't actually shown us any properties in over a month."

My pulse quickened at the thought. We'd caught China in another lie? Finally, we might have caught a break. Before I could stop myself, the words gushed out of my mouth? "So nobody in your company was viewing properties with her?"

"No." He chuckled, then ran his hand over the back of his neck and smiled. "As a matter of fact, we had an afternoon tee time Monday. We were playing golf at O'ahu Country Club."

I gaped at Tommy. "Together?"

"Well, yes. That's how it usually works."

I swear I heard the sound of air whooshing out of a balloon. Or maybe that was just our case against China Gaardner.

33

IN THE FIVE MINUTES SINCE I'd met Tommy West, I'd learned several things about him. The most important being that he was a man not easily flustered. I could see him running for political office someday. Who knows? I might even vote for him.

"Sorry, guys," Tommy said. "I only have a few minutes. My next appointment is going to be here soon, but I can tell you this. If you're thinking China had something to do with Kenji's murder, think again. She's a hard worker, smart as a whip, and doesn't even get parking tickets."

"Do you play golf with her often?" I asked.

"When we have a deal to work on."

Chance sat a little straighter and looked at Tommy. "What deal are you working on now?"

Tommy chuckled. "Kudos for trying, but I can't tell you. We're still in negotiations. That's why we're not considering any properties right now."

"Was she working for you the night she appeared at the City Council meeting?" Chance asked.

"Which one? She's been our representative there several times."

"The night they decided to proceed with Kinohi Village."

Leaning back in his chair, Tommy contemplated both of us for a few seconds. Finally, he shrugged and put his elbows back on the tabletop. "What the heck? It's no secret I was opposed to Kenji getting the project. For me, it was a lost opportunity."

Finally, we knew who the mystery client was. Out of curiosity, I asked, "How so?"

"Homelessness is a huge problem here in Honolulu. But I didn't think that particular plot of land was the best place to be creating that kind of development. I thought there were better uses for the property."

"Where would you have them go?" Chance asked.

Tommy made a face and sighed. "Kind of a moot point, isn't it? There are places. City Council didn't see it our way. That's all."

Chance steepled his fingers. "Was China's job to get the powers that be to understand there were better alternatives?"

"Unfortunately, she got all riled up. I've made enough mistakes to know you don't let your emotions get in the way of things. My first wife taught me that lesson."

"So you're on number two?" I asked.

Tommy smirked. "She didn't work out so well either. I'm settled down now. I have a good relationship with number one and see our kids all the time. I'm finally in a place where things are good."

Amanda appeared at the door. She gave Tommy a little wave. "I'm sorry, but your next appointment is here."

"Okay, guys. My time's up. If you have any more questions, let me know. I'm happy to help."

"Just one more, if you don't mind?" I said.

"Sure. If it's quick."

"At the City Council meeting, China said her client had other plans for the property. What were you planning on doing with it?"

Tommy turned toward the wall and pointed to one of the artist's renderings. "It was to be a combination of housing and commercial development. People could work and live in the same area. Lots of greenspace. It would have been a shining example of what's possible with good planning."

I regarded the drawing. There was a large park with ribbons of green—most likely walkways—meandering throughout. The artist had done an excellent job of making the entire project appear very attractive and walker friendly. But, it didn't seem like the kind of place the middle class could afford.

We thanked Tommy. Told him the project was a real gem. A loss for Honolulu. I was sure to leave off the part about it being good for the Honolulu wealthy, not the workers. Then, we all stood and Amanda guided us back down the hall. A black woman I recognized from one of the photos in Tommy's office passed us. She wore a hibiscus-flowered sundress and had a matching flowered purse slung over her shoulder. Even without her high-heeled sandals, she would have been about my height. As it was, I had to look up at her when we passed. She gave me a cordial smile as she swayed down the hall toward Tommy's office.

With the glass doors closed behind us, I said, "You suppose she's on track to be wife number three?"

Chance chuckled as he punched the elevator button. "Could be. Did you see the family photos?"

"Yes. She was with Tommy and his two kids from wife number one. This guy really gets around."

"That he does. And he's a good salesman for his project. What he left out was the cost of those homes and that most of those businesses were retail."

The elevator arrived, we entered, and I waited to respond until the doors were closed. "There's no cheap real estate in Honolulu; I get that. But that rendering? Wow. If I had a spare million bucks and was in the market for a new residence, I'd have been devastated, too, when the City Council made their choice. As it stands, I still think they made the right decision."

The elevator stopped to pick up additional passengers on two of the lower floors, and that put a damper on our conversation. The problem was, after talking to Tommy, I felt even less confident that we were going to make any further headway. I was beginning to wonder if we'd ever untangle this spider's web.

"Anywhere you think we should go?" Chance asked when we were in the car again.

"Home. I'm stumped for now."

"Next stop, Sunsetter Apartments."

We were five or six miles from home, a trip that would take less than fifteen minutes with no traffic, but it was late afternoon and the H1 was a mess. I noticed that Chance seemed to be checking his rearview mirror more than normal. I dismissed it, thinking he might have a tailgater dogging him. Never having driven the Ferrari, I had no firsthand knowledge about that sort of thing, but it seemed a reasonable assumption.

We arrived at the Sunsetter Apartments at quarter to four. Chance followed me to my place and after I had opened everything up, told me to check the answering machine. I really was dead beat and in no mood to deal with whacky tenants, but punched the button anyway.

"Hi, my name is Jessica Black—oops, I mean Ho. I just got married and haven't adjusted to my new name. Anyway, I'm calling about the apartment. If ya'll still have it available could you call me back? My husband and I just got married and we want a place near the water. We both have good jobs and when I saw ya'lls ad I got really excited, but we were flying back from our honeymoon and…gosh, I'm sorry. I'm rambling. I have a tendency to talk too much."

She left her name and numbers, both work and cell.

"Bubbly," I grumbled. "And southern."

"Excuse me?"

"She has a strong southern accent and she married a guy named Ho."

"What are you so grumpy about? She sounds nice. Don't let a couple of bad tenant interviews get you down."

"Three. It's a record."

"McKenna. You're sounding like an old fart."

I wanted to be angry at Chance, but I couldn't. He was right. I had been. I laughed, then said, "That's because I am. Fine. I'll call her, but if this one doesn't work out, you're renting the apartment."

Chance dismissed my grumpiness and went to the kitchen table, sat, and tapped on the keys of his laptop while I called Jessica with the two names. I got her right away, and just as I was finishing the conversation, Benni arrived. She waved to Chance and me, then went into the bedroom to drop off her things. By the time Benni reappeared, my spirits had lifted. I was almost hopeful again. After having struck out three times, I wasn't ready to jump for joy until someone signed on the dotted line.

Benni and I exchanged a quick kiss, then she asked if the caller was a new tenant.

"It sounds promising and she said they would come by tomorrow night after work. They'll be here by five-thirty at the latest."

"See? You get to meet the bride and the groom," Chance said.

Benni's eyebrows went up, as did the interest in her voice. "They're newlyweds?"

"Just got back from their honeymoon." I crossed my fingers and held them up. "Here's hoping for the best. By the way, we also had a meeting with Tommy West."

"You met with the competition?" Benni planted her hands on her hips. "Really? Tommy West is out for nobody but himself. He's got two ex-wives and a girlfriend. He cheated on both wives."

"We heard about the wives, but not the cheating. He left that part out." I raised and lowered my eyebrows a couple of times, then added, "He lives for the thrill."

Benni glared at me. "Don't get any ideas."

"No worries. I'm a one-woman man." I cleared my throat and looked at Chance. "What are you working on?"

"I was just doing a little checking because of something Derrick Tanaka said. He told us he wanted to go to work for West Construction because the pay was better. I was hoping to find something that might confirm that, but from what I can tell, they're both union."

Unless Chance wanted a job as a carpenter, I was having trouble seeing his point. "Meaning the pay would be the same. But what's that got to do with anything?"

"As you would say, McKenna, it's an inconsistency." Chance stood, closed the lid on his laptop, and regarded Benni. "Sue gave you access to the books, right?"

"Yah. McKenna asked me to snoop around for anything suspicious."

"I didn't say snoop," I said defensively.

"Same difference," Benni chuckled.

"Like blackmail?" Chance asked.

Benni nodded. "There have been a couple things that popped up. That payment to Joe Taylor was one."

"What else have you found?" I asked.

"People are pretty fed up with the government wasting money by reinventing the wheel. Kinohi Village is a public-private partnership that appears to be very efficient and cost-effective. There was a lot of interest in Kenji's expertise in setting up these kinds of projects because it went so smoothly."

"And that's a problem?"

"You know Honolulu, McKenna. Our government has had… a colorful past. Fortunately, this was handled perfectly. In fact, Kenji was working on the project for free and all company resources were being donated."

Chance's eyebrows went up. "That part about the colorful past sounds interesting." He raised his hand and wiggled his fingers. "Do tell."

Benni explained that she had been a baby when Honolulu's mayor was indicted on charges of accepting a $500,000 bribe. A few years later, by the time she was in Mrs. Nakamura's class, there were plenty of scandals filling the news. From murders to government contracts awarded based on payoffs, teachers like Mrs. Nakamura made sure their students learned the truth. "The charges were eventually dropped against Mayor Fasi, but those days will always be a part of the city's history."

Benni's comments reminded me of China Gaardner's outbursts at the City Council meeting. Was she alleging that we were seeing a return of graft in government? Payoffs of public officials? What if there was a bit of truth in all those accusations?

34

DINNER TURNED OUT TO BE a surprise for me that had been arranged by Benni and Lexie. We sat at a white metal table for four in Flour and Barley, a restaurant on the third floor of the International Marketplace. We'd come early to avoid the crowd and had scored a table overlooking Kalākaua Avenue. Below us, pedestrians swarmed the sidewalk on both sides of the street. Sitting here with Benni and our friends, the day seemed far away indeed.

"I've been dying to come here," I said.

Benni laughed. "I know. Award-winning gluten-free pizza. Once you heard about it, you talked about it nonstop for a week."

My face warmed at the memory. "I may have gone a little overboard."

"A little?" Benni scoffed.

"Okay, a lot." I took a sip of my glass of Zinfandel and savored the notes of blackberries and chocolate.

Overhead, lights hung in rope slings beneath a dark open-beamed ceiling. The exposed air conditioning tubing had been painted a matte black. It was all a very contemporary design.

Leaning over, I kissed Benni on the lips. "You're right. I did talk about this place a lot. And I'm glad you took the hint."

Benni laughed and looked across the table at Chance and Lexie. "McKenna's hints are kind of like a marching brass band. They're hard to miss."

My ears felt like they were about the color of the zin, but I didn't care. This was going to be a great night with no talk of murder—at least, that's what I hoped. After dinner, maybe we'd stroll around and enjoy the tourist version of paradise. Developers had spent a fortune turning the International Marketplace into a shopper's dream. Directly targeted at travelers with money, what had once been a bargain-hunters shopping haunt had gone upscale and was now well out of my league.

Lexie, bubbly as usual, said, "Let's talk about the wedding. Benni told me you guys agreed to keep it simple and small. Yah?"

"McKenna got confused when Auntie Asuka tried to sell him on a big ceremony. We got that straightened out." She looked directly at me. "We did? Didn't we?"

It was time for me to commit publicly to a decision. "Yes. If that's what you want."

Benni's face fell. She didn't have to say a word for me to realize that in my efforts to hedge my bets, I'd screwed up—again.

"What I meant was, yes, that's what we agreed on. And…" I jerked when someone kicked me under the table.

Chance smiled at me. "You were saying?"

226

It wasn't the most subtle form of communication, but I got his point. Shut your mouth while you're ahead. "I'm delighted with the decisions we've made." Even if I did have to find a way to unhire the musicians Benni had found. "So Lexie, what have you been up to?"

She rolled her eyes, took a sip from her glass, and exaggerated a groan. "Other than arguing with my dad?"

Chance frowned at her. "About what, babe?"

"You, mostly. And your investigations. He thinks it's dangerous."

"He's right," I blurted. Uh oh. Wrong thing to say. I was on a roll tonight. "What I meant was, there is a certain element of danger, but you girls don't have to be exposed to it."

Peeved. That should sum up the reaction from Benni and Lexie. And Chance? He was trying to ignore the whole thing by focusing on his beer.

"Okay," I said. "Maybe there have been some…incidents. Chance, help me out here."

"You don't need my help. You're digging a hole for two quite nicely all by yourself."

"Thanks," I grumbled. Then, sitting up straight, I pretended to search the restaurant for our server. "You think our order's almost ready?"

"McKenna, really? You're going with the bailout strategy?" Benni nudged me in the ribs, then put her hand on my shoulder and whispered in my ear. "I still love you, anyway."

"A fight with your dad's not good for two reasons," Chance said. "First, I never want to come between the two of you. I really like your dad, and I'm surprised he thinks I'd let anything happen to you."

There were times when I'd swear Bennie and Lexie operated on some sort of telepathic wavelength. This was one, because in unison, they said, "But…"

"How do you two do that?" I asked.

Lexie giggled, then said, "It's a girl secret."

"That's right," Benni added. "Don't worry your pretty little head about it. Neither of you have the right parts to understand." She gave me a sweet smile, then turned to Chance. "And you, you're not off the hook either. What's the other reason?"

Chance swallowed hard. Turned to me for help. I just raised my hands. "You didn't come to my aid. You're on your own. Besides, I have no idea what your other reason is." Unless it had to do with Lexie's sudden desire to have kids.

"It has to do with Tommy West," Chance said.

Okay, didn't see that coming. "What's he got to do with this discussion?"

"He's a member of the O'ahu Country Club."

I threw my hands up. "So?"

"So's my dad," Lexie said.

"Spit it out, buddy. What are you getting at? Do you want the councilman to invite Tommy to play golf or something?"

"Not exactly." Chance turned in his chair so he was facing Lexie. "Tommy told us he was playing golf with China on Monday afternoon. I was hoping your dad might check a tee time for me."

Now I got it. OCC was a prestigious club, and they'd laugh us out of the building if we showed up and started asking questions. But Councilman Ashbrook was a member and could get the answer with a simple phone call. Lexie's response was not what I expected.

She shook her head. "That's not a good idea, babe. My dad's super concerned right now. I made the mistake of telling him you were investigating Kenji's death. He asked me to see if you'd just let the police handle it."

"You know, Chance, this didn't start out as a murder. We were supposed to find Kenji. And then we were supposed to be checking out a few rumors. But, murder…"

Chance's jaw dropped. He locked his gaze on mine. "I thought you were on board, McKenna. We agreed that we should do this for Sue."

"I think that today convinced me we're going to make some serious enemies if we keep going. Maybe the councilman's right and we should think about letting the police handle this. They'll find the killer."

"And what about Kenji's reputation? They won't care about…" Chance's eyes flicked toward the entrance. A frown creased his brow, and he pushed his chair back. "There's something I have to do."

He stood abruptly and weaved his way toward the entrance, sidestepping servers and patrons who got in his way.

"You really made him mad, McKenna," Benni said, then reached out and took Lexie's hand. "You okay, Lex?"

Her voice cracked when she tried to speak. "I don't know." She bit her lower lip and watched the direction Chance had gone. "He's been acting so strange lately."

I let my gaze follow Lexie's. Chance had disappeared from view. Turning back to Lexie, I saw tears welling in her eyes. There was something going on between Chance and Lexie. Maybe it was her dad, or her desire to have kids, or something completely different that I knew nothing about. No matter what the reason, I felt as though I should take the blame for Chance's sudden exit.

"I don't know that I've ever seen him angry. I shouldn't have surprised him by backpedaling. Not here, anyway." A few seconds later, I added, "Do you think he's coming back?"

My question was met with silence. No one at this table wanted to hazard a guess.

"Let's give him a few minutes to cool down," Benni said.

We waited quietly in the midst of organized chaos. All around us, friends and family laughed and talked loudly. The aroma of baking bread and tomatoes and cheese should have made the entire evening an event to remember. Instead, we seemed to have fallen victim to one trap after another.

After a short wait, Lexie pushed back her chair and took a determined breath. "I should go see if I can talk to him."

"No. Let me. I'm the one who set him off," I said and started to stand.

Benni grabbed my forearm and squeezed. "Neither of you have to go. Here he comes."

I crossed my hand over my heart. "I'll be on my best behavior. Promise."

Lexie watched Chance approach, her concern obvious. "He's super upset. I can see it on his face."

I snuck a peek at Chance. Lexie was right. He wore the same frown that had been there just before he ran off. And he kept glancing over his shoulder.

"Sorry," Chance said as he sat. He kissed Lexie, then rearranged his napkin on his lap. "I thought I saw someone...that I know."

"Who's that, babe?"

It was an admirable attempt at sounding upbeat, but Lexie could only hide so much.

"I'm sorry about what I said, Chance. We don't have to stop the investigation. We'll continue. Full speed ahead and all that."

Chance's shoulders slumped as he faced Lexie. "I never wanted to put you in danger. You have to believe that."

"I know. Please, tell me what's wrong." She took his hands in hers and waited.

He shot one final glance across the restaurant toward the entrance, then let out a heavy sigh. "I don't think I can do this anymore."

"Can't do what, babe?"

"Keep this a secret."

"Oh my God, are you breaking up with me?"

"What? No! But you might want to stay away from me for a few days."

Tears welled again in Lexie's eyes. Next to me, Benni cocked her head and stared at Chance. I was having trouble figuring out what alien had taken possession of his body. By his own admission, he was madly in love with Lexie. Why would he do this?

"You are making no sense at all," I said. "Take it from someone who knows how to screw up a relationship. You need to come clean. Now."

He took several deep breaths, the concern on his forehead etching deeper with each. Finally, he straightened up and said, "Okay. The truth is—somebody's following us. We've been under surveillance all afternoon."

35

FLOUR AND BARLEY WAS FILLED to capacity with diners whose anticipation and satisfaction were off the charts, but at our little table for four, the mood had soured. Chance's revelation that we'd been under surveillance sent a rash of creepy-crawlies down my spine, but it was the fear on Benni's and Lexie's faces that worried me most.

"You're positive?" I finally asked.

Chance sighed as he massaged his forehead with his fingertips. "Yes. A blue Toyota pulled out behind us when we left the Finance Factor Center. It stuck with us all the way home."

"You never said a word. I never saw them."

"I didn't want to alarm you, and then they drove past the Sunsetter, so I figured it wasn't a big deal."

Lexie rested her hand on Chance's. "Just before you ran off, you said you saw someone. Was that them? Watching?"

"I spotted someone taking a picture. Of us."

I found myself inspecting the faces of every person in the room. Instead of good times and celebration, each table now constituted a potential danger. "Are you sure? Do you have any idea who it is?"

"No. He was wearing a hat and black tee and jeans. He's kind of a little guy, but there might be others."

"So someone's spying on us." My shoulders slumped. All I wanted to do was turn back time so I could change that moment when I'd agreed to help Chance find Kenji.

A body appeared at my side, pulling me back from my short lapse into self-pity. It was our server, not a hired killer. Not a reason to panic, but an opportunity to eat. She cleared a spot in the middle of the table.

"Here's your order," she said as she set down two pizzas, one gluten-free for Benni and me, the other regular for Chance and Lexie.

I bent forward and breathed in the heavenly aromas—the San Marzano tomato sauce, pepperoni, basil, and mushrooms, topped off with mozzarella and fontina cheeses. Under normal circumstances, it would have been enough to make me drool freely, but with Chance's bombshell, this felt more like a last meal. At least it would be a good one.

Unlike most gluten-free pizzas, whose crusts tend to be a close relative of cardboard, this one was thick, light, and crunchy. A pizza lover with Celiac couldn't get much closer to heaven. And when I took that first bite, my eyes glazed over. There was no more talk of spies or murder or weddings until after we'd polished off the last pieces and the check arrived.

Lexie snatched up the bill and handed it to Chance. "This is on me," he said. "We'll call it a pre-wedding present."

Benni and I thanked Chance for his generosity, but that seemed to be the end of our respite from the evening's concerns.

Lexie craned her neck to look around, then whispered to Chance, "Is he gone?"

"I hope so."

Terrific. We were trapped in the world's best pizza restaurant. On the bright side, we might not sleep, but we wouldn't go hungry.

On the way out we took the glass elevator using the rationale that we could all watch in different directions for the person following us. While good in theory, the reality was that we were shoehorned in with a bunch of overeager shoppers and diners. If this was supposed to be reverse surveillance, our mission was an epic failure.

The sun was slipping below the horizon when we arrived home. Streamers of pink, gray, black, and mauve crisscrossed the sky in subtle, abstract patterns that changed with each passing minute. We all decided to take a walk on the beach, so we left our slippahs at the edge of the grass and walked barefoot across the sand.

Benni squeezed my hand when I took hers. It was hard to believe we would soon be man and wife. The realization started out as a tiny little thing, something about the size of a pea in my brain, but rapidly grew into an elephant-sized force that dominated my thoughts. When Benni asked if I was okay, I gazed into her eyes and kissed her.

"It just hit me, in about a week we'll be married."

Her eyebrows went up and even in the pale twilight I could tell she was trying not to laugh. "You're just figuring that out?"

"Sorry, that's not what I meant. I was thinking of it in the context of the fact that someone's following us." Watching

Lexie, I added, "Now I understand how your dad feels. Chance and I shouldn't be messing around in a murder investigation. Is it always the same person? The one who's watching us?"

Chance let out a deep sigh, his forehead furrowed and he shook his head. "I don't know. I never got a close enough look at the driver of that Toyota. And I haven't seen him since dinner."

Lexie hugged herself and shivered. "You think it could be the killer?"

"Maybe McKenna's right," Benni said. "When I asked you guys to find Kenji, I thought it would have taken you a few hours, maybe a day. I never expected—I'll talk to Sue in the morning."

Unfortunately, I didn't think that was going to work. "I don't know if we can stop. We're in too deep. We've obviously come to somebody's attention. If it's the killer, we'd be a whole lot better off finding him. Otherwise, we'll never know if or when he'll strike."

"What if it's not him? What if it's somebody else?" Lexie asked.

A sliver of color still lined the horizon. And, though pretty, it offered me no solace. "That would be nice, Lexie, but who would bother? If I could forget Kenji Ito tomorrow and have things go back to normal, I'd be delighted. The truth is, I think we need to finish what we started."

Lexie put a hand on Chance's arm. "He's right, babe. Whether you guys want to stop now or not, you probably can't."

Chance pulled Lexie into a loose embrace and held her gaze. He sighed, then said, "You're okay with me continuing, then?"

"It's not up to me. You're the one who has to decide what you want to do with your life. If I tell you to stop, you'll resent me for it. No, this decision has to be up to you two."

235

"Where does that leave us, McKenna?" Chance asked.

"That depends on Benni." I turned to face her. She was so beautiful she took my breath away. I couldn't—wouldn't—do anything to endanger her. "What do you think? Next week, you're supposed to take me for better or worse. Marrying you is a dream come true for me, and I don't want to screw it up. So, I'm willing to go either way. You tell me—what would you like me to do?"

Benni grimaced. She looked first at Lexie, then Chance, then me. "You're putting me in an unfair position, McKenna."

"I know. And I'm sorry." Off in the distance, a commercial jet departing Honolulu International climbed and banked away from the island. Visitors leaving. It was a regular event in a tourist destination, yet one that reminded me of another secret I'd been keeping. "There's something else you should know."

She let out a little huff. "Why not? What else is there?"

"Andi's coming."

"What? No, she said…"

"I know. She's got a tour. Obligations."

"I asked her to come," Benni stammered. "She said the wedding was only two days after her last US concert. A couple days later she flies to London from New York."

"We might have…um…worked something out." I cleared my throat, then glanced involuntarily at Chance. "It was supposed to be a wedding day surprise."

Benni did the full-on gaping routine—her mouth open, her eyes wide. She swallowed a couple of times. "I don't understand. What did you do?"

Lexie grabbed Chance's arm and shook it. "Spill, babe. What did you do?"

"I called my dad. He's been a huge fan ever since I told him about her. He volunteered to fly Andi here on the company jet right after her concert. She'll arrive the day before the wedding."

Benni's jaw dropped. "Your dad is flying her on his corporate jet? For free?"

Chance gave Benni a sheepish smile. "Not exactly. They're making a stop in LA to pick up him and my mom. You might say Andi's going to have to do a very small private concert on the plane." He paused, then added, "Basically, she's flying for a song."

"I'm not sure whether I should hug you or smack you, McKenna. You did all of this behind my back?" Benni crossed her arms over her chest and tried to sound angry, but there were tears in her eyes. When I nodded, she threw her arms around me and kissed me, then pulled away and bit her lip.

"You just realized the implications," I said. "Now we're not just talking about Chance and me being in danger, but there's the potential for someone to come after all of us—and that could include Andi. If you want me to stop my part in the investigation, I will. It would make perfect sense to me."

Benni pulled away and let the trades blow her hair across her face, then hung her head. "I don't know what to do."

I got it. Even I wasn't sure that continuing was the right decision, which left me with a dilemma. Here I was, in paradise, just footsteps from the ocean where the rhythm filled my senses. Since moving here, I'd discovered there was no more soothing lullaby. I never wanted to give it up. But even more than that, I never wanted to give up this woman. I'd do anything for her.

"Whatever your decision, I'm okay with it. I won't hold it against you if you want me to stop."

Standing tall, Benni donned a grim smile and brushed windblown strands of hair out of her face. "No. You were right. If you two are being followed, someone could be coming after any of us. We have to fight back. I just hope you catch this person before they do something. And before Andi gets here."

36

AT SHORTLY AFTER EIGHT THE next morning, Chance appeared at my door. His hair was a mess and he had bags under his eyes. I couldn't recall him ever being this bedraggled and realized he hadn't been out surfing that morning.

"Rough night?" I asked.

"Lexie said she needed to think about whether she should ask her dad to check that tee time at OCC. If she won't do it, we'll have to find another way. I'm fine with that, but she got super quiet on the way home. I might be losing her, McKenna."

Figuring it could only make things worse, I wasn't about to mention Lexie's fear about them breaking up. I handed him a mug filled with coffee and sat at the table. "I'm sorry. I know how much you love her."

"Let's get this stupid case solved so we can get on with our lives." He took a long drink from his mug before he continued. "Do you still want to talk to Sue? You said you thought we might get something out of her."

"She should be in by now. Benni's got a meeting with some aging rocker who flew in for a little R&R. Now that she's doing work here and on the Big Island, she's talking about expanding the business. Hiring a couple of part-timers."

"That's good for her," Chance muttered.

"You're really down."

"I don't want Lexie to have to choose between me and her dad. But that's exactly the spot I put her in. It was stupid."

"You're telling the wrong person. Call her. Tell her you're sorry and that you were…well, yeah, tell her you were being stupid. That always works for me."

"You know what? I think I'll do that. Do you mind? I might need a few minutes."

I gestured at the lānai. "I have a nice phone booth out there. Good view of the ocean. Natural air conditioning."

While Chance made his call, I tackled the morning kitchen cleanup. When he returned, he appeared less down.

"She agreed," he said as he slid the screen door closed.

"To talk to her dad?"

"No, that I was being stupid. We'll get it worked out. Come on, let's go talk to Sue."

According to Chance, we were not followed on our short drive to Ito Development, but I couldn't shake the feeling that he might be trying to make the best of things. We found Sue at her desk, her face buried in her hands and muttering to herself. When we walked in, she swiped at her cheeks with her fingertips. She had dark circles under her eyes that weren't from smeared mascara. Apparently, sleepless nights were going around.

"Sorry, I was just thinking about my dad," she said.

I felt like the world's biggest jerk for intruding on her time of grief. "You have nothing to be sorry about. We didn't mean to bother you. If this isn't a good time, we can come back."

"No. I'll have all day to think about him. Have you got news?"

"Actually we have more questions than when we started. There are so many things that don't go along with who we originally thought Kenji was."

Sue sighed. Then gestured at the chairs in front of her desk. "I received a very upsetting email. I can deal with it later. Have a seat."

We told her about Kelly's disappearance, what seemed to be some sort of collaboration between Kelly and Celeste Campbell, our conversation with Tommy West, and finally, our suspicions about China Gaardner. When I mentioned China's name, the soft line of Sue's jaw hardened.

Bitterness tinged her voice as she spoke. "So you think this China Gaardner's the one who killed my dad?"

"We don't know yet. Like I said, we have questions. Do you know anything about her?"

"Read this." Sue turned to her computer, tapped on the keys, and brought up an email. She turned the monitor so both Chance and I could see it.

This sham of a project you say will improve the lives of a few homeless people in Honolulu is a disgrace. You have ruined what was to be a magnificent development for the working class in this area. By your actions, you also nearly destroyed my company. My family almost became homeless because of your greed. I know what you're up to and I'm determined to stop you!

Sue's brown eyes gleamed with the fire of someone bent on revenge. "She sent that the day my dad went missing."

"Have you showed this to the police?" Chance asked.

"I just found it last night. I couldn't sleep and started going through his old emails."

"The police need to see it," he pressed.

"What if they want to take the computer as evidence?"

"They might. They might want a forensic expert to examine it."

"I can't afford to be without this computer. It's got all the business records on it. If I don't have this, the entire business stops. The police aren't going to care about that."

I told myself she wasn't thinking clearly. Her emotions were guiding her. She hadn't been sleeping. I tried to sound firm, but consoling. "It's evidence, Sue. You have to tell them about it."

She sat, absently stroking the back of her hand with her fingers, once again lost in a world of memories.

"Is the business your real reason for not wanting to show this to the police? Or is there something else going on?" I asked.

"I'm only worried about the business."

Her eyes teared up, pooling with a mixture of anger and hurt. What was it she really wanted to say? While I'd have loved to find out, I couldn't bring myself to press her for more information.

"Is there anything we can do to help?" Chance asked, his voice soft and soothing.

Again, her jaw tightened. Her breathing became more pronounced and determined. Controlled. Bitter. "Find the person who killed my dad."

"We're working on it," I said. "But to do that, we need more information. Like I said, we have more questions now than we had when we started. It seems everywhere we turn, there are people who didn't like your dad. We've heard complaints about all sorts of things. The only person who didn't complain about him was Tommy West."

"I hate that man."

Well, that caught me by surprise. "Did he have it in for your dad?"

"No," she scoffed. "Tommy and my dad go way back. They were friendly in the old days. But over time, Tommy became more focused on making money than doing good things. My dad always taught me to consider people when you make decisions. Tommy West never considers how what he's doing might affect someone else."

"Are you talking about his live-work project?" I asked.

"The one that was supposed to be the best thing ever for working people?" Sue smirked, then continued. "Like Tommy West ever cared about them."

"He gave Chance and me quite the sales pitch. I wasn't impressed."

"It would have been a disaster," Sue said. "Anyway, him and my dad stopped being on good terms ten years ago when we got the contract for a big project in Honolulu. Our bid was higher than the one from West Construction, but we showed the property owner how our approach was going to save him money in the long run. That set the tone for everything that's happened since."

"What about the City Council meeting?" I asked.

Sue raised her hands and gave me a blank stare. "What about it?"

"China Gaardner was working for Tommy West the night she let loose at the council meeting. Were you aware of that?"

"No. I figured she was working for someone, but didn't know who."

243

"That email from her?" I pointed at the computer screen. "It goes to motive. If she was really damaged like she claims, she might have wanted revenge."

"And then there's her injured hand," Chance added. "She told us she hurt it in yoga, but the teacher said she showed up at class with her hand wrapped."

"I've never met her. Never even heard of her until Dad came home and started complaining about this lunatic woman who made all sorts of allegations in public. Thank God the Council didn't believe her."

"We've got a couple of others we're focusing on. Graham Tynsdale, for one."

"The activist?" Sue shook her head. "No way. I'm sure he's harmless."

"Why?" Chance and I asked at the same time.

"Because he's a wannabe. Dad talked to him once. He said the guy wasn't all there. He's good at one thing—getting people fired up. But even at that, he starts to wear thin soon. He can never keep the same set of protestors going for more than a week or two."

"He's still out there. Still has people with him," I said.

"Look at the faces. You'll see they're different every week or so."

Sue turned the monitor around and began working her keyboard. When she turned it back to face us there were six photos of the protest line in front of Kinohi Village. The photos were crystal clear, their sharpness and composition, excellent. It was almost as though they'd been taken by a professional. Someone like Kelly Atkinson.

"Where'd you get these?" I asked.

"Each week one of them came to my dad's email from an anonymous address. Notice how the same people only show up in one or two photos?"

"When did the last one come in?" I asked.

Sue peered at her computer screen, then her eyebrows went up. "They all came in on Thursdays and the last one was a week ago."

"Your dad got one every week on Thursday, and then they suddenly stopped this week?"

"That's right. Why? Does it mean something?"

Chance and I both nodded, but for the life of me, I wasn't sure what to say. It was entirely possible we'd found why Kelly Atkinson had gone on the run. Now, if we could just figure out which side of the fence she was on, we might actually be able to determine what happened to her.

37

AFTER SEEING THE PHOTOS OF the protestors, I was convinced that Kelly Atkinson had stumbled across something she shouldn't have. On our way back to the car, I shared that thought with Chance.

"I agree with you," he said. "The problem is, we'd have to find her to know what she discovered."

"Maybe there's a way to do that."

"What? Are you going to use your old skip tracing skills?"

I chuckled. If only it were that easy. Tracking down a skip could take days or weeks. Precious time we didn't have. "Nothing that involved. Why don't we just talk to the last person who saw her?"

"Celeste Campbell?"

"Exactly."

Chance's face lit up. He raised his hand and we exchanged a high-five. "That's brilliant, McKenna. Celeste should be easy to find—call her work."

"How about if I tell her we've got a hot tip? That way we can get her out of the office and away from the gatekeepers. She might talk more freely is she's on neutral territory."

"Good idea, but what's this tip? It would have to be pretty good to have her drop whatever other story she's working on."

"Head to Ala Moana Center. I've got it covered."

Luring Celeste out of the office was easier than I'd expected. She started out wary, but with just a little exaggeration of what we'd done so far and what damaging evidence she might get from us, she was ready to drop everything. Chance and I both knew this was a ruse, and once Celeste found out, I could see her going ballistic, which was another reason I wanted to meet in a public place.

There were two Starbucks at the mall. The one I chose stood on its own between high-end jewelry and high-style fashion. Lush tropical landscaping bordered a long line of bistro tables. We found an empty table and snagged an extra chair, then waited under the shade of our dark green umbrella, which blended in perfectly with the tropical landscaping.

I recognized Celeste immediately, but avoided making eye contact. She wore fashionable jeans and a gray turtleneck sweater. Even though the temperature was more than eighty degrees, she seemed perfectly comfortable in what most tourists would consider winter wear. I'd scoffed at the locals a lot during my first year here. Now, acclimated to tropical days and nights, I felt the urge to bundle up when the temps dropped into the seventies.

After Celeste scanned the area and glossed right over us, I was satisfied she didn't know who we were. I raised my hand and waved. She caught my signal, pursed her lips, and came forward.

Her hair was cut at the shoulder and her natural brown color was highlighted with blonde streaks. I felt certain she spent more on hair styling products in a month than I did in a year. Then again, she was on TV. I wasn't. At least, not unless she'd snuck a camera crew in here somehow.

Though it wasn't obvious, I could tell she was sizing us up as she approached. We did quick introductions, then Chance offered to buy her whatever she wanted.

"If I want something, I'll get it." She pasted a business smile on her face, reached into her back pocket, and pulled out a cellphone as she sat. "Mind if I record this?" She watched my face as if she were daring me to say no.

"Not at all," I said casually. "You, however, may not want this conversation on record."

The smile fell away. "You said you had information about Kinohi Village."

"That's true. I believe you were the last one to see Kelly Atkinson before she disappeared." I didn't think my tone was accusatory, but Celeste reacted as if she'd been slapped.

She hissed, "Who are you two?"

"Now, now. You're in public," I cautioned.

Celeste put the phone back in her pocket, pulled in a breath, and buried her anger under the mask she'd perfected for onscreen interviews. "I should walk away right now."

"If you do, you lose control of the narrative," I said.

She paused, perhaps to consider storming off, but must have decided the risks of leaving were greater than staying. "I'm listening," she said.

"You interviewed Kelly Atkinson on camera prior to the arrival of the police at a murder scene. We're curious how you got there so quickly."

Celeste tugged on her sweater, then rotated the ring on her finger slowly. It would seem we'd found a weak spot. "I've changed my mind," she said. "Would you get me a venti mocha with an added shot?"

"Of course. I'll be back in a few minutes." Chance stood, snuck a wink at me, then sauntered away.

A ringtone reminiscent of the old *Twilight Zone* TV theme song blasted from someone's cell phone. I eyed Celeste, convinced it must be hers. She closed her eyes and sighed.

"You want to get that?" I asked.

She shook her head. "It's my mother. She calls at the worst possible times. She'll leave a message."

"I'm okay letting you deal with family business first if you need to. I know how difficult parents can be." It wasn't exactly a lie—I had known once.

"Leave my parents out of this," she snapped. "I'll deal with them later."

"Okay. Then let's go back to how you arrived on the scene before the police."

Tiny crows feet around the corners of Celeste's almond-shaped eyes crinkled as she forced a polite smile. "I was in the van when the call came through," she said smoothly. "We weren't that far away."

Celeste was way too cool under pressure, which, I suppose, could be a consequence of her time on live TV. Still, she had to be lying. I could almost smell the untruth. In the old days, being a skip tracer meant being a professional liar, so I knew well that even a simple lie could spiral out of control. If I pressed further, would this one fall apart? Maybe, if I could leverage her fears. And I'd bet one of those was losing her job to someone younger.

249

In addition to the crows feet, Celeste also had tiny lines at the corners of her mouth. She was in her early forties, which was not a good age for a female TV reporter. But it provided great ammunition to use against her. "I see you every night on the news. I've been watching you since you joined the network, in fact."

The compliment had its intended effect. She sat a little straighter and held her head up. I even got a little bit of a smile.

I continued, "You've had a good ride. But, if you don't mind my being brutally honest, you're at an age where you're vulnerable."

Oh, man, if looks could kill. "Your point?" Celeste snapped.

"You need to keep the stories coming or the higher ups will find a way to get rid of you. How did you get to Kinohi Village so quickly? And please, don't lie to me about being close by. Did Kelly call you before she called HPD?"

Chance arrived and handed a cup to Celeste. She took a sip, bit her upper lip, then said, "All right, Kelly has done some work for me before. She and I got along well, so when she came across the body, she called me before she called the police."

"That explains a lot," I said. Simple enough. Too simple, actually. It was the kind of throwaway line a practiced liar would use as a distraction.

To my surprise, Chance wasn't focused on Celeste, but on something in the distance. A chill ran down my spine and I wondered if our stalker was back. Even if he was, I couldn't let that distract me. Celeste was my priority—and I wasn't letting her get away with a partial lie.

"After Kelly called you, how long did she wait before she called HPD?"

She sat, staring at her cup, rotating it in her hands. "I'm not saying anything else unless you two tell me who you are. Are you cops? I haven't done anything wrong."

"That's an interesting comment. Why would you assume we're accusing you of something?"

"I'm a reporter. You call me and tell me you have a tip. When I show up, you start grilling me with all these questions. You know what? I'm done here."

The metal legs of Celeste's chair screeched on the concrete floor as she pushed it back. The noise pierced the dull hum of milling shoppers and drew attention from people at other tables. It seemed to be the last thing she wanted.

"You're free to leave," I said. "But you know how it works. We're giving you the opportunity to tell your side of the story. If you want to turn yourself into a victim, that's your choice."

Acting like I didn't care if she walked away was a huge gamble, but I'd learned long ago that with the right pressure friends would rat out friends and even family members could be talked, or sometimes tricked, into giving up their loved ones. And someone who wanted to avoid blame? They'd talk every time. Sometimes, a lot.

She sat straighter, brought her chair closer to the table, and hissed, "Who's behind this?" If her intent had been to come across as more imposing, she'd failed.

"Doesn't work that way. Just tell me how long she waited."

"Why don't you ask her?"

"Because I'm asking you."

She took a sip from her cup and watched my face, seeming to weigh her options. "Kelly has been following the project for a long time," she said.

Not exactly what I was looking for, but it would do. "Since the City Council meeting? We heard that's where you two met."

"That's right. We did. She called me the next day to pitch this idea she had. She wanted to provide the photos, and I'd write the story. She said we could expose all the corruption behind the project."

"Wait. She called you? It wasn't the other way around?"

Celeste laughed. "I've already got a cameraman. We work together all the time. Why would I hire an amateur? This way, I could keep tabs on that story while I worked my official assignments. Besides, she was obsessed with the thing and I figured if she came up with something, I could get my editor to approve me covering it."

"So you could take advantage of the resource and work the story with a minimum of effort."

"That's right. But the longer she was out there, the more reckless she became. After a while, the project manager told her she couldn't come on the property during work hours anymore. That's when she started going out after the crews finished for the day."

"By project manager, you mean Julie Edgeworth?"

"Yes."

The tension in Celeste's shoulders softened. She was obviously delighted to be pointing the finger at someone else— anyone who kept her from being the center of attention. Chance apparently hadn't noticed; he was busy darting glances off in the distance.

"You said she became reckless. What do you mean by that?"

Celeste quirked her cheek and gave me a little shrug. "Kelly started out being very good about staying out of the way, but the longer she was there, the more comfortable she got. At the end, she was doing dangerous stuff."

"Like?"

"Getting too close to workers. Climbing ladders to get a better shot."

Or sabotaging things to get a photo? Was that why she'd disappeared? "So while she took photos, you were working on the narrative?"

"We both thought it would be a good way to gain the exposure we needed."

"So that's why you were willing to work with her. Your career needed a boost and Kelly was your ticket to security."

"You were right about my job. Nobody will say it, but the higher ups don't think the public wants to watch a middle-aged woman report the news. They want young and perky." Celeste huffed. "I needed that story to prove my skills were better than anyone else's, so when Kelly came to me, I asked her to be my eyes and ears on the project."

"Where did she hear about all this corruption?" I pressed.

"You're messing with my career."

In a way, she was right. But the fact of the matter was, she still hadn't left. And that could only mean one thing. Celeste Campbell had a lot more to hide than just a news story.

38

CELESTE WAS GETTING MORE AND more uncomfortable the longer she sat, and I wasn't absolutely positive I could keep pumping her for information before she'd leave. The only option might be to make her choose between saving herself and giving up Kelly. True, we didn't have much to go on, but for someone who'd bluffed more times than a professional poker player, I knew half the game was in using a bait-and-switch technique to turn up the heat.

"You didn't like Kenji Ito, did you?"

Her jaw worked from side to side. "It's not that I didn't like him. My job is to find the news."

"About that, I've done some research on your career. You survived two rounds of layoffs at O'ahu Publications, but when you finally did get laid off, you made the jump to TV news almost immediately. How did you pull that off?"

"I had connections."

I fingered my chin and contemplated what was clearly another BS answer. "So did every other news reporter who got laid off, but you survived. That's impressive. I'd bet with your connections you wouldn't have gotten laid off if you hadn't kept pushing a story about Ito Development."

Celeste took a long sip from her coffee. Now I got it—she was using the coffee as a delay tactic.

"I'd had a lead from a guy who worked for Kenji that said he was working with the yakuza. I went to my editor and he gave me a green light to go further. I did a huge amount of work on the story."

True, the yakuza had tremendous influence in the construction industry—fifty or so years ago. On their way out the doors of power some of the yakuza's moguls had made substantial real estate investments in Hawaii. Just based on Kenji's age, he was too young to have ever done business with them. And Celeste should have known that. Still, she was talking, and I was willing to let her lie herself into a corner.

"Go on," I said calmly.

"I spent weeks doing research and when I turned in the story to my editor, he told me they weren't going to run it. He never did tell me why, but I heard that the big boss knew Kenji from Vietnam. He didn't think Kenji was the kind of guy who would do anything dishonest. The next time they laid off people, they included me."

"So you felt wronged by the powers that be because you wasted time on a story and then got fired for it."

"Laid off," she shot back, then she brushed back her bangs, sat up straight, and transformed herself into the same person I saw on the news almost every night. "Kelly came to me with all this research she'd done. It went all the way back to when Kenji first started. I thought, wow, my research was correct. There really was something to my story."

"Was it the story or your career you wanted to boost?"

Apparently, I'd hit a chord. Celeste's body language exuded anger like sap from a tree.

"Are you still working with her?" I asked.

"I haven't heard from her since we did the interview. She was okay on camera, but afterwards, when the police were talking to her, she freaked out."

I planted my elbows on the table and narrowed my gaze. "Enough that you thought she might have killed Kenji?"

"What? No!"

"Why? You just said she was acting strange with the police."

"I don't think Kelly had any reason to commit murder."

"I see. Did you?"

Celeste's hand went to her heart. "Did I...no! Absolutely not."

"If you didn't do it, and Kenji was already dead when you got to the scene, how do you know it wasn't Kelly?" Other than the fact that he'd already been dead for twenty-four hours, I thought.

She sat, staring at one of the planters. A pair of young girls, probably kids ditching high school, walked by. Their movement caught Celeste's attention. She sipped from her cup and watched them until they disappeared in the crowd. "I don't know," she said. "It's possible, I suppose. When I got there, I was with my cameraman, so I don't know what Kelly did before that. She could have been there for thirty, maybe forty, minutes."

I wasn't surprised she'd chosen to sacrifice Kelly. What I didn't know was what she'd do when I started to pick apart her story. "Who told you about the yakuza connection?"

Celeste's jaw tightened and she stood. "No. I've said way more than I should have." She pushed her chair back, again making that loud screeching noise of metal on concrete. This time, she stood and walked away.

I watched her leave, her stride hurried. "Oh, crap. I pushed her too far."

Chance watched until she'd disappeared into a mass of shoppers. "It was worth a try. That's not our only problem. We've been under surveillance since she arrived."

"Double crap." I wanted to take a gander, but knew that was the worst thing I could do. "Where are they?"

"To your left, maybe a hundred feet away. Small guy. Black tee. Jeans. Baseball cap."

"Same one from last night?"

"I think so."

I took a sip from my cup. Made a harrumphing noise. "There have to be fifty guys who fit that description walking around here."

Chance chuckled. "By my count, about ten of them walked by while you two were talking."

"No wonder you were so quiet."

"I kept trying to figure out if there was real danger or if this guy was just watching. The good news is I don't think he'll want to do anything with this many witnesses around."

"Do you think he was with us when we came in?"

"Don't know. I didn't see him until after Celeste showed up."

"So maybe she was playing us? Trolling for a story?"

"You didn't ask if she brought someone with her."

"You're right. What do you want to do about this guy who's following us? Got a plan?"

"I was thinking we might want to lay a trap."

"Are you out of your mind? He could be a killer."

"What better way to find out?" Chance waggled his eyebrows a couple times and threw me an infectious smile.

I wanted to scream. This was insanity. And Chance was being way too flip. "This is not a game. Or a movie. What if…what if Celeste is right about Kenji's past? He might be a member of the yakuza."

"We'd be dead already. Right? And there wouldn't be just one."

"You might not be bothered by the idea of dying today, but I have a wedding coming up." I shook my head and added an emphatic, "No way."

"You have a better plan? I'm listening." Chance raised one hand to his ear and turned his head slightly. "All joking aside, this is the only way."

I recognized the intensity on his face. Complete focus and determination. I'd seen him like this a few times, and each time it happened just before he used some kung fu voodoo move to take down an opponent. He was in the zone. The place where total concentration pushed aside any other thoughts. "You're doing this no matter what I say. Aren't you?"

"Yes." His face was impassive. No fear. No anger. Nothing but pure determination.

If only I could be strong like Chance. I'd been called a lot of names in my time, most of which were derivatives of four-letter words. Fearless had never been one of them.

My heart pounded in my chest. I couldn't change what was going to happen, so I took a deep breath. "I suppose somebody has to stop this guy. Whoever he is. Alright, I'm in."

"You sure?"

"Don't try and talk me out of this." I gave Chance a wry smile. "What do we do?"

"All you have to do is sit here and enjoy your coffee."

"Wonderful. I'm the bait."

"It'll be okay, McKenna. I'm going to pretend I have a phone call and head toward the exit. You sit here and enjoy your mocha. I'll circle around and come up on him from behind. With any luck, he'll still be watching you and I can surprise him."

It didn't take the intellect of a genius to see the fallacy in the plan. "You're assuming he doesn't know that we know he's watching."

"Don't go down that path, McKenna. There are too many options. If I can't get the guy easily, I'll back off and we can try something else. Give me one minute, then get up and start to pace like you're nervous or something."

"That shouldn't be hard to pull off," I grumbled. "I am nervous. For you."

"McKenna." His stern tone was all I needed to know he wasn't happy with me.

"Sorry, but I hate the idea of you taking this kind of risk."

"It's the only way. We have to find out who this guy is."

What the heck? If Chance wasn't concerned, why should I be? "Be careful, okay? Benni and Lexie will kill me if you get hurt."

"No worries," Chance said as he pulled out his phone. He began talking, then stood and walked toward the exit as though he were deep in conversation.

I raised my cup as if I were going to take a drink, then put it back on the table. After one minute, I stood, pushed in my chair, and started to pace. On my first about-face, I peeked at the exit. Chance was gone. The clock was ticking.

The number of shoppers was picking up—from individuals to couples to families, everyone seemed to be focused on anything but where they were walking. I dodged a group of teens as they jabbered in Pidgin. Two of them were laughing so hard they had no idea who was in front of them. Getting around them gave me a chance to try and spot our stalker, but the crowds were way too thick and I couldn't see a thing.

A mother with three kids, one in a stroller, walked by me and sat at the table I'd just left. While she fussed with the infant, the two overactive boys started a game of tag, using shoppers as obstacles and barriers. One of the kids narrowly missed a woman who was talking on her cellphone as she walked. Mom made a half-hearted attempt at reining in the two brats, but they ignored her pleas to come sit next to her.

Still carrying my cold mocha, I crossed traffic to get to the nearest store. My concern grew with each step. I did an about-face. Chance should have gotten in position already. No sooner had the thought crossed my mind than I heard a commotion further down the mall, which was immediately followed by Chance's voice.

"Come back here!"

Sure enough, he was chasing our stalker. They were running my way. The little guy in front, Chance not far behind. Fixated, I watched the pair dodge people in their way. Some shoppers sensed danger and froze in their tracks; others tried to jump out of the way. It was complete chaos in an already busy environment.

"You! Stop!" Chance yelled.

But the little guy didn't stop. He slipped between a family of four, leaving Chance behind. I had to give this guy credit, he was nimble. To my left, the boys had decided hot pursuit was an even better game. Their mother yelled at them as they rushed into the line of traffic. I made a quick turn to stop them. And bumped into a security guard. An easy three-hundred pounds of solid... something.

I bounced off like a ball on a wall. The mocha flipped out of my hand.

The landing drove the air from my lungs. I lay there. Watching. Watching.

The mocha did a full somersault before it landed with a loud smack against the tile floor.

The lid exploded and a small lake of chocolate-flavored goo spread across the tile.

The stalker tried to sidestep the mess, but missed. His shoe skidded on the tile and down he went.

His cap landed in the goo while she slid to a stop a few feet away from me.

Yes, she. I was staring into the face of Kelly Atkinson.

39

THE SECURITY GUARD GLOWERED DOWN at Kelly and me as though we were a pair of reprobates who had deliberately caused the chaos around us. Then, without warning, he seized each of us by an arm and hoisted us up. With hands the size of a catcher's mitt and the strength of a vice, the possibility of escape evaporated. Kelly's shoulders sagged as the reality sunk in.

Chance, standing a few feet away and shaking his head, was doing his best impression of an irritated parent. "McKenna! I had him...her."

The guard fixed Chance with an irritated stare. "No, brah, you didn't." He watched as shoppers gave me stink eye and trudged through the mess, creating a sea of brown footprints.

"Look what you guys did! I oughta call the cops on all three of you." He turned his full wrath on me. "If it wasn't for you, this wouldn't be so bad. What'd you got to say for yourself?"

I scrunched up my face and tried not to sound too whiny. "Cleanup on aisle 5?"

He wasn't amused and escorted the three of us to the nearest exit. Outside, he admonished us in the strongest possible terms—at least the strongest terms he could use on the job—to take our personal business elsewhere.

Kelly was still holding her camera to her chest, exactly as she had when she'd fallen. Had I not seen the way she clutched it when she went down, I might have been surprised it could have survived such a fall. As it was, I knew she'd used her body as a cushion. For all I knew, that was the professional photographer's mantra—always save the equipment.

"How long have you been following us?" I demanded.

She averted her gaze, then heaved a heavy sigh. "Since you broke into China Gaardner's office."

"China's...how do you know..." Chance gaped at Kelly. "Are you the one who set up the webcam?"

She nodded.

"And you picked us up on Nuuanu Street?"

Another nod.

"Young lady," I said, "we're going to need a lot more than head nods to answer all the questions we have. Right, Chance?"

"Right," he said uncertainly. "But we have a problem, there's no place to talk. We're banned from the mall. The Ferrari seats two."

I grimaced, not sure what to do. Transportation was a huge issue. Another conundrum, as the policy makers were fond to call it.

Kelly put one hand on her back and cringed. "I need to change. I've got coffee all over my back and butt."

She turned so we could see. Indeed, her formerly black jeans and tee were stained brown, and despite the heat and the trade winds, they'd be damp for awhile.

"The problem we have is we can't trust you." I turned to Chance. "Any ideas?"

Kelly pulled a keyring from her front pocket. "I have clothes and a towel in my car. That's where I've been living."

Chance snatched the keys from her hand, then handed them to me. "Where are you parked?"

"A row over from you. That Ferrari's pretty easy to follow."

I resisted the urge to shoot an I-told-you-so smirk at Chance. "Fine. Let's go. You can change in the car."

Kelly led the way. Once there, we unlocked the door, rolled down the windows, and waited with our backs against the rear end of the car while Kelly changed.

"What do you want to do?" I asked.

"Find a place where we can talk to her. We need to know why she disappeared. Why she's been following us."

"Tell us what she's found out. If this was Celeste's idea. Yada, yada."

"For once, I agree with that, McKenna. Yada, yada. I wonder if she's got any other webcams out there?"

The question stopped me cold even though we were standing in a parking lot with the sun beating down on us. What if Kenji's murder was only the tip of the iceberg? Okay, I admit it—I had water and ice on the brain. My body felt like a plant wilting on a hot day, but in my mind, a very clear picture had formed.

"Ala Moana Park," I said.

"What?"

"The park isn't far. We can interrogate her there."

"What the heck?" Chance said. "It's not exactly like we have a lot of choices."

The car door slammed, and Kelly walked toward us. She'd changed out her black tee for a tank top and her jeans for a wild pair of cropped yoga pants. I could see why she'd chosen the jeans for her surveillance. Nobody could miss those pants, even in a crowd. She'd also replaced her cap and pulled her auburn hair through the opening in the back. "Where are you taking me?"

"To the park." I handed her the keys, told her she was driving, and that Chance would follow us. When I sat in the passenger's seat, I realized what a mistake this was. The car was hot, humid, and smelled of stale coffee and junk food.

"What are you guys going to do to me?" Kelly asked as she navigated toward the exit.

"That depends on what you've done. You were the one to find Kenji's body, but instead of calling the police, you called Celeste Campbell and got yourself an interview. At a minimum, that seems like obstruction of justice to me."

Kelly slouched forward and took a few deep breaths. The smooth skin of her forehead puckered with fear. "Am I gonna go to jail?"

"I don't know. That's up to the law. What I don't understand is why you ran."

"Because your guard dog was chasing me," she snapped. "I was scared."

"I get that. What I meant was, why'd you run after you reported the murder?"

Kelly's shoulders shook as she laughed. "Are you kidding? I wasn't running. I was doing the same thing you guys are. Trying to find out who killed that poor man."

"Wait a minute. When we first met you, you painted Kenji Ito as the villain. You didn't consider him a 'poor man' then."

"I didn't know who you guys were at first. You walked into my studio and tried to pass yourselves off as cops with that fake ID. What was I to think?"

Ouch. So much for Chance's ID tricking people. I wondered how many others had come to the same conclusion. "You might have thought we were trying to find a killer."

"Ha! Like people do that." Kelly jammed on the brakes for the signal light. When the car came to a stop, she sneered at me. "That's up to the real cops."

"Okay, Miss Smarty Pants, since you have all the answers, why don't you tell me the whole story rather than making me play guessing games?"

The light changed, Kelly made a left, then merged to the right. In the passenger's mirror, I saw Chance behind us. He was close enough that Kelly couldn't lose him at a light, and that gave me comfort.

"It started the night of the City Council meeting. I showed up there because I knew the project was gonna generate a lot of interest. I figured there'd be protestors, and that maybe they'd wind up in a confrontation and I could get some good shots. I'm always looking for new contacts and I thought if had the right photos, someone would want to buy them."

"That's the night China Gaardner went ballistic."

"Totally. Celeste was covering the meeting for the paper. I thought it would be cool to get a shot of her and her photographer."

I remembered the story and it's obvious bias. "Go on."

"When Celeste saw me taking photos, she gave me her card and told me to call her the next day. She said she had a long-term assignment for me. At first she said there wasn't any money in it, but when I told her I couldn't work for free, she said she'd see what she could do. She also said it could turn into something big, so I started following Kenji because her sources told her he was doing something illegal."

"Did she tell you what this illegal activity was?"

"She didn't have anything specific. Her source told her she'd have to find the proof on her own."

"So she put you on the job. Did you know she was leveraging you to help her own career? You were just a resource."

Kelly's grip on the wheel tightened. She kept watching the traffic ahead, but started blinking faster as her eyes teared up. "She was using me?"

"That's what she told us at the mall. Here's the turn."

"I know," she snapped. "What...what else did she say?"

"If this is going to be a two-way exchange, you need to come clean first. Tell me what you've done, then I'll share what I can."

She pulled into an open parking space, turned off the engine, and hung her head. "I've been so stupid. She used me. I thought we connected..." Her voice trailed off and her breathing quickened. "She told me how she lost her dad and how she was working when it happened and..."

"When did she tell you about her parents?"

"When we met."

"I have more bad news for you, Kelly. Celeste's parents are alive and well."

"What?"

"Celeste got a call from her mother while I was talking to her. She's been lying to you all along." And, most likely, to us.

40

SITTING IN THE DRIVER'S SEAT of her old Toyota staring into space, her face devoid of any emotion, Kelly had the appearance of a disillusioned child. "I feel so stupid," she croaked.

"I'm sorry." I didn't know what else to do or say.

"She never intended to give me a break, did she? It was all just a big act so I'd feed her information." Kelly's shoulders shook and a tear dripped down her nose onto her yoga pants.

I'd spent my entire career chasing down people who tried to take advantage of the system, but seeing someone like Kelly become a victim still upset me. There was a small pack of tissues on the seat next to me. I pulled out one and handed it to her.

Chance approached, saw Kelly crying, and stopped. I tilted my head toward the door, eager to get out of a car that was rapidly turning into an overripe steam bath. Chance helped Kelly out and guided her to a nearby picnic table. A stand of coconut palms towered overhead, shrouding the table in dappled shade. While they were getting settled, I returned to the Ferrari and grabbed my water bottle. On the way to meet them, I stopped and surveyed the area.

Ala Moana Park was a sea of green grass, which was slowly being overtaken by people. With activities from lawn bowling to tennis and everything in between, there was something to do for everyone. Families with keiki flocked here to let the kids frolic while mom and dad talked story with friends. All this activity made our reason for being here feel so incongruous.

I was relieved that Kelly had recovered from her meltdown—well, mostly recovered. All because she'd been duped. As had we all. It didn't seem possible, but we'd started out looking for a missing businessman and now we were investigating a murder. Or corruption. Or…what?

"Kelly? Why did you bug China's office?" I asked.

She sniffled a couple of times, then wiped her nose with the tissue she'd been clutching in her fist. "Because Celeste told me to."

"Did she have you bug anyone else's office?"

"Ito Development."

Crap. We'd been so focused on Kenji that we'd missed the big picture. And big it was if I was correct. "I see. A webcam?"

"Yes. Celeste told me to put them in the HVAC vents."

"So you bugged two offices for Celeste. How did you get in?"

"She had a key for Ito Development. I was so eager to score points with her that I never questioned how she got it. I never even told Barbara what I was doing until about a week later. She had a fit and told me I was being an idiot. She said that if I got caught, Celeste could just deny she ever told me to break the law."

269

Chance put a consoling hand on Kelly's shoulder. "You realize you've committed about a dozen felonies?"

I rolled my eyes, determined not to burst out laughing. We had at least twice that many to our credit.

Kelly laid her forearms on the table and rested her chin on top. "What am I gonna do? I can't go to jail."

I was tempted to tell her she should have thought of that before she started breaking the law. Of course, there again, who was I to talk? "We need the whole story, Kelly. Don't leave anything out. And remember, if you lie to us, Celeste will find a way to make you the fall guy for Kenji's murder."

While Kelly pulled herself together and rehashed what she'd told me with Chance, I let the trades work their magic. I felt better just sitting on this picnic bench in the midst of so much history. I'd learned that history from Benni's brother, and today I was glad I'd paid attention because it felt pertinent to our investigation.

"Did you know this park used to be a wetland?" I asked.

Kelly stared at me as though I'd gone mad.

Chance turned to her and snickered. "Don't worry. He does this. It's either a random stroke of genius or a random glimpse of senility." Smiling at me, he added, "No, McKenna, I didn't know this park was once a wetland. Do tell."

I screwed up one cheek, sneered at him, but continued. "Almost a hundred years ago, this park was overgrown and the city used it as a garbage dump. Somebody got the bright idea to turn it into a park, so in 1931 the Parks Board did that. Here's a little tidbit for you. President Franklin D. Roosevelt visited Hawaii and participated in the opening ceremonies."

The reaction from both of them was underwhelming.

"You two do know who Franklin Roosevelt was. Don't you?"

"Yes, McKenna, we know who Roosevelt was." Chance smiled at Kelly, but her eyes got wide.

"History was never my strong subject," she blurted. "Wasn't he like the crippled guy in the White House?"

"Oh, dear God," I muttered. "Close enough. Anyway, it wasn't until 1947 that the park's name was changed to Ala Moana, which translates roughly to path to the sea."

Cocking his head in my direction, Chance said, "This is where we find out whether it was genius or senility. So, McKenna, what's this got to do with anything we've been talking about?"

"Nothing. It has to do with what we haven't been talking about."

"Okay," Chance sighed. "I think he's actually lost it. Sorry, Kelly. Now…"

I cleared my throat and shook my head slowly. "I haven't lost anything. Give me two minutes. If this isn't worthwhile, I give you permission to dunk me out there." I gestured at the beach.

"That could be fun," Chance said. He pulled out his phone and started a timer. "You're on. Go."

Jeez. I never thought he'd actually time me. Whatever. I wasn't going to lose this bet. "Celeste told us you were obsessed with the project, Kelly. While she didn't come out and say it, she intimated that you wanted to prove there were problems. Is that true?"

"No way. I told you. I got involved because I thought I could sell my photos. Celeste is the one who was so obsessed."

"A minute forty-five," Chance snickered.

I set my jaw, determined not to fail. "You're going to be so sorry." I quickly turned my attention back to Kelly. "Why did Celeste have you take her bio photo?"

271

She shrugged and shook her head. "I dunno. I think it was like a pity job. I'd been telling her how slow things were and that I might have to find more work. She asked me to do a photo session with her and then got me a couple other jobs."

"Do you think she was feeding you work just so you'd keep on the Kinohi Village story?"

"Maybe. I kinda thought that at the time, but I needed the money."

"Apparently, it worked."

"It totally worked."

"Do you see now that she even got you to break the law?"

Kelly groaned and slumped forward. "Don't remind me. That's what Barbara told me, too."

"Barbara's a smart girl."

"One minute." Chance smiled and winked. "Just saying."

I continued, undaunted. "You said you planted webcams in Ito Development and in China Gaardner's office. There were no others?"

"It was only the two."

"You didn't plant one in the trailer at Kinohi Village?"

"She never asked me to."

Chance had been so busy watching the timer that he hadn't thought through my line of questioning. That made what was about to happen all the sweeter. "What if China's office was a diversion?"

It only took about two seconds, but Chance's smile fell away and he muttered something under his breath.

It was my turn to smirk. "Gotcha."

Chance's phone went back into his pocket, after which he put his hands in front of him and bowed a couple of times.

"What?" Kelly demanded. "What's the big deal about that?"

I raised my hand, indicating that Chance should explain.

He sighed. "If Celeste was trying to prove Kenji was doing something against the law on the project, she'd have bugged the construction trailer, too."

I sat a little straighter and smiled.

"I still don't get it," Kelly said. "What's the trailer got to do with anything?"

"Celeste has been going after Kenji for a long time, and yet she never asked you to bug the most likely place to get information about Kinohi Village. I don't think she cared about the project. What she cared about was his development company. That's why she had you plant the webcam there. She was determined to prove he was corrupt, so she told you to plant a webcam in China's office. It was only a smokescreen to make you think she was searching for the truth."

"But she said she wanted both sides of the story."

"Exactly. With you, she had instant credibility. Now, the last time we talked to you, you showed us a photo of Kenji talking to three men. One of them was Joe Taylor. At the time, you said you didn't know what was going on. Are you standing by that statement?"

"Kenji was pulling him aside to fire him. He was really polite about it and told me they needed privacy. Right after that, Julie called me into the office. She was super mad and told me I was banned from the property."

"Let's go back before that. You spent a lot of time at the job site. You met most of the workers. What were your impressions of them? Were they happy to be there?"

"Of course. They just wanted to do a good job. And most of them liked what they were doing."

"Any exceptions to that rule?" I asked.

"Maybe Derrick Tanaka. I saw him going out toward the protest line. I followed him one time. He was talking to Graham Tynsdale. I couldn't hear them, but from a distance it looked like they were totally getting into it."

"Did you get a picture of them?"

"Of course."

Chance leaned forward like an attentive student in one of Mrs. Nakamura's classes and raised his eyebrows. "What are you thinking, McKenna?"

"That Kenji was the victim of Celeste's conspiracy. And, that we might have just found a way to make Derrick Tanaka tell us the truth. Oh yeah, and that you still haven't called me a genius."

41

CHANCE WASN'T HAPPY WITH MY suggestion that we take another run at Tanaka. I couldn't blame him. The man was a terrible snitch. Completely unreliable. But this time, we might have something even better than Chance's broken plexi-whatever.

"The reason I think it's worth a try is that several of the players have a long history with Kenji. China Gaardner seems to have gotten fed up with Kenji being on the winning side. Tommy West has been Kenji's rival for years." Turning to Kelly, I added, "And Celeste has written a number of negative stories in her little crusade."

"She said she'd written about it before. But I just kinda thought it was like part of her job. I never went back and checked out what she'd done. I totally should have." A deep frown etched Kelly's forehead. "Do you think she's the one who killed him?"

"I'm not sure. The problem is they all have alibis. The one that makes the least sense is Celeste. She's got something against Kenji and this project, but we have no idea what. Of course,

275

people commit murder for the most bizarre reasons, so if she was convinced she couldn't stop him any other way, that could have been her motive."

"What about Graham Tynsdale?" Chance asked.

"He's on my list, too. I think it's too soon for us to start zeroing in on any one person, but I would like to know more about the relationship between Tynsdale and Derrick Tanaka. Speaking of those two, Kelly, did you ever see Celeste talking to them?"

She thought about my question briefly, then shook her head. "Not together. Celeste did say she was gonna interview some of the protestors."

I snapped my fingers. "Of course. We've got all these different players out there with this common agenda. Tynsdale, China Gaardner, even Celeste, and they all wanted to bring down Kinohi Village. Celeste would have to talk to all of them for a story. It's the perfect cover. Especially if you'd gotten tired of waiting for a story to happen and wanted to manufacture one."

"So you think Kenji found out what she was up to and confronted her?" Chance said enthusiastically.

"Exactly. The other thing is that we asked where she was when you discovered the body, but we didn't ask where she was on Monday. What we need is a way to flush out Celeste's real agenda—and I think I have just the way to do that. It'll mean putting Tanaka on the back burner for now, but he can wait."

The plan was simple. Thankfully, Kelly had bought a prepaid phone when she went underground, so she would call Celeste and say she'd found a link between Derrick and Graham. If Celeste was conspiring with one or both of them, she might panic and reach out. We all agreed Celeste wouldn't use the company phone to make contact, which meant she'd either use a burner or go to see them in person. It was the latter option that we were hoping for.

Fifteen minutes after Chance left to stake out the lot where Celeste parked, my phone pinged with a message telling me he was in position.

I gave Kelly a thumbs up. "He's ready. Dial. Put her on speaker."

When Celeste answered, Kelly's voice was velvety smooth. "It's me."

"Just a minute."

There was a long silence, during which Kelly fidgeted and I worried she might decide to bail on this whole endeavor. After what felt like the longest hold ever, Celeste returned to the line.

"I can talk now. What do you have for me?"

"I was out at Kinohi Village and noticed that Graham's got some new recruits. I took some photos."

"You called me for that? Get real, Kelly. I need something more substantial. You're supposed to be focusing on the project's defects, not those who are trying to stop it."

"The thing is, that construction worker we talked about? His name's Derrick, right? He came out and was talking to Graham. They went off away from the others and it looked like they were getting along."

"They met? Near the project?"

"It totally looked like they were planning something."

"When did this happen?"

"Not that long ago."

The line was so quiet that I thought we'd lost the call. "I'll get back to you. Don't tell anybody about this. Do you have a photo?"

Kelly glanced at me for guidance. I nodded, just sure we had Celeste hooked.

"Yeah, but I can't send it right now. I'll do it when I get a wifi connection."

Celeste huffed an irritated, "Fine," then hung up.

Kelly regarded me from across the table. "She sounded mad. Like maybe she was ticked off at me for wasting her time. Do you really think she'll go see them?"

"I hope so. And I don't think it's you she's mad at. Let's see what Chance has to say." I dialed his number and filled him in. "What do you think?"

"This shouldn't be too hard. She drives an old clunker with a broken taillight. I've got her in sight, so if she leaves, I can tail her, but this really is a long shot, McKenna."

"What would you do if you were in her shoes and your plan was falling apart?"

"Assuming you're correct and she's trying to create the news, I'd go knock some heads together. Wait!" The excitement in Chance's voice came through loud and clear. "She's on the move. Holy smokes, this crazy plan might just work."

I gave Kelly a thumbs-up. "Try calling Celeste again. Tell her you butt dialed her if she answers."

Kelly called and listened for about thirty seconds, then hung up. "Voicemail."

"Did you hear that, Chance? Celeste didn't answer her cell."

"Got it. She's on Kapi'olani. If you're right and she's involved in some sort of conspiracy, she might have left her phone behind to avoid being tracked by the GPS."

"No matter what you do, don't lose her."

"That won't happen. Traffic is light, so I'm giving her room. I don't want to be easy to spot."

"You're driving a fire-engine red Ferrari, Chance."

"Okay, I'll keep my distance. Maybe you two should pick this up for a while?"

Kelly pumped her fist once and muttered, "Yes!"

"On the way," I said.

We hurried to Kelly's car and made an abrupt U-turn. By some miracle, we caught the green light and didn't get hung up with the traffic heading into Ala Moana Mall.

"She's got to be on the way to the project," Chance said. "Which one do you think she'll meet with? My money's on Tynsdale."

Chance's tone had turned giddy, and that made me nervous because he was expecting her to do the predictable. On the other hand, I expected her to do the unpredictable. "Just focus on her. We'll worry about who she's meeting when it happens."

Kelly took Ala Moana Boulevard past the mall. Traffic was heavy the other direction, but we were moving quickly and I was becoming convinced the traffic gods were on our side. The way this was going, we'd catch up with Chance and be able to take over the chase. My pessimism suddenly felt ill-placed.

"She just turned left on Beretania," Chance said. "I don't undertand why she didn't turn right. She could have gotten on the H-1. Oh, maybe she'll take Punchbowl. If you two can stay on Kapi'olani you can pick her up there and follow her on the freeway."

"Maybe she's working a story," Kelly said.

I shook my head. "She would've answered her cell. And she'd be in the van with her cameraman."

"Unless she's meeting him there."

"Then why didn't she answer when you called?"

"Oh, right." Kelly hunched forward and gripped the wheel.

279

The drive from the mall to the park had been short and I hadn't noticed it, but now that I was seeing the way this girl drove, just watching her made me nervous.

I pointed at a car directly ahead. "Don't get too close. We don't need an accident."

Kelly continued to close in on the rear bumper.

"You're tailgating. You need to…"

"Shut up," she snapped. "You're freaking me out."

My hand went to my seatbelt. I checked to make sure it was secured. Good God, we'd be riding in the poor guy's trunk if we got any closer.

"What are you? Like the world's worst passenger?"

"He is," Chance said. "Ignore him."

"Hard to do when he's ranting in my ear."

I crossed my arms over my chest and gripped my sides. "Fine. I'll just sit here quietly. And if you say another word, Chance, I'll end the call." I quickly added, "Not everyone likes freeways, you know. Personally, I hate them."

Chance laughed. "I knew you couldn't stay quiet. You don't have to drive, McKenna. All you have to do is watch the scenery go by. And try not to freak Kelly out too much."

"I'm warning you, Chance."

Kelly's face contorted into a mask of irritation. "Could you stop that?"

"What?"

"Gripping the seatbelt like it's some kind of lifeline."

I glanced down. Oh. White-knuckle grip. I hadn't even realized it. My bad. I released the belt and rubbed my hands on my thighs. When I got another dirty look, I stuck my hands under my armpits—right when the light ahead of us turned yellow.

Kelly hit the brakes. My chest slammed against the seatbelt, which locked up at the sudden deceleration.

"It feels like somebody did ten minutes of CPR on me." The next thing to pop into my head was that my stops weren't that bad. I was proud of myself, however, because I didn't say it out loud.

"Sorry," Kelly said sheepishly. "You're making me super nervous. It's worse than driving with my grandpa."

Ouch. That one hurt. "New drivers make me nervous." It seemed like a decent enough apology to me, but Kelly wasn't happy.

"I'm not a new driver," she barked.

"You're new to me."

"Hey, will you two quit bickering and get your butts over here? It's only a few blocks to Punchbowl."

"Maybe you need to get closer, Chance," I said. "You know, just in case we don't make it."

"I don't want to do that. She might spot me."

"You're right. I can't say that I've ever seen two red Ferrari's on the road at the same time."

The light changed. Kelly hit the gas. "We're on Ward and King is coming up."

"King?" Chance said. "That's one way."

Kelly gritted her teeth and grumbled. "I hate all these one-way streets. I can never keep them straight. We'll turn onto Beretania and catch up from behind."

It wasn't a perfect plan, but it would work. Beretania was a major street. There'd be a dedicated left turn lane. A few seconds later, with a half block to go, I pointed it out. "There it is! If the light cooperates, we can zip right through...crap. It's no left turn."

Kelly gaped at the no-left-turn sign as we cruised through the intersection. The next street was Kinau. One way to the right. And we were in the left lane.

"Where do I turn? Where do I turn?" Kelly yelled.

"I don't know. Don't panic. We'll figure this out." Wow. Me, the voice of reason. In a car. Who would've thought?

And then it was over.

We were on the wrong side of the freeway.

Kelly's shoulders slumped and she hunched forward in her seat. "I'm lost."

"If you don't make it, I can keep this under control," Chance said. "No worries."

"We just passed over the H-1," Kelly said. "Can I get on from here?"

Really? I'd seen the traffic. It was stopped. It would take us ten minutes to get on the stupid freeway. "Chance? I hope you're still with her. You're going to have to do this on your own."

"No. No, no. Don't stop you idiot!"

"What happened?"

"Celeste bypassed Punchbowl and the car ahead of me stopped for a yellow light."

"You mean she's not taking the H-1?"

"I don't think she's even going to Kinohi Village. Either she spotted me or she's got a whole different agenda than we thought. We're screwed."

42

BETWEEN OUR STRUGGLES WITH ONE-way streets and impatient drivers, it had taken Kelly forty-five minutes to drive me home. All the while, Chance circled the streets of Honolulu in search of Celeste. As if that wasn't enough, Chance called just as Kelly and I were approaching the Sunsetter Apartments.

"I've got a problem," he said. "Councilman Ashbrook has invited me to dinner."

Personally, I didn't see how that was a problem. Chance had been to the Ashbrook home for dinner before, and while it would take him off the case for the rest of the day, it wasn't the end of the world. I told him to have a good time and that I'd try and do some work on finding Celeste.

"You don't understand, McKenna. The councilman has never called and invited me to dinner before. That's always been up to Lexie. And this wasn't like an actual invitation, it was more of a directive."

283

Hard as it was for me to see the humor in much of anything right now, I managed a chuckle. "You mean it was one of those be-there-or-be-square invitations?"

"No. I mean be there or you're dead to me. This can only mean one thing—he's laid down the law with Lexie and told her we can't see each other anymore. Lexie told me how he did that with one of her older sister's boyfriends. Nobody ever saw the guy again."

"Seriously? Councilman Ashbrook is a prominent citizen. He's not going to grind you up and put you in the meatloaf. Relax, it'll be fine."

"You're not helping things, McKenna."

There was a bite in Chance's voice I seldom heard. He really was panicked and I hoped I could calm him down. "This is no big deal for you, buddy. Go to dinner. Be yourself. You'll be fine. I have to go. Kelly's waiting for me to get out of her car so she can head home."

I disconnected the call, unbuckled my seatbelt, and turned my attention to Kelly. "You are going home. Right?"

"When I tell Barbara what I've been doing, she'll be furious, but she'll be glad to see me."

I gave her a thumbs-up and got out of the car. Before I closed the door, I said, "Who else would know Celeste? Is there anyone you know that would be close to her?"

"Her cameraman? His name is Pablo. We met at the council meeting, but that's all I know about him."

"Thanks. I'll track him down. Now, go home and make up with Barbara. You'll be happy you did."

Kelly smiled at me, then drove off hunched forward in her seat with the windows down. As she pulled onto the street, I had the strange feeling she wasn't heading home. Then there was

Chance. I felt kind of sorry for him. He was most likely still stuck in traffic and sweating about his dinner invitation. I didn't want to distract him by calling, and I most certainly didn't want to tell him my suspicions about Kelly. The poor guy had enough worries right now.

Besides, it was time I gave up on trying to fix other people's relationships. My job was to deal with the one I had. I went to the apartment, noticed immediately that the place was still closed up, but called Benni's name anyway. When she didn't answer, it hit me how lonely this little apartment felt without her. I'd lived alone for so many years, and now I couldn't imagine going back to that lifestyle.

With all the windows open and the trade winds blowing through, I pulled out my laptop and set up at the kitchen table. Perhaps Celeste's old news stories would help me find Pablo's last name. I started through the list. Sure enough. Pablo Lupica was given photo credit on most of Celeste's old stories. I couldn't tell if he'd been laid off at the same time as Celeste, so I called the paper hoping he'd simply been reassigned. What I got was bad news—nobody by that name worked for the company.

"Why can't anything be easy?" I grumbled. Searching the Internet turned up a photographer by the same name in Los Angeles. Fortunately, the man had a website. My first impression was that he'd been relegated to wedding and portrait photography. So much for his days chasing all over the island in search of newsworthy photos. There was also a phone number. It was going on five p.m. in LA, so I took a chance and dialed.

A deep voice said, "Lupica Photography."

I introduced myself, told him why I was calling in very vague terms, then asked, "Are you the same Pablo Lupica who used to work with Celeste Campbell?"

"Yeah, I worked with Celeste for a few years. I got laid off because of her."

The note of dissatisfaction in his voice gave me hope he'd be willing to gossip. "Would you mind telling me what happened?"

The man snorted, then paused. "What's this about?"

"We're investigating the death of Kenji Ito."

A groan.

"Celeste was on the scene of the murder before the police." I let the statement stand on it's own, hoping Pablo would feel an obligation to fill the empty space.

"This is kind of a difficult subject. You know?"

"Why's that?"

"Celeste was always obsessed with breaking the big story. She thought it would eventually get her into the big time. She wanted a lot more fame and money than Honolulu could provide."

"Is that why she was so interested in Kinohi Village?"

"Basically. She thought if she could bust something wide open, the job offers would come flooding in. I tried to tell her it didn't work that way, but she was…well, convinced she knew better."

"Especially with Kenji Ito?"

"Yeah. Especially with him. She latched onto him based on some tip she got."

"Do you know who she got the tip from?"

"She'd never talk about it. Said it had to be kept a secret. I have to go. A client just walked in."

I disconnected the call and stood at the lānai screen door. The ocean, a gray-blue this afternoon, was heavily dotted with caps of white. The trades were up. That might mean we had a storm coming. Maybe the weather reporter on the news could get that one right tonight.

The reminder I'd set on my phone dinged and I realized my prospective tenants were due here any minute to check out the apartment. I was in the middle of filling a glass of water when there was a knock on the door. I took a deep breath, donned my best welcoming smile, and went to answer.

A young couple stood holding hands. She was petite and blonde with blue eyes. The logo on her khaki shirt was from a local plant nursery. The young man stood about six inches taller and wore a muted hibiscus print shirt that couldn't quite hide the fact that he was muscular enough to benchpress his wife quite easily.

"Mr. McKenna? Hi, I'm Jessica and this is my husband Donny." Her voice, just as it had been on the phone, was bursting with enthusiasm.

I pushed open the screen door, shook hands with them both, and said, "Please, call me McKenna. I've got my keys right here. Let's get you into the apartment."

After putting on my slippahs, I led the way. No sooner had I stepped out the door than my landline rang. I ignored the call and let it go to the machine. As we walked toward Apartment 6, I explained the amount of interest I'd had, but left off the part about the others being complete losers. That was only my opinion, of course, but in this case it was the one opinion that mattered.

"I am so thrilled that ya'll could fit us in this afternoon. We're just so anxious to be near the beach. Isn't this an ideal location, honey?"

Before Donny could answer, Jessica continued to prattle on. By the time we'd reached the apartment door, I was convinced

Donny's voice would atrophy within their first two years of marriage.

How many times had I performed this ritual since I'd taken this job? Key in lock. Open door. Wait for some sort of response. "It's a bit stuffy. Most of the tenants like to leave at least one window open even when they're gone."

Jessica stepped inside and stopped. Okay, she actually gawped the living room and the kitchen with her mouth hanging open. Uh-oh. Not what she expected. I was going to need another ad.

"It's adorable! Honey, look, the kitchen's open so we can talk while I'm fixing dinner and there's room for that big screen TV you want." Without waiting for Donny to reply, Jessica darted into the bedroom.

As Donny passed by, I whispered, "She likes it."

He rolled his eyes, but kept a smile on his face. While the newlyweds explored the apartment—which Jessica gushed over constantly—I opened the living room window. Unless I was mistaken, I had my new tenant. And, this was going to take awhile.

I went into the bedroom to open it up and let in fresh air and found Jessica telling Donny where they could put the bed, a dresser, and about a dozen other items. The minute I pulled back the drapes, Jessica was right beside me, her hand over her heart.

"Oh my God," she said. "Honey, you've got to see this view!"

"It's Diamond Head," I said.

Donny took a quick peek. "Sure is."

I smiled at him. "You must be *kama'āina*?"

"Born and raised. Third generation. My grandfather and my father were both in the Navy." Donny's eyes misted over. His voice cracked when he said, "My grandfather died at Pearl Harbor."

In that instant, I knew. Donny was a good guy. Jessica loved him dearly. And my search for a new tenant was over. I gave them a couple of minutes alone, then returned to the bedroom, saw the delight on Jessica's face, and gave them a thumbs up. "So, when would you like to move in?"

43

SIGNING A LEASE IS TYPICALLY a very predictable process. The renters are eager. So am I. They have questions. So do I. But in this case, Donny and I let Jessica do the talking. She'd ask a question and, about two seconds later, would come up with an answer. Since she was never that far off, I let her handle both sides of the transaction. She also gave up far more information than I'd ever asked any tenant—all without me ever saying much more than 'uh huh'.

Donny and Jessica left before Benni arrived. Jessica, of course, had to give me all the details on where they were going for dinner to celebrate their new apartment. While I was delighted to have the unit rented, I was also exhausted and convinced Jessica would take some getting used to.

When Benni arrived, she kicked off her slippahs, plopped down on the couch, and sighed. "I'm beat. All I want to do is have dinner and curl up on the couch."

"I rented number six," I said.

"Awesome. That's great. That couple who called last night?"

"Yes. And I'll warn you, she's a talker. You don't want to do laundry at the same time as her."

"Oh. One of those." She winked at me. "Better that than, who was it? The guy you said was a looney wannabe spy?"

I could see where this was going. Benni might be exhausted from a long day, but she was ready and willing to engage in a verbal jousting match. Right now, all I wanted was a little time to unwind, so I suggested she rest on the couch while I prepared dinner. It was a suggestion she thoroughly loved.

After dinner, we parked ourselves on the couch to watch the evening news. The couch was perfectly positioned so I could keep my arm over Benni's shoulder, engage with her in conversation while I alternated between watching the TV and enjoying a sunset filled with shades of gold, red, gray, and purple. This was the only way to watch the evening news. The first story was covered by a reporter I'd never seen before. "She's new," I said.

"I'm not surprised. They have lots of turnover."

"Why?"

"Hawaii's a small market. The stations can't pay that much and you know how high the cost of living is here."

I shifted sideways so I could get a better look at Benni. "What about someone like Celeste Campbell? She's been around a while."

"When she switched to TV news, she basically started at the bottom. I'll bet she's not making more than fifty or sixty thousand—if that."

As I watched the next news report, one thought returned over and over—Celeste paid Kelly Atkinson a lot of money—a full portrait package, some webcams, and even though she hadn't

291

mentioned it, maybe a little something for Kelly's time. How had she afforded it?

There was only one way to get answers. "Excuse me, I have to call someone." I slipped my arm from around Benni, grabbed my phone, and dialed Kelly's burner. After four rings, the call went to voicemail. I left a message and returned to the couch.

"Who were you calling?"

"Kelly Atkinson. It seems to me that Celeste paid her a lot of cash. At the time she told me about it, I assumed Celeste was making enough to afford it. But if she wasn't…"

"Somebody with deeper pockets was making the payments for her?"

"Exactly. We were thinking Celeste was trying to turn Kinohi Village into a career-making story, but what if she was nothing more than another hired hand?"

"It's possible, I suppose. She's on TV all the time. She seems nice enough on camera, so maybe she's just totally focused on her career. You know how some people get, McKenna. You had to chase them for money for years."

"You're right. I always had to figure out which ones couldn't pay their bills and which ones had other priorities. I'm surprised I didn't see this sooner, but I think Celeste is really good at taking advantage of other people's resources. At Starbucks, she said she'd buy her coffee, but then she let Chance get it. She drives an old beater, except when she's in the company van on her way to a story. And she must spend a fortune on beauty services."

"Personally, I don't think she's that good." Benni shrugged. "She doesn't have a real spark. But if she wants the spotlight and a job at a larger station, she's going to need something super big."

"And what better way to get it than breaking—or maybe manufacturing—a huge story?" I grinned and kissed Benni on the cheek. "I think we just figured out what role Celeste played in this whole question of whether Kenji was a good guy or a bad one."

Benni pointed at my phone, which I still held in my hand. "Maybe you should call Chance?"

"I'm going to wait. He's having dinner with the Ashbrooks. I'd hate to interrupt his shot at bonding with his future father-in-law."

"My, my, aren't you optimistic? Next thing you know you'll be planning their wedding."

My cheeks flushed. I was doing the same thing as Mrs. Nakamura. Getting myself wrapped up in someone else's life and wanting to make changes. "You're right. I've got enough issues of my own to deal with. In fact, there's one I haven't told you about that you should definitely be aware of." I didn't wait for Benni to respond, but charged ahead, knowing that if I didn't, I might chicken out. "I've been contacted by a man who claims to be my half-brother."

Benni's eyes widened and she blinked a few times. "This is a joke. Yah?"

"No joke. I'll show you the letter." I pulled out my wallet, extracted the now worn paper and unfolded it, then snuck a sheepish glance at Benni. "I received it a couple of weeks ago."

She nodded knowingly. "So you've been carrying this around for two weeks? Why didn't you tell me? Were you afraid I'd be appalled and leave you?"

"Nothing that bad. Let's just say I was being stupid. Again."

"You're not stupid."

I held up my hands to stop her. "It was wrong to not tell you the truth right away."

"Is that why you were so uncomfortable at Sue's presentation?"

"Yes. This possibly having a family is something new for me. It feels so weird."

Benni brushed back her bangs and smiled. "The last time I checked, having family was an either-or proposition. You either do or you don't have a brother."

"Part of the problem is I'm not sure I believe him."

"Why would a man write to you for no reason and claim to be your brother? You're hardly rich—" She raised her eyebrows. "Wait, do you have a fortune you've been hiding from me?"

"If only. What I have is this job, my meager savings, and a social security check. I also have a bunch of questions about Celeste Campbell."

According to the clock on the wall, it had been thirty minutes since I'd called Kelly. Why hadn't she called back? I dismissed the thought, thinking she might still be talking to Barbara.

I'm not a believer in coincidence, but I do believe in karma, so when the landline rang, I chalked it up to the universe eking out a tiny amount of revenge for my relationship faux pax. I checked CallerID. It was a number I didn't recognize, so it could be another wannabe tenant. Then there was the flashing light on the machine, which was reminding me I still hadn't listened to the voicemail from the previous caller. If I was lucky, this was the same person and I could give them the bad news, thus saving myself a callback.

"Sunsetter Apartments, McKenna speaking."

"Thank goodness you answered!" The voice was female, somewhat familiar, but I couldn't place the person behind it. "I called Chance, but he didn't answer, so I called you and left a message almost an hour ago. Didn't you get it?"

"I'm sorry, but I don't usually answer this phone after hours." And, I shut off the beeper so I didn't have to listen to the stupid thing all night.

"Sorry, I didn't know. You left me your card. This is Barbara Valdez." When I didn't respond immediately, she added, "Kelly's spouse."

"Oh. Hi, Barbara. How's Kelly? She did make it home okay, didn't she?"

"She called right before I called you the first time. She said she has a lead on the murder investigation."

The back of my neck tingled with that feeling of little creepy-crawly things running across the skin. I rubbed the spot, but it was of no use. "What do you mean, she has a lead?"

"She told me she was going to see Celeste Campbell and that Celeste was the one who killed Kenji Ito."

Forget about creepy-crawlies, the thought of Kelly accusing Celeste of murder on her own sent ice through my veins. There was no telling where that conversation might go. "Do you know where this meeting is taking place?"

She rattled off an address. I told her to not worry, that we'd get there right away. The problem was, my regular ride was at dinner.

I laid down the receiver, closed my eyes, and tried to come up with a solution. I had none. Benni came to stand before me, concern etched on her face. There were no good choices here. If I didn't enlist Benni's help, Kelly might get hurt. And if I did, I could be endangering both of us.

Taking a deep breath, I said, "I have a problem."

44

BEFORE BENNI AND I LEFT for Celeste's home, Benni suggested I forward the landline to my cell in case Barbara called back. And sure enough, we were most of the way to Celeste's home when a call came through—but it wasn't Barbara, it was Derrick Tanaka. Tempting as it was to let it go to voicemail, I didn't want to risk letting him have a change of heart. My best case scenario was that Celeste had told him we were closing in and he wanted to be the first to rat on his friends.

Derrick didn't waste time getting to the point. "You still want information on Kinohi Village?"

"I thought you told us everything you knew," I said sharply.

"I…uh…discovered a few things, brah. Like about how things was goin' wrong on the project."

"Are you saying you know who's behind the sabotage out there?"

"Yeah. I know."

I'll bet he did. And that he would try and pin the blame on someone else. Unfortunately, if he gave me Kelly's name, I might just believe him. "Here's the deal, Derrick. You have exactly thirty seconds to tell me the truth or I'm going to turn the photo I have of you talking to Graham Tynsdale over to Julie Edgeworth. I'm pretty sure she'll fire you on the spot. So what's it going to be? The truth or more BS?"

"I was trying to stop him! I didn't want none of the guys to get hurt."

"Stop who?"

"Graham."

"Are you saying Tynsdale was behind all of the sabotage?"

"Yeah, brah. He caused it all."

The voice of the GPS blasted through the car's speakers. "Take the exit."

"Who's that?"

"The GPS. You caught me on the road. You know what, Derrick? For once, I believe you." At least, I wanted to believe him.

"Turn left at the signal."

"Where you going?"

"None of your business. I have to talk to Chance. We'll get back to you." I disconnected the call.

"Sorry about that," Benni said. "But I don't want to get us lost. I'm not out here very much."

"No worries. That was Derrick Tanaka. He told me Graham Tynsdale was behind the sabotage at Kinohi Village."

"The protestor guy? What a scum."

"Right you are," I said, but was drowned out by the GPS as it announced our next turn. It butchered the pronunciation, which caused us to burst out laughing. I read the street name displayed

297

on the screen and chuckled. "Too many vowels, not enough consonants."

Celeste Campbell lived in a small house near the Kalihi Kai district. It was a standard two-story home with a carport and main entrance on the first floor, bedrooms on the second. Even in the twilight, it was apparent the place needed repairs. Built long before the advent of modern residential housing codes, the only lighting on the street came from entryways and windows.

"Not exactly the kind of place I'd want to walk at night," I said.

Benni shuddered. "Me, either. Are you sure you want to go in there?"

"No, but I'm worried about Kelly. I'll text Chance and let him know where we are." His reply came immediately. They'd just wrapped up dinner and he was on his way. "He said he can be here in thirty minutes."

"Do you want to wait?"

"No. If Kelly's in there alone, she could be in danger. At least with two of us, Celeste will have to think twice before she does anything stupid."

"If you think you're going in there and leaving me out here alone, you're crazy. I'm going with you." Benni popped open the door, got out, and stood in front of the car.

"I sure wish Chance was here," I said when I met her at the front bumper.

Benni nudged me in the ribs. "Don't worry, I'll protect you."

"No problem. But who's going to protect you?"

She stood a little taller and took my arm. "Haven't you heard? I'm a woman. I can do anything."

We marched toward the front, Benni leading the way, me following. Even outside, we could easily hear two women's voices who sounded very much like they were engaged in a full blown let's-tear-each-other-apart type of argument. At best, I considered Benni's statement about being able to do anything sketchy on this one.

"Let's see if we can keep things under control until Chance gets here," I said.

"Works for me." Benni turned and rapped on the screen door.

The argument turned into a one-sided series of accusations from Kelly, but Celeste came to the door and peered at Benni through the screen. "Who are you?"

I stepped forward and grabbed Benni's hand. "She's with me."

"Oh, you. What do you want?" She turned and yelled over her shoulder, "What did you do? Bring reinforcements?"

"She had no idea I was coming. Can we come in? It sounds like you two need a mediator."

Celeste rolled her eyes. "Whatever. Just get her out of here. She's twenty kinds of crazy. Door's open." She turned and stalked away.

The inside of Celeste's place wasn't much better than the outside. With empty walls and a worn couch as the only place to sit in the living room, it was obvious Celeste hadn't spent much on decorating. Not that it would have taken much, space was very limited.

Kelly's face flushed bright red when she saw me, then she did a masterful job of avoiding my gaze. I interpreted her reaction to be embarrassment, not anger. She snuck a peek at Benni, but didn't ask who she was.

With two potential suspects in the same room, my biggest dilemma was how to get them to rat out the other. Then again, based on the nasty looks they were exchanging, it might not be hard at all.

"It sounds like you two were having quite the discussion," I said to Celeste. "And for the record, you lied to me earlier today."

"I didn't lie. It's not my fault you didn't ask the right questions."

"Not amused," I shot back. "And neither will you be if you get charged with murder."

"I didn't kill anybody!" Fire rose in her cheeks, but it was quickly replaced by a trembling in her lower lip.

"Why did you lie at the mall?"

Celeste stood, her weight over her back leg, her left out in front, her arms crossed.

Kelly jabbed an accusing finger in her direction. "Because she killed Kenji to hide what she'd been doing!"

"You don't know anything." Celeste snapped.

"Rein it in, Kelly. Now. So why don't you tell us the whole story, Celeste?"

Benni crossed the room and put her hand on Celeste's shoulder. "I get it. You're afraid of losing everything. Aren't you?"

Celeste's white knuckles clutched her sweater. Benni stepped closer and pulled her into a hug, and the last of Celeste's resistance crumbled. She choked back sobs and put her arms around Benni. They held onto each other while Kelly and I watched from the sidelines, exchanging glances that indicated neither of us understood what had just happened.

When Celeste pulled back, she said, "He tricked me."

"Who tricked you?" Benni asked. "Kenji?"

"No. Graham Tynsdale. He told me he'd get me the story I've needed for five years." She paused and her watery eyes sought out mine. "My career. It's all I have."

"You've had to fight for everything, haven't you?" Benni said.

Celeste sniffled, then glared at me. "When men get older, everyone says they're distinguished. But when women get a few wrinkles or gray hairs, everyone says we just look old. I've only got a couple of years left on camera. I needed a story so big they wouldn't worry about my age."

"That's what he promised you?" Benni asked.

"Yes. He said the story surrounding Ito Development was going to be the biggest scandal since Kukui Plaza. And it was going to be all mine. I'm the one who would have broken it. Everybody would have wanted me on their team. I could have gone anywhere."

"Why would you believe anything Graham Tysdale told you?" I said. "The man's nothing more than a sign for hire."

Celeste shook her head and smirked. "Don't kid yourself. The man's connected. He knows everyone and everything that goes on."

Even if the story were true, her aspirations were out of proportion with reality. One story about contracting payoffs and political corruption on an island three-thousand miles from the mainland was not going to land her a job in LA or New York. This woman was living on fantasy island. "And what story did you get?" I asked.

"I got nothing." Celeste indicated Kelly with a lifting of her chin. "She knows. She bugged Kenji's office for me."

"And China Gaardner's," Kelly grumbled.

301

I shot a warning glance at Kelly. "Celeste, I understand why you bugged Ito Development, but how did you get in the office?"

"Graham gave me a key," Celeste said. "I didn't ask how he got it."

I blew out a long breath, then fixed her with a determined stare. "Fine. If you thought there was something going on at Kinohi Village, why didn't you have him get you a key for the construction office out there?"

Celeste snickered. "Because the story was never about Kinohi Village. It was about kickbacks and payoffs from Ito Development to government employees and politicians. The webcam Kelly put there was supposed to help me find out what he was doing on all of his projects. For decades, every governor that came in promised to clean up the pay-to-play corruption in construction, but there were always loopholes. It's a lot harder now, but Graham had information about how Kenji was manipulating the system."

"I don't understand. If Ito Development had to bid everything, how were they manipulating anything?"

"They didn't," Celeste said glumly. "Ito Development is clean. Everything Graham Tynsdale told me was a lie."

45

WITH CELESTE'S CONFESSION THAT SHE, too, had been duped, Kelly growled like an angry dog. I'd have expected her to have some empathy since she was in the same boat, but apparently she was fresh out of that. Benni and I exchanged a look—one that, at least for my part, was filled with my own anger, confusion, and frustration with all of the players and their games of deception. It baffled me how a seasoned reporter like Celeste could be fooled so easily. Unless she hadn't.

"Enough," I snapped. "I can see why Kelly's so angry with you. I'm about ready to call your competitors and turn them loose on you. See how you like that side of things."

Celeste slumped down onto the couch and buried her face in her hands. "Graham and I met at the City Council meeting where they green-lighted the project. He told me he'd been watching my coverage of Kinohi Village and liked my potential. He said Ito Development had won the vote because they'd bribed the mayor. When I told him I needed proof for a story like that, he said there was a way we could get it. But it would take time and resources."

"I can't believe your editor would approve you working on a story like that without some sort of verifiable evidence."

"He didn't. He told me to leave it alone. According to him, the paper didn't want reporters chasing windmills. He didn't say it outright, but he made it sound like if I didn't back off, I'd be caught in the next round of layoffs. I've been fighting so long just to keep my job that the idea of getting laid off scared me to death."

That part, I got. Who hadn't been in fear of losing their job at some point? "What did you do?"

She paused, let her attention flit from object to object in the room, then sighed. "I went to visit Graham and told him what I was up against. He asked how bad I wanted the story. He told me again it was another Kukui Plaza. I said if he wanted me to take this risk, he had to provide something concrete. He handed me two grand and said he'd give me more when I took steps to prove I was on-board. I was dumbfounded. I've never had anyone who believed in me that much. Later, he gave me money for the equipment. He's the one who paid for my photo shoot and for Kelly's time."

I scowled at Kelly. "You were being paid? All along? So while you were complaining about how tough things were with me and Chance, you were getting money from Graham Tynsdale?"

"Equipment's super expensive," she muttered. "I thought she was paying me."

"The two of you are a real pair. You know that? You both worked for the same man, have taken his money, and now neither of you trusts the other for doing exactly the same thing."

A frown darkened Benni's brow. It was a subtle change, and it amazed me that without saying a word she'd made me realize I was letting anger cloud my thoughts. I had to refocus. And get Celeste to tell the truth. I gave Benni an almost imperceptible nod before taking a deep breath and turning my full attention on Celeste. "What made you change your mind about Ito Development?"

Celeste put her hand to her mouth, then ran it down her neck. "The fire that almost destroyed two homes."

"What fire?" I asked innocently.

"Someone torched two of the houses that had just been completed. It happened after the webcam was in Kenji's office. He was devastated when he heard about it. The story never made the nightly news because there wasn't that much damage. But the more I listened to him talk on the phone, the more I realized he really was trying to accomplish something good. And then I'd watch the feed for China Gaardner and it was just the opposite. Whenever she talked to her clients, it was all about the money. And then I overheard her talking to Tommy West. That's when things kind of clicked for me."

Sometimes, it just pays to be lucky. Especially when you miss the obvious. We'd known Tommy West was the mystery client. We'd also known he had all kinds of people working for him.

"What's up, McKenna?" Benni asked.

"Pieces of the puzzle just fell into place."

Benni raised her eyebrows and gave me a questioning look.

"I'll explain later." I no longer thought either Celeste or Kelly had murdered Kenji, but guilt is a wonderful thing and because Celeste felt guilty enough to talk, I planned on taking full advantage. "Let's suppose that I believe you. Why did you bug China Gaardner's office in the first place?"

"I figured China had to be working for someone, and I had to do something to convince Kelly I was trying to get both sides, so I bought the webcam and told her I didn't have a key. I knew she'd get resourceful."

Kelly wore a smug smile and seemed all too eager to brag about what she'd done. "I waited for the janitor to open the door one night. She had the office open and had to go get more plastic bags. That's when I slipped in and hid under China's desk. I had no idea that it was going to be so easy."

"You were lucky she ran out of bags when she did."

"Nope. I went by the cart while she was vacuuming inside and took the ones she had."

"Clever. Celeste, when you were listening, did China ever mention Derrick Tanaka?"

"No."

"What about Graham Tynsdale?"

"No. Never."

My phone pinged with a text from Chance. He was only a few minutes away and wanted to know if I was in danger. I handed the phone to Benni and asked her to let him know the situation. She began typing right away.

If Celeste was telling the truth, this had been a very compartmentalized operation. Tommy brought in China to handle the real estate deal and had Graham organize everything else. With those two on the front lines, Tommy was able to hide in the shadows and direct everything. It was a brilliant plan.

At least I knew who the players were now. It was time to fall back on McKenna's Skip Tracing Secret #5—*the best defense is a good offense.* And Kelly was, in my opinion, the one most likely to crack.

I narrowed my eyes and glowered at her. She sat up straight and sucked in a breath.

"Why did you call Celeste first when you found Kenji's body?" I demanded. "And don't lie to me or I'll turn you both in for obstruction of justice—and conspiracy."

She started to look at Celeste, but I moved between them.

"I'm asking you. Answer me." Celeste started to speak, but stopped when I pointed a finger at her. "And don't you say a word if you want to avoid prison."

"I...I..." Kelly swallowed hard. "I didn't know what to do. I saw this shoe sticking out of the ground and I freaked out." She swallowed again. And the little bit of color that she had in her cheeks drained away as she continued. "My first instinct was to run. I've...never seen a dead body before. I knew Celeste had, so I called her to ask what I should do."

Turning my attention to Celeste, I said, "And what did you do? Tell her to wait for your signal before she called 9-1-1?"

"I'm not proud of what I did," she said. "But I needed that story."

"How did you know it was Kenji?"

"I didn't, but he hadn't been in his office. The man was a workaholic and the body had been buried in an area where there was nothing going on. I figured it had to be him. And if it wasn't, I still had a story."

"Were you with your cameraman the entire day?"

"From the time we left the office. Our news director had us chasing down a domestic violence story out in Kaimuki Kai. When Kelly called me, I told my cameraman we had something way better. I told him I'd take the heat if it didn't work out. He wasn't happy, but he went along."

"You realize I can easily check your alibi."

Celeste appeared unconcerned as she shrugged. "Go ahead. Call my cameraman if you want. Talk to my news director. They'll both confirm it."

I was also convinced Kelly hadn't killed Kenji for one other reason. It might seem stupid, but I'd seen her drive. The odds of her being able to operate a backhoe were about the same as me being able to run one.

"I don't believe either of you were involved in the murder, but you did delay reporting a crime. If HPD finds out about this, you'll both be facing charges. And you, Celeste, you'll lose your job."

Kelly's shoulders sagged and she remained silent as Celeste pleaded with me to not tell anyone.

"For now, I'll keep this quiet. But if I find out either of you has lied or interfered in any way, I won't hesitate to call HPD and tell them everything I know." I looked across the room at Benni. "Ready to go?"

"Wait! Why were you asking about Tynsdale and Tanaka?" Celeste asked.

"Because I believe they're working together. Actually, I believe all of you were ultimately working for Tommy West." The expression on Celeste's face told me more than any words she could say. "You had no idea, did you?"

"No," she croaked. "I knew there had to be things Graham was leaving out, but I...so I was just a pawn in some game?"

"Yes."

"For what? The land?"

"That's all you get for now."

I cocked my head toward the front door. Benni gave me a curt nod, but then marched over to Kelly, grabbed her arm, and pulled her to her feet. "And you—you're going home. Now."

Wow. So that was mom-power? I definitely wanted lessons on that skill.

46

CHANCE HAD PARKED BEHIND BENNI'S car. The contrast of a completely practical Toyota Corolla against a pulse-raising machine like the Ferrari made me chuckle. Both doors opened, and I realized Chance had brought Lexie with him.

I met them on one side of the car while Benni huddled on the other with Kelly. When Kelly nodded, mumbled something, and got in her car, Chance gave me an appreciative smile. "I see you found another source of muscle."

"She's tough," I said.

"And don't you forget it," said Benni as she approached.

"She looks sad," Lexie said as she watched Kelly drive away.

"I told her if she values her relationship with Barbara at all, she'd better go home and be honest with her. Kelly's starting to realize how close she came to ruining her life. I also told her McKenna would call Barbara and assure her that Kelly was on the way."

"That's one call I'll be happy to make," I said and pulled out my phone. "Let's hope our little photographer doesn't interfere anymore."

"I don't think she will. I also told her she needed to get herself together. She's a good girl. She just got taken in by Celeste's greed."

"Sorry to bring you all the way out here for nothing, you two," I said. "There was so much guilt between Kelly and Celeste that it was easy to get them to talk. How'd dinner go?"

Chance didn't even try to hide the smile on his face. "You're not the only one with information. Councilman Ashbrook was very helpful. He told me a few things about O'ahu Country Club."

"Did he tell you anything about Tommy West?"

"As a matter of fact, he told me a lot about him. Not much of it was good, either. I'll tell you on the way. Lexie and I agreed she'd go with Benni and you can come with me. You and I have a stop to make."

"Where are we going?"

"To see China Gaardner."

"She's not working at this hour."

"Oh yes she is. She thinks she's meeting a client who's flying out in the morning. She'll be in her office."

"You are a man full of surprises." I got in the Ferrari and dialed Barbara's number, determined to do my part to straighten out Kelly's behavior.

As Chance had predicted, China's office door was unlocked. We found her at her desk. The color in her cheeks turned fiery red when we walked in. Call me a chicken, but I felt this was Chance's show and was prepared to let him take the flack.

"Before you say anything, there's something you need to know. And it's going to be worth your while to indulge me." Chance picked up one of the side chairs and crossed the room to the HVAC vent. He stood on the chair, opened the vent, and pulled out the webcam Kelly had planted. I thought China's eyes might pop out of her head when she realized someone had been spying on her. Her mouth worked, but nothing came out.

"Courtesy of Tommy West," Chance said.

Somehow, I kept a straight face. Don't ask how.

"What do you mean? He sent you?"

"No. He's been spying on you."

It wasn't exactly the lie I would have gone with, but I was proud of the kid—it was a doozy.

"Why would he…he's my client…"

"Given the stakes on this project, did you really expect him to have complete trust in you? Besides, if he needs someone to take the blame, you're there."

"For what? I haven't done anything illegal!"

"Murder. Conspiracy. Attempted bribery." Chance inched closer to China's desk. "You want me to continue?"

"No. No, no, no. I am not taking the fall for that man."

"What fall?"

"For the bribes," she blurted, then added, "Wait, why are you here? What do you want?"

I love it when someone panics. It's like they open the candy jar and beg you to stick your hand in.

"You can start by telling us about these bribes," Chance said.

"Oh my God. You didn't know." China squeezed her eyes shut and took a deep breath. "I need a lawyer."

"I'm sure you will," Chance said, then turned to me. "You've got the latest. Why don't you take this?"

"Sure. Before you make any phone calls, China, let's play a little game called Save Yourself First. We know you were hired by Tommy West to help disrupt the development of Kinohi Village and broker a very lucrative land deal when the project fell through."

"How do you know that?"

I continued without slowing down. "There's plenty more where that came from. So let's make this easy. You get one opportunity. After that, you become Tommy West's number one sacrifice. You can stop that if you tell us why he wanted Kinohi Village to fail."

China's jaw tightened. Her breaths now came short and shallow. "He wanted to eliminate Kenji Ito's influence in this town. My job was to make sure nobody else got to bid on that property."

"And the bribes? Is Tommy still trying to get government contracts with the old pay-to-play methods?"

She gritted her teeth, then blurted, "Tommy's been having trouble ever since the last time they tightened up the government procurement laws. I told him the political contributions weren't doing him any good, but he said they'd pay off in the end. It was his money, so I figured, what the heck, let him spend it how he sees fit."

"And you didn't think that knowing about those payoffs would make you an accomplice?"

China chewed on her lower lip as she gazed at the photo of her family.

"She never thought she'd get caught," Chance said. "You have bigger problems though than conspiracy, China. You have no alibi for the time of Kenji's murder."

"I was at OCC with Tommy."

Chance picked up the webcam and turned it over a couple of times. "No. You two left early. We have witnesses."

At first, I thought China might actually try to lie her way out of her predicament, but she was fixated by Chance's little prop. If this hadn't been the worst possible time, I'd have high-fived him and told him it was a brilliant move.

"Screw him. Fine. Tommy got a call on the twelfth hole from Kenji. He said Kenji wanted to talk to him, and then he told me I was going to have to get to work on the land deal. He didn't want any delays, so he insisted I come back here and double-check everything. He wanted me ready to move forward on taking over the land."

"Is that what you did?" Chance asked.

"That's right. I came back here."

Chance held up the webcam. "If you're lying, the video surveillance can disprove your alibi."

She shook her head. "Go ahead. Check it. I was here from four until after seven. When I got home I was dead tired, said goodnight to my family, and went to bed."

"How'd you hurt your hand?" I asked. "We know it wasn't at yoga."

Her cheeks flushed and she bit her lower lip. "I was so mad about Tommy cutting off the golf game and ruining my night that I wasn't paying attention and slammed the trunk lid down on my fingers. It was stupid. I should have been happy because everything I thought we were trying to accomplish was going to come to fruition. Instead, I was angry because my golf game got cut short."

For once, I believed something China had said. "Why'd you lie about it?"

She pointed at the miniature camera in Chance's hands. "If I'd have known about that thing I never would have. When I heard about the murder, I called Tommy. He said we could alibi each other. If I told the truth, I wouldn't have had an alibi and I might have become a suspect."

I regarded China, tempted to remind her that we'd come to exactly that conclusion because she had lied. Instead, I acted like an adult and said, "I see."

Chance gave me a raised-eyebrow look. "We've gotten everything we needed here. Unless you have other questions."

"I'm good."

"Then we have another stop to make." He winked at me on his way out the door.

I hurried after him, not sure who we'd be going to see next, but quite sure Chance hadn't wanted to disclose a name in front of China. When the elevator door closed, Chance punched the button and held up his hand to exchange a high five. I slapped his palm with mine.

"We're going to crack this sucker tonight," he said.

"That would be nice. What's this other stop you want to make?"

"Graham Tynsdale."

I hate looking stupid in public, so it was my good fortune that we were the only people in the elevator. But when the door opened and we were on our way out the building exit, there was still a question that had been burning a hole into my psyche. "How did you find him?"

Chance chuckled. "Councilman Ashbrook, again. Graham has quite a reputation. And the lesson here is very simple—it doesn't pay to make enemies of almost every good cause in town. People complain to someone like Councilman Ashbrook.

He says something to someone at HPD. They talk amongst themselves. And the next thing you know, everybody knows right where the guy lives."

"Impressive work." I held up my hand, palm facing out to exchange another high-five. "You really are turning into a boy wonder. If I could make a suggestion, get serious about your license. Stop dinking around with an old skip tracer."

Chance remained silent during the rest of the walk to the Ferrari. Perhaps he'd been thinking exactly what I'd suggested. Or maybe he was caught up in his own type of fear. Either way, I let him keep his thoughts to himself until we were back on the road.

The night wind felt good blowing through my hair. During the day, driving in an open convertible was like being in a sauna, but once the sun went down, the experience could be exhilarating. Tonight, in fact, was a perfect night for a drive. Evening trade winds refreshed the land with their constant flow. They brought with them the fresh scent of the sea.

Silvery clouds rode across the sky like ships sailing a dark ocean. Despite the urban glow accentuated by everything from streetlights to skyscrapers, a few stars twinkled overhead. It was as though every sense in my body had come alive, and as Chance drove I relished the experience. That is, until he broke in on my thoughts.

"It wasn't my good work, McKenna. It was my future father-in-law's. Oh yeah, Lexie wanted to ride with Benni because she wanted to tell her the news. I proposed and Lexie accepted."

"Congratulations! So you're going to settle down. Next thing you know, you'll be buying a house so you have room for a few keiki."

"Don't rent my apartment yet. That's still a ways off. Here's our turn."

Chance pulled to a stop in front of a fourplex that, based on the Mid-Century Modern architectural style and overhead spider web of utility wires, had most likely been here for more than fifty years. Despite the drone of traffic on the H-1, a woman sat in a chair outside one of the downstairs units while two keiki played hopscotch on the sidewalk in front of her. It amazed me how normal life went on even in the shadows of an Interstate.

"Tynsdale lives here?" I asked.

"So I'm told."

"It's straight out of the 50s and 60s. The freeway wasn't even a distant vision when the owner bought this lot. And now, these people practically live on top of it."

"I'll bet this was a nice area in those days," Chance said.

"Maybe. But now it's just tired and old. As the manager of a much nicer complex, I can tell you this is the kind of apartment people rent when they can't afford something better."

"You do what you've gotta do to get by."

Wow. Those were pretty smart words coming from a rich kid. "You still want to talk to this guy before we turn him over to the police?"

"If we're going to give Sue closure, we have to. Come on, let's see if he's home."

47

THE WOMAN SITTING OUT FRONT eyed us suspiciously as we dodged traffic to cross the street. Her two keiki, who were dressed in old tees and shorts, did the opposite and continued their game of hopscotch until Mom gave them a stern warning.

"Let the men by, you two."

The kids dutifully stood to the side while we stepped around their chalk markings on the concrete. The boy gazed up at me with the biggest, saddest brown eyes I'd ever seen.

"You here for the wallet, Mister?"

I knelt next to him. "What wallet is that?"

"The one the nasty man threw in the garbage."

Their mother approached, her slippahs beating out a slow rhythm on the bottoms of her feet. She eyed us both, letting her suspicion flick from me to Chance, then back again. "Who are you?"

"My name's McKenna. This is my associate Chance Logan. We're here to see Graham Tynsdale."

"Nasty haole," the woman spat out. "That man cause trouble for everybody."

"Ma'am, what's this wallet your son mentioned?" Chance asked. "Was it blue and tan? It would be pretty fancy. And expensive."

She sneered at the upstairs apartment door. "I knew he stole it. Phillip, go get this man's wallet."

Phillip ran off, his slippahs clip-clopping like a trotting horse's hooves.

"Good kid," I said.

She watched as the boy disappeared into the house. "Mahalo. I'm Maile. Phillip's got a lot of his father in him." She shot another nasty look at the second floor, then continued. "He saw that no-good throw it in the garbage. When he brought it home I told him it was going to bring trouble. I made him put it away."

My eyes widened when Phillip returned. He handed me a blue-and-tan resin wallet. A wave of emotion rushed over me when I ran my fingers over its buttery smooth surface. I was holding Kenji Ito's wallet, one of his favorite possessions. "This is it." I whispered. "How much do you want for it?"

Maile shook her head. "It not right to charge money so someone can get their things back."

I contemplated the kids. Their mom. My eyes misted over. This woman was trying to raise two children with a solid belief in right and wrong. How often did she get to see them? At dinner? Did they get Christmas presents? "You work, what? Two jobs?"

She smiled, but her eyes betrayed her. "We get by."

"You have no idea what this wallet will mean to our friend," Chance said.

"Her father died and this was one of his favorite possessions," I added. "I certainly admire you for your principles. But this wallet is precious to someone else, and we'd like to give you a reward."

Chance nodded, pulled out his wallet, and folded two bills in half, then in half again. He reached out and pressed the bills into Maile's hand. "Believe me, you deserve this."

Maile started to protest, but I quieted her with a polite, "Take it for the keiki."

She sniffled, blinked back tears, and her voice cracked. "I was short on this month's rent. Thank you." She pocketed the money without looking at it.

We said our goodbyes to Maile, Phillip, and his sister, then took the stairs to the second floor. The old wooden treads creaked as we climbed. The nearby concrete wall was still warm from the day's heat. Add to that the fact that we were on the wrong side of the building to get the benefit of the trades, and the air we breathed reminded me of a sauna filled with stale exhaust.

"Let's get this over with," I said.

"Agreed. I'm so tired of this guy."

Down on the first floor, Maile and Phillip were playing jump rope with Phillip's sister. The little girl, who was in the middle, hopped up and down as they chanted and laughed. I hoped Chance had given Maile a good reward—it wouldn't dig her out of poverty, but it might keep them off the streets for awhile.

Chance rapped on the door three times. A voice from inside yelled at us to be patient. When the door opened, the man behind it kept the security chain pulled taut.

He scowled at us from the other side. "What'd you want? I'm busy."

I took a small step back, practically bowled over by the smell of stale booze on his breath. One thing was for sure—Graham Tynsdale was no less prickly in person than he was from a distance. His dirty white cotton tank top was, in my opinion, on the bottom of the fashion ladder. And those flowered shorts? They left an equal amount of style and elegance on the table. No matter how 'connected' this guy might be, he had loser stamped on his forehead with a capital L.

Chance flashed his wannabe-PI ID and pocketed it in one smooth motion. Tynsdale tried to follow the move, but the alcohol slowed him down too much. "Lemme see that again."

"We have some questions for you about the murder of Kenji Ito," Chance said.

Tynsdale's reaction came slowly at first, but then he seemed to get the gist. "What? I didn't have nothing to do with that."

I held up the wallet. "You were in possession of a custom wallet you stole off Kenji Ito's body. We think you had a lot to do with it."

"Get outta here or I'm calling my lawyer." He slammed the door shut.

Stunned, I said, "He has a lawyer?"

Chance stared at me for a second, then shook his head and pounded on the door again. This time, there was no answer.

"Great," I said. "We'll have to think of another way to get to him. Maybe wait until morning?"

"Too easy to miss him. We have to flush him out."

I snapped my fingers and tugged on Chance's sleeve. "Follow me."

We went to the end of the walkway, which went past the next unit. As I'd hoped, there was a second set of stairs. "We can wait for him here. When he comes out, you grab him and make him talk."

"Seriously? Are you trying to land me in jail? You go back to the car. There's a small case in the trunk. It contains surveillance equipment. I can attach a microphone to the window. I'm betting he'll call Tommy for help." He shoved the keys to the Ferrari in my hand.

I gaped at the key ring. Holy crap. This was not a good idea. "What if I drop these? Or scratch the car?"

"You're not going to do anything like that, McKenna. All you have to do is open the trunk and pull out the black, plastic case. It's about this size." He made the shape of a small rectangle with his hands.

"I'll stay here. You go get it." I tried to shove the keys back at him, but he pushed my hand away.

"If he tries to leave, what are you going to do? Argue him to death? Go. And grab my water bottle, too. I need to wash the taste of that slime out of my mouth."

Keys in hand, I swallowed hard and went down the stairs. The game of jump rope had finished. Maile and her keiki were inside. The only evidence of the family's presence was the chalk diagram on the walkway.

We'd jaywalked on our way in, but I wasn't feeling nearly as bold this time. I went to the corner, pushed the button for the light, and waited for the little man to signal it was safe for me to cross. While I waited, I glanced over my shoulder once. Chance stood there, moving his hand in circles. Got it. Stop dawdling.

By the time I got to the car, Chance had gone into pace mode. I understood why he wanted to be the one to stay behind. If Tynsdale made a run for it, he could stop him. But I hated being in charge of the keys for a car that cost more than some ungodly multiple of my annual salary. Nevertheless, I persevered. I got the trunk open and even found the plastic case Chance had described.

I was about to close the trunk when Benni called. Knowing she'd be worried if I didn't answer, I felt I had no choice. "Hey, what's up?"

"Has Chance told you? He and Lexie are getting married."

"He did. But I can't talk right now."

Two cars rushed by, one of them loud enough to drown out the conversation.

"What was that?" Benni asked. "Where are you?"

"We're at Graham Tynsdale's apartment. We believe he killed Kenji, but we want to talk to him before we turn him into HPD. We want proof that all the accusations against Kenji were part of some big conspiracy."

"McKenna, don't be taking chances. Call the police."

I checked on the second floor again. Chance was still pacing. I resolved to tamp down my own ridiculous fears. I wasn't going to hurt Chance's car. I was going to carry my weight. I'd been sent to get two lousy items. By God, it was time to get it done.

"Sorry, but there's a lot of traffic noise. We'll talk later."

I disconnected the call and closed the trunk, then went to the passenger side of the car. Even stretching across the seat, Chance's bottle was just out of reach. "Rats."

The traffic light at the corner changed to green. Two cars charged off the line and roared by the Ferrari. They had to be doing thirty-five and were accelerating. I might have decided to carry my weight, but I wasn't going to get killed doing it. I set the plastic case on the floor and got into the passenger's seat. This time, I was able to wrap my fingers around the bottle.

I raised my prize high in the air and shot a triumphant glance at the second floor. Just as the body of Graham Tynsdale flew out of his open front door and plummeted to the concrete walkway below.

48

I WATCHED, PARALYZED BY FEAR as Chance came running from the stairwell. He stood in front of Tynsdale's door leaning over the railing. A shadow emerged from the open doorway, its arms hoisting a large object in the air.

"Chance!" I yelled. "Behind you!"

The attacker brought down the object. Chance ducked to avoid the blow, but went down hard. I sucked in a breath when the man turned to run for the stairs. In the stairway lighting I clearly saw the face of Tommy West.

Maile and a couple of the other tenants burst out of their apartment doors and rushed to where Tynsdale lay. They were so busy poking at the body that they missed the lone man running to the street.

On the second floor, Chance stood unsteadily, keeping his hands on the railing. West had made it to a BMW across the street from where the Ferrari was parked. I felt so useless. All I'd done was sit here gaping at the action like an idiot. West was about to get away, and once he was gone, he could vanish—or manufacture an alibi just as he had for the time of Kenji's murder.

I had no way to stop him. He was younger, stronger, and more agile. I fumbled with my phone. My only tool. But even that would be too late. Except—I did have another weapon. On the seat. Right there. Inches away.

My heart pounded against the wall of my chest. It was my only option. I took one final look at the second floor. "Sorry, buddy. I hope you can forgive me."

I snatched up the keys and wormed my way into the driver's seat.

Ignition key. In hand. Check.

I jammed it in the lock. Hundreds of horses roared to life. The tachometer zipped past six-thousand. Just like that? Holy crap.

West closed the BMW's door. A row of vehicles rushed by. Five cars. Four. I was running out of time.

Anxiety burned inside me. If I screwed this up, Chance would never forgive me. And West would be free.

I narrowed my focus. Car in gear. Hands on wheel.

Three cars.

Turn signal. Check.

Handbrake. Where was the stupid handbrake? Got it. Off. Check.

Two cars. One.

I jammed my foot on the gas. The side of my face lit up with approaching headlights.

Horns blared. Tires squealed. The smell of burning rubber filled the air. And in the middle of it all there was the thunder of the Ferrari's engine.

My personal rocket roared across the road. I locked my sights on the BMW. All I could do was ride this baby. Straight into Tommy West's $100,000 BMW.

To my credit, I must say my aim was perfect. I nailed the driver's door. Bullseye, in fact.

Chaos erupted around me. Drivers yelled obscenities. More horns. Sirens.

Oh crap. Sirens.

HPD must be on the way. So much for my chances of ever driving again in this state—or any other.

And then there was Tommy West. Who was currently fighting his way out of a sudden encounter with an airbag. By the time he freed himself from the white ghost clinging to him, HPD had arrived. So had a very angry Chance Logan.

Ewww. I wouldn't want to be on the other end of his temper right now. Oh wait, I was.

When the first HPD officer, a young guy who could have been fresh out of high school, arrived at my door, I extended my arms above my head. Might as well make it easier for him to cuff me. At least in jail I'd be safe until Chance cooled down.

"Lock me up," I said. "I deliberately rammed that car."

The cop did a full body scan of the Ferrari. He started at the front end, made his way to me, and eventually got to the rear end. When he was done with his visual inspection, complete disbelief clouded his face.

Eventually, HPD got their act together. Okay, it wasn't entirely their fault. My brief stint at driving might have complicated things a bit. But they did get the detectives who'd been working on Kenji's murder to join the party. They quickly realized some of the crimes were out of their jurisdiction and called in the FBI, who then called Homeland Security. We soon had a smorgasbord of federal crime-fighting organizations swarming the area with interests in everything from murder to attempted bribery of public officials to financial crimes.

I'm not sure which one of them impounded Tommy's car, but it was definitely HPD who secured the Ferrari. And it was only because Chance called Lexie, who called her dad, who called the police chief, that I avoided spending the night in jail. It wasn't until the following morning that I realized how lucky I'd gotten.

Benni and I were still sitting on the lānai sipping our morning coffee when Chance and Lexie showed up and joined us on the lānai. Chance didn't have any visible wounds, but he did have quite a headache and, for the first time since we'd met, he sat gingerly.

I felt terrible that I hadn't been there to warn him and that I'd… "I'm sorry about the car."

"Sorry? Do you have any idea how dangerous that stunt was?"

"Well…I didn't have a lot of time to plan things out."

Chance held his thumb and index finger about an inch apart. "You were this close to getting T-boned by two oncoming cars."

My shoulders slumped. Yup. I definitely felt awful. "It was the stupidest thing I've ever done."

"I agree with that," Benni said adamantly.

"You're right," Chance said as he rubbed his neck. He winced, but then chuckled.

"What's so funny, babe?" Lexie asked.

He shook his head slowly and smiled. "It was pretty epic. There was smoke coming out of the back end of the Ferrari. Cars were going every direction. And here's McKenna, making a beeline across traffic to stop the bad guy. I've never seen anyone so focused on being a one-man demolition crew."

"It's the concussion," Lexie said apologetically. "I should take him home."

"No, babe, I'm fine." Chance smiled at me. "You haven't had the news on this morning, have you, McKenna?"

"I'm on a news fast. I prefer to avoid my own press coverage."

"Well, you should be watching. Last night is the big news of the day."

Lexie laughed. "When my dad turned on the TV this morning, the first thing he saw was a video of Chance's car stuffed into the side of West's BMW. Then the news reporters started in. According to them, Kenji's murder is just the tip of the iceberg. They're speculating there's all kinds of scandals coming. My dad started making phone calls, and let me tell you, by the time he was done, he was almost apoplectic."

"We should tell McKenna. He deserves to know," Chance said.

"Well…"

Lexie stretched out the word and I, despite my morbid fascination with the possibility of me going to jail, edged forward in my seat. Benni waited, her coffee mug poised at her lips, her eyebrows raised.

"My dad got a call from a friend who works for West Development. He said the business has been in trouble for years. It all started when Tommy took over from his father. Tommy was never satisfied and was always scheming on how to make more money. A few years ago, he lost a development opportunity to a competitor. Six months later, the competitor went bankrupt because of a series of so-called accidents."

The result sounded all too familiar. I took a sip from my mug. "Was Tommy behind these accidents?"

Lexie nodded eagerly. "There's no proof yet, but that's what the president of the company always claimed. The really big news is my dad got a call from HPD this morning. They were giving him a heads-up because they found the microchip hidden in Kenji's wallet. They won't give out details, but said there's going to be a full review by the FBI of West Development's contracts."

"Councilman Ashbrook told Lexie something else," Chance said. "It was Kenji's reputation for bidding honestly that was the main reason things went so smoothly for him with Kinohi Village. The other reason was that it addressed a need and the company wasn't making money off the project."

"So Tommy showed up on a social call and decided to throw Graham off the balcony?" I asked.

"Tynsdale is saying Tommy came there to kill him," Chance said. "My theory is he was trying to blackmail Tommy. The truth may not come out until the trial."

"That's totally it," Lexie added. "My dad found out Tynsdale kept business records for every meeting he had with his clients, so he was a lot smarter than anyone thought he was."

I took in a satisfied breath. We'd gotten the bad guy, at last. Even if we had taken a twisty path to get there. Over the weekend, it became obvious that Tommy West was going to be up to his eyeballs in trouble. Tynsdale's story had come out and was making news headlines. He'd learned about the microchip during the argument between Tommy and Kenji. When Tommy exploded and killed Kenji, they decided to bury the body using a backhoe. While Tommy was getting the backhoe, Graham stole Kenji's wallet hoping to find the microchip. He went through the wallet that night, didn't find the chip, and threw it away.

It was his bad luck that Maile's son was watching. His plan might have even worked if he hadn't been so focused on blackmailing Tommy and gone back Tuesday evening to dig up the body and do another search. By the time he figured out a backhoe was a lot more complicated to operate than a car, he'd made a mess, which is what Kelly saw.

By Monday, Celeste Campbell had been fired and China had cut a deal to avoid prosecution. Even Derrick Tanaka was under investigation. The kicker happened on Tuesday when Kelly called me complaining that HPD had confiscated the computer with all of her photos of Kinohi Village. I reminded her that those who played with fire sometimes got burned. Predictably, she hung up on me.

The really good news was, Benni and I were getting married on Saturday. As long as nothing else happened.

49

I STOOD ON THE GRASS at Wai'alae Beach Park hugging the shade provided by a stand of coconut palms. Though it was only ten a.m., the sun was already intense, which made me glad we'd opted for the colorful sunshade 'altar' Sarah, our officiant, had recommended.

My heart swelled with love and joy at the sight of the small group gathered around for the ceremony. Chance stood next to me. Our classic Aloha print shirts and white shorts could have come straight out of a movie. Our other guests, Benni's brother Alexander and his wife Kira stood with Mrs. Nakamura. Next to her was Benni's daughter Andi. All were dressed casually, as is so often the custom with island weddings.

As I thought about each person here, I realized the part they'd played in my transformation. Prior to moving here I'd let myself become mired in self-pity. What I'd discovered in the years since I'd fled to the islands was that location changed nothing but the scenery. For many of those years, Alexander had been my only friend. How he'd put up with me, I still didn't know.

Dear old Mrs. Nakamura, who stood next to Alexander, reminded me of a diminutive doll. Although she'd always felt like a thorn in my side, I realized now that in her way she'd been teaching me how to live life again. Then there was Andi, whose disappearance on the Big Island had been what brought me together with Benni. Even Chance and Lexie had helped me become the man I was today—the one good enough to marry Benni Kapono.

A short distance away, Benni and Lexie took up their positions. Unlike an indoor service where the bride could be sequestered until she walked down the aisle, this venue had no such option. There was no traditional aisle. No walls. No doors. We'd both wanted it that way.

Standing here now, I realized there was nothing to prevent me from thoroughly enjoying the star of the show's approach. Her white cotton dress, with its fitted waist and tiered skirt, was simple, yet elegant. White wedge heels and a purple orchid Haku around her head completed her ensemble.

My breath caught and I whispered, "She's beautiful."

Chance agreed, but his gaze was fixed on Lexie. I had to admit, Lexie was lovely, but my heart was taken by the woman wearing the purple head lei.

At a nod from Sarah, Chance and I took our places. Andi began to play *Here Comes the Bride* on her guitar. As Benni walked toward us, I saw the misting in her eyes. She gave me a smile, then stumbled on an uneven spot in the grass. Lexie caught her elbow, they laughed, then resumed their approach.

Sarah waited until Benni and I were standing next to each other to begin. "Aloha, Benni and McKenna. We are here with your friends and *'ohana* to share this ceremony joining you in marriage. We'll begin with an exchanging of flower leis." She gestured to Mrs. Nakamura, who tottered forward with two handmade flower necklaces in her arms. Benni's was made of white orchids and red roses; mine was also white orchids, but accented with a strand of ti leaves.

"Presenting the flower lei is a gesture of love, aloha, and respect," Sarah said as she accepted the leis from Mrs. Nakamura. She gave one to Benni, the other to me. "These hand-picked flowers represent an ancient Polynesian tradition. Your lives will now become one. This is the true meaning of aloha. The lei symbolizes the love and aloha that you share as you begin a new life together."

A new life together. It was hard to believe we'd met only a short time ago. For my part, it had been love at first sight. It seemed impossible that this wedding wasn't a dream. After all, I'd always considered myself to be more of an acquired taste, not the kind to sweep a woman off her feet.

"Who has the rings?" Sarah asked.

Chance stepped forward. Handed the rings to Sarah. She then asked Alexander to bring the koa wood bowl he held in one hand. In the other, he held a ti leaf. Sarah dipped the ti leaf in the water and shook it over the rings three times as she chanted in Hawaiian. When we'd first met, she'd given us a loose translation—the ti leaf represented prosperity, health, and blessings.

My fingers shook as Sarah handed Benni's ring to me. I prayed I didn't drop it in the sand. It was wet and slippery, but as soon as it was on Benni's finger, my breath returned. The biggest surprise happened when Benni took my hand and slipped the ring on my finger. I hadn't been able to move, talk, or even think.

Even breathing seemed an impossible task. I just stood, dumbfounded, staring at it until Sarah spoke the words I'd waited for.

"You may now kiss the bride." Sarah then pronounced us man and wife, had us turn to face our 'ohana. Andi began to play *Somewhere Over the Rainbow*. I'd never thought much about the song, but as I listened to the words, I realized it was about dreams, beauty, and a world filled with love. I'd never have selected the song, but right now it felt like the perfect choice.

When the ceremony was over, Chance slipped away. I watched him hurry to the parking lot where his rental car was parked. He still hadn't exploded at me about totaling the Ferrari, but maybe that was to come after the honeymoon. When he returned, he carried a small decorative box.

At a nod from Benni, he handed it to me. "This was Benni's idea. It's really a present from Benni, but Lexie and I helped with the research. We haven't had a lot of time, so it's not complete, but we've gone back two generations."

I inspected the package and shook my head. "Generations? I don't understand."

"Open it," Benni said, her voice tentative.

I opened the box and my jaw dropped. I ran my fingers over the gold letters embossed on the front. "The McKenna Family," I whispered.

"It's the beginning of your family genealogy," Benni said. "We all thought that since you're starting a new life, you should have something to remind you of how you got here."

"How did you do this? When did you have time?"

Benni winked at Lexie. "Lexie's been a very busy girl."

"My dad called in a favor with a printer who's done a lot of work for him and got him to rush the printing and binding."

I opened the cover and found the first page. Wilson McKenna. Wife, Benni Kapono.

Andi stood at my side; her fingers touching the inscription. "That's awesome. What a great gift, Mom." She kissed me on the cheek. "Congratulations...Dad."

Oh my God. I hadn't given it much thought, but I was now a dad. I sucked in a breath. My parents' names were in the book. So were theirs. "Holy cow, this is the best gift ever."

"You really mean that?" Benni asked.

"At Sue's presentation, I was afraid of what I might find in my past. Now, I'm not. I'm actually looking forward to doing more research."

"That's good," Lexie said. "Because I didn't hear about your brother until the last minute. I tried finding him, but couldn't come up with anything."

He wasn't listed, nor was there a placeholder for Stephen, McKenna's Potential Half-brother. Right now, that was for the best. "I can always add him in later."

"I'm sure you'll do a better job than I did," Lexie said.

Maybe. Assuming the guy was real. Now that I had a family, I had more reason than ever to find out.

"You did a great job, Lexie," I said. "You all did. This is a wonderful gift."

Benni nudged me in the side and, with a sly smile, said, "If you do decide to check him out, try to stay out of trouble this time."

I kissed her lips, gave her my best Cary Grant smile, but skipped the impression. "Don't I always?"

www.ingramcontent.com/pod-product-compliance
Lightning Source LLC
Chambersburg PA
CBHW061927170626
46813CB00006B/2329